# 

# NIKKI CASTLE

Cover Design: Bitter Sage Designs

Editing: NiceGirlNaughtyEdits

*This book is for those who think their identity and self-worth are wrapped up in just one thing.*

*You have so much more to offer the world.*

# TRIGGER WARNINGS

This book contains references to depression, grief, anxiety, substance addiction, thoughts of self-harm, thoughts of suicide, and death of a parent (mentioned)

# AUTHOR'S NOTE

Dear Reader,

If this is your first time reading one of my books: you picked the perfect one to start with. This is, by far, my favorite book I've ever written.

But if you've read me before, I wanted to give you a little notice before you dive in. Because this one is a little different than my usual. It still has all the banter, realism, and character-heavy story that you probably expect from me, but there is one difference: it has less spice. If you're reading this one expecting a Chapter 8 (a reference to my book "3 Count"), you might want to skip this one. Due to Roman's injury, the spice in this love story needed to be handled a little differently. It's still in there, but it's less, and it's softer. Personally, I absolutely loved writing a love story in which spice wasn't in the foreground, but I recognize that it makes this book a little different than my usual. So I wanted to be transparent about it.

If you continue reading, I hope you love Roman and Liliana as much as I did.

With love,
Nikki

# PART ONE

# 1

## ROMAN

"And your winner, fighting out of the blue corner... *Roman Ward!!*"

The cheers are deafening. The lights are blinding. The adrenaline coursing through my body is overwhelming.

I wouldn't have it any other way.

As the ref lifts my arm in victory, a huge grin breaks across my face. *One step closer.*

I feel someone clap me on the back, and when I turn, it's one of the commentators ready to interview me. His eyes light up with excitement as he extends his hand for a shake.

"Roman, congratulations on an incredible victory," he says, his words reverberating around the arena as he speaks into his microphone. "How does it feel to know you're officially the number one contender in the light heavyweight division?"

My grin widens. "It feels fucking amazing, Joe. Even knowing it was inevitable, it feels amazing."

He shakes his head, but he looks more dazed with admiration than anything else. "That confidence has carried you far," he says. "Would you say that's been the secret to your success? To being 12-0 in one of the most stacked divisions in the world?"

I sober and lean into the microphone to give him a serious answer. "It's definitely contributed, but I'd hardly call it a secret. And it's not the only contributor. Hard work, incredible teammates, and the smartest coaches in the game have been just as important."

Joe nods his approval at that answer. Then he shifts so he can look toward the giant TV screens in our view. "Well, all of those things combined have created a very successful night for you, that's for sure. Talk us through some of these moments during the fight."

I look at the screen just as a slow-mo video of me starts to play. I watch myself evade my opponent's punches, ducking into a double leg takedown that slams him to the ground. As I drop elbows onto his face, I say into the micro-phone, "Wrestling was a big part of my training camp for this one. I knew he was feeling good about his striking after his last few fights, so I brought in collegiate wrestlers to help me work that part of the game plan."

Joe turns his stunned gaze toward me. "So you went into this *planning* to beat his wrestling, even though he's one of the greatest collegiate wrestlers? Is that what you're saying?"

I shrug. "I know what I'm capable of."

As Joe watches another clip on the screen, this time of me defending my opponent's takedown right before ragdolling him with a takedown of my own, he says dazedly, "Yeah, I'd say you certainly do."

I feel a smug sense of pride as a third clip plays, this one from the last round of the fight. My opponent was running on fumes, exhausted and dejected by his repeated attempts to beat me with his striking, and then with his wrestling. But I was just getting warmed up, teeing off on him, never giving him a moment to rest, or even to guess what was coming. Beating him with athleticism and force of will.

"So...title fight next?" Joe finally asks with a grin.

"Damn right," I affirm with a nod. Grabbing the microphone, I look square into the camera as I say, "You hear that, Baker? Keep that belt real warm for me, because I'm coming to take it from you. I'll see you in London, baby."

The arena explodes with cheers as I walk off with those parting words. I embrace my team and wave to the crowd, then show off my sponsors in the cameras as I exit the cage. And the whole time, the high of adrenaline buzzes along my skin. *I fucking love this shit.*

"*Fuck* yes, that's what I'm talking about!" one of my teammates exclaims as we file into the locker room. "That was *incredible!*"

When the door closes behind us, I take a deep breath, the privacy and support of my team allowing me to fully relax for the first time all night. When I let it out, my reality seeps into my consciousness, and a slow smile spreads across my face.

I just won my fight.

I just broke a division record with my undefeated record.

I just became a title contender.

*I just became a title contender.*

I am *thisclose* to winning that belt and achieving the thing I want most. The thing I've spent every waking second dedicated to for the past decade. I'm so close to victory, I can taste it.

"So how soon before Lorenzo calls, do you think?" another teammate asks, practically bouncing in his seat. "There's no way they don't offer you the fight soon. I mean, Baker can deny it all he wants, but he's been training for you for months. And you're uninjured, even though you just fought. They could schedule that fight next month and you'd be prepared."

"Speaking of uninjured..." my striking coach says, jumping into the conversation with a concerned frown. He gestures at someone behind me. "Doctor needs to check you out. Let him take a look."

When the doctor indicates that I should sit up on the massage table along the wall, I sigh but follow directions. Every fighter will tell you that this is the worst part, because more often than not, you end up going to the hospital—even if you won the fight.

But it's mandatory, so I sit patiently as the doctor does his exam, even knowing the only thing he'll find are some bumps and bruises.

"Incredible," the doctor murmurs, pulling his stethoscope out of his ears. "You're consistently the most uninjured fighter I look at." He gives me a look of incredulity. "How is it possible that you just fought a fifteen-minute war with one of the toughest bastards on the UFC roster and all you have is a black eye?"

I can't help my smug grin. Shrugging, I say, "I don't like being injured. It disrupts my life."

Chuckling, he shakes his head. "I hope for your sake you never get a bad injury, Roman. I'm not sure you'd know what to do with yourself."

I snort. "You got that right. No thank you. I prefer being healthy and pain-free."

Closing his bag, the doctor turns to my coach. "He's all good, Dom. I'm clearing him."

"Great, thanks, Marty," my coach says, shaking his hand.

Marty waves at me and at the room as he leaves. "Have a good time celebrating tonight, boys. And Roman, good luck with the title fight."

The sounds of whoops and cheers follow him out of the room, my teammates once again riled up by his words. I think they might be running on more of a high than even I am.

Proving my point, Dustin jumps up from his chair and starts to shadowbox right there on the warmup mat, too amped to sit still. "Speaking of celebrating... Where we going tonight, champ??"

I wince. My version of celebrating is a little different from my teammates'. "Dude, I'm tired. I really don't feel like going to a strip club tonight and spending my bonus on a bunch of girls, just so *you* can take one of them home."

"Rude," Dustin sniffs, not stopping his shadowboxing. "I don't need your money to convince a girl to come home with me."

"Perfect. Then *you* go to the strip club. I'll be home reviewing fight footage."

At that, he finally stops and puts his hands on his hips. "Come *on*, seriously. You can't just go home and study after a win like this! You need to celebrate! You just became the most dominant fighter in division *history!*"

I sigh, feeling my defenses crumbling. The truth is, I haven't given myself a night off in months. I've been working to the bone even before I got offered tonight's fight, partly because I wanted to give everything in pursuit of my goal, but also because it takes a lot for me to convince myself I deserve a break. I rarely do anything that's not training, recovering, eating, or sleeping.

"Alright," I concede. Already, my teammates are cheering. "But not tonight. I'm serious. I feel like I'm going to drop into a coma as soon as I leave this locker room and the adrenaline wears off. You know how hard I've been pushing my body."

Dustin can't argue that. Begrudgingly, he nods. "Okay, fine, not tonight. Tonight, we'll celebrate in your honor."

I wave him off as I take a big swig of Pedialyte. "Works for me. Have at it."

"But we're planning a night next weekend," Dustin demands, pointing a finger my way. "You can pick the spot, but we *are* going out. I'm not taking no for an answer."

"Fine. Next weekend. Tonight, I'm celebrating *my* way."

And by that, I mean going *home*. Where I can be by myself, in silence, until I eventually fall asleep without having to set an alarm for the first time in months. Maybe years.

Knowing that's what I have to look forward to has me rushing through all the obligatory post-fight press, then sending a silent *thank you* to the promoters for scheduling tonight's fight in my hometown. Being able to go from the arena, straight to my penthouse and sanctuary, is a relief in itself.

As soon as I'm home, I toss my gym bag down in the entryway and immediately grab a cold bottle of water from my fridge. Since I already showered at the arena and changed into sweats, I don't have a single other thing on my to-do list. Now, I finally get to relax.

Stepping up to the floor-length windows, I take a sip of my water as I look out over the city. With a deep breath, I release every remaining bit of stress, nerves, and adrenaline from the day.

As my heart rate slows, so does my breathing, and I clear my mind of everything but this moment. I'll watch my fight tomorrow, pick apart every mistake I made and everything I could have done better, but for now, I'm allowing myself to revel in the simple fact that I won—and dominantly.

The sound of my phone interrupts my meditation. Since

I have it on Do Not Disturb, that means the message can only be from one of my emergency contacts, so I reach into my pocket and pull out my phone.

> Mom: Congratulations, Roman. I'm so
> proud of you <3

I smile and text back a quick, *Thanks, Mom,* making a mental reminder to call her tomorrow.

But once I have my messages open, I can't help seeing how many other texts I have rolling in. Four hours after my fight, I have over a hundred in my inbox. Muttering a curse, I read a few.

Most are just the usual congratulatory text, but some are from people I haven't talked to in years, sending congratulations and following it up with a *we should catch up sometime.* Others are from women I've hooked up with, asking me to let them know when I'm free for some *celebrating.*

I huff an amused laugh as I power off my phone and toss it on the couch. A lot of people would probably be over-whelmed, but I've always loved the praise.

Pulling in another deep breath, I turn my attention back to the city skyline before me. It's times like this when I feel like I'm literally on top of the world: I'm rich, I'm adored, and now the entire MMA world knows that I'm also the biggest threat in the light heavyweight division. Only one more fight before I can prove I'm the biggest threat in its *history.*

I can't help the slow, self-satisfied grin that stretches across my face at the thought.

*God, I love my life.*

**2**

___

**ROMAN**

Dustin's 'team celebrating' lasts approximately twenty minutes.

Because that's how long it takes him—and the rest of the guys—to find a group of girls to chat up.

Sighing, I stretch my arm along the back of the booth and settle deeper into my seat. Not that I'll be here much longer; drinking doesn't hold the same appeal it used to. Nowadays, I stay away from anything that doesn't make my body feel better. And with half my teammates gone, I'm not exactly itching to hang around in a loud bar for no reason.

But then, I see her.

She's standing at the bar with her back to me. From here, all I can take in is her blonde hair down to her waist, and the tight black mini dress she's wearing. But then she pushes up onto her heels to yell her order in the bartender's ear, and the position perfectly accentuates her shapely legs. My focus immediately zeroes in on her ass.

*Fuck*, I want to bite it.

Once he takes her order, the bartender shoots her a wink and walks off to grab her drinks. The attention causes her to duck her head with a smile, her hand reaching up to tuck her hair behind her ear. The motion is adorable.

I take a sip of my whiskey, my eyes glued to her. She takes the four shots of clear liquor from the bartender and turns to her girlfriends standing behind her. With a big smile, she passes them out, then clinks her glass to theirs. The wince that pinches her face as she downs the shot tells me drinking isn't really her favorite thing to do, either. When one of her friends gestures to ask if she wants another, she shakes her head with a laugh.

Downing the last of my own drink, I decide this is my opening.

It occurs to me on my way across the bar that I can't remember the last time I approached a woman. With my name growing bigger and bigger—and with there being minimal damage to my face throughout my career—it's not usually me who's initiated dates or hookups. Being the one to approach feels weirdly foreign.

But she's gorgeous, and that smile is doing something to me. I'm slightly more forceful than I need to be as I push through the crowd.

As I slide in next to her, she's still facing her friends, her back to the bar top, which means we're side to side but turned in opposite directions.

Keeping my gaze trained forward, I lean over to speak softly into her ear. "You know, I can recommend a great mocktail if you're interested."

I don't plan to look at her when she inevitably turns to face me, but...I can't help it.

She's fucking breathtaking. I knew she had a great body and an infectious smile even from across the bar, but seeing her up close? Looking into those blue eyes?

It stuns me for a moment.

With only inches between us, I can see the surprise in her eyes and the way her hair sticks to her damp neck from the heat. Can smell the lingering tang of tequila on her breath, along with her subtly sweet perfume. And I take my time registering all of it.

But when she doesn't answer, and her gaze continues to travel over my face, I eventually quirk an eyebrow in question.

Her head jerks as she snaps out of her study. "Sorry," she blurts out. "I don't think I've ever heard the word 'mocktail' come out of a hot guy's mouth. Threw me for a second."

A grin slowly pulls at my lips. "You calling me hot, gorgeous?"

She blinks, then slaps a hand across her eyes. "I can't believe I just said that out loud. See, *this* is why I can't drink tequila."

I let out a loud laugh, which has her hand lowering and a small smile peeking up at me.

"Well, that just brings me back to my mocktail offer," I say with a chuckle.

Her expression sobers, and she turns toward me fully as she cocks her head to the side. "You don't drink?"

I shrug. "I do. Sometimes. I just like to put healthy things in my body more."

She nods in understanding. "Same. Blueprint cookies are my exception."

I glance back at her friends. "So does that mean tonight's a special occasion?"

A proud smile overtakes her face. "Mmhmm. My best friend just passed her nursing exam, and *I* passed the NPTE." When that only gets her a blank stare, she explains, "It's the National Physical Therapy Exam. It means I'm now officially a licensed physical therapist."

Impressed, I let out a whistle. "Wow. That *is* worth a celebration."

"It really is," she says on a heavy exhale. "I thought for sure the past three years were going to kill both of us."

I wave down the bartender.

"Hey, Roman. What can I get you?"

Glancing beside me, I ask, "Are you okay if I order that drink for us? I promise it's delicious."

I love that she only hesitates for a beat before she nods. "Sure."

Turning back to the bartender, I ask, "Can we get two orders of a mint berry smash?"

He's already reaching for the cocktail shaker. "You got it, boss."

When I turn my attention back to the blonde, she's looking at me with a curious expression.

"If you don't drink often, how does he know your name?"

I could tell her that I get recognized more often than not in this city, especially by men. But for some reason, I don't feel like going into my pseudo-celebrity status with this girl.

Instead, I say, "I just realized I still don't know *your* name."

For a moment, I expect her to push the issue. But then she says, "It's…Liliana. Lily."

I don't hide any of the heat from my gaze as I take that in. "Liliana," I murmur, tasting the syllables on my tongue. "That's a beautiful name."

And we're still close enough that I can see the way her cheeks pinken, her eyelashes fluttering when she says quietly, "Thank you."

I open my mouth to flirt some more, when we're interrupted by the bartender appearing in front of me.

"Here you go, two mint berry smashes," he says, sliding the drinks across the bar with a grin aimed my way. "No charge."

I give him a nod, pulling cash from my pocket and dropping a twenty in his tip jar instead. "Thanks, man, I appreciate it."

When I slide one of the drinks over to Liliana, she's got that same curious look on her face from before. "So, he knows your name, *and* you get special treatment." She cocks her head as she studies me some more. "But I don't think you're lying about the not drinking a lot, because you held strong eye contact when you said it."

My lip quirks. "Are you sure that physical therapy degree wasn't a psychology one?"

She chuckles and pulls her drink closer. "Sorry, that one's all me. I like people watching."

Letting out a thoughtful hum, I turn to face her fully. "Alright then. Any other observations, Doc?"

"I'm not a doctor," she says, aiming an amused smile at me.

Lifting an eyebrow, I tell her, "I've met enough physical therapists to know you need a doctorate to get there. Ergo...doc."

That earns me another curious look. "So, you work with physical therapists, and the bartender knows your name, even though you don't drink. Not to mention, nobody has that many muscles without a good reason." Her eyes narrow. "You're a professional athlete, aren't you?"

And even though I wasn't planning on leaning on the pro athlete card to get her attention, I can't help smirking at her accurate guess. "How badly does the physical therapist in you want to study my body to find out?"

A blink of surprise, then...

She bursts out laughing.

"I was expecting a line, but *that* was more than I could have hoped for," she says between giggles.

I school my expression to one of affront. "Not exactly the reaction a guy wants to hear after he buys a pretty girl a drink, Liliana..."

"*Technically*, the bartender bought my drink," she teases with a pointed look.

"*Technically*, the bartender bought *me* drinks," I counter with a sniff.

She collapses into another fit of giggles, which is enough to make me smile. I'm still smiling like a fool as I watch her try the drink.

"Oh *yum*," she says emphatically, licking her lips as she turns wide eyes to me. "That's delicious."

I nod at the drink. "Told you. Beckett knows how to make 'em."

My gaze stays locked on the way her lips wrap around the straw as she sucks down more of her drink. By the time she straightens again, her glass is half empty and my jeans are a little tighter.

"So the not drinking thing..." she starts, oblivious to my staring. "That's because of your career?"

I roughly clear my throat. "Yeah."

"And what's your sport?"

"MMA."

Her mouth forms an O. "That's a rough one."

"It's not that bad," I say with a shrug.

Her eyebrows pinch together slightly. "You've never had a bad injury?"

I shake my head.

"Why do I have a feeling that your idea of a bad injury and mine are two very different things?"

When that only earns her a grin, she rolls her eyes playfully.

"So why MMA?" she asks. "How'd you get into it?"

"I don't know, it just kind of happened," I answer, twirling my glass on the bar top as I recall the memory. "A new gym opened down the street when I was sixteen, and I was curious, so I tried it out. I got addicted my first class and never stopped."

"Which naturally leads to getting in the ring and later going pro, of course." She nods in mock-seriousness.

"Something like that." Chancing a hip check, I volley the question back to her. "So why physical therapy?"

She takes a lazy sip as she thinks it over. "It sounds cliché, but I just wanted to help people. Specifically, with their quality of life. I mean, working with someone to make them healthier? It's"—she sighs happily—"everything."

"Sounds fulfilling," I remark honestly.

"It is," she says with a nod. Then she lets out a loud laugh. "The fact that I come from a family of thrill-seekers who are prone to injuries probably played a part in it, too. But I'm going to say that was my secondary reason."

That piques my interest even more. "Thrill-seekers, huh? What kind of activities are we talking about?"

She waves her hand. "Oh, you know, the usual. Skydiving, mountain biking, hiking the biggest mountains in the U.S."

My eyebrows lift. "Damn. I kind of thought you were going to be exaggerating."

I'm bumped from behind, the bar starting to fill up. But since it moves me closer to Liliana, I don't even mind it. Especially when it causes her to bite down on her lip in an attempt to hide her smile.

"So do you join your family for these crazy hobbies?" I

ask her, letting my gaze drift down to her glazed lips for a split second.

"Of course," she says with a fond smile. "Although that will probably change now with my degree. I'll probably be too focused on my career to do the impromptu stuff that my chaos junkie older brother comes up with. But family vacations are always really fun."

"I can imagine," I say with a chuckle.

"What about you?" she asks. "Any crazy hobbies? Outside of the obvious, of course."

I shake my head. "Nope. MMA pretty much fills my quota of crazy."

Her lips twitch. "What about normal hobbies, then? What do you do when you're not fighting?"

I mull it over for a second. "Nothing. Fighting is all I do."

That makes her frown. "*Nothing?* Your entire life is fighting? Sunrise to sunset?"

I shrug. "Yeah. It's kind of a full-time gig."

"Nothing is *that* full time," she argues, leaning closer as she asks, "What do you do to relax? You have to have time to relax after fights."

Her proximity makes it hard to think straight as I answer, "I'm actually post-fight right now. So I guess...this." I gesture around the bar. "Celebrating with my teammates."

"But we've already established that you don't drink, so clearly this wasn't *your* idea of a good time." Then something occurs to her, and she quirks an eyebrow. "Unless you came out to meet women."

I hold her gaze as I slowly shake my head. "Believe me, that was just a happy coincidence," I tell her. "I was on my way out when I saw you."

Her throat bobs with a swallow, eyes not leaving mine.

"Suddenly, I'm not as annoyed with my teammates for dragging me out here," I murmur.

That earns me a blush. It takes her a few seconds to respond, and she stumbles over her words when she says, "So, um, we've established you don't like partying." She clears her throat. "What *do* you like? We still haven't figured that out."

I take another chance. "Talking to you," I say evenly. And it's the truth.

Her blush deepens as she glances away. "God, and you're not even *lying*," she blurts out quietly.

I can't stop my grin. "No, Liliana, I'm not. In fact—"

I look toward the dance floor, flashes of my usual 'move' appearing before me. How I would ask the girl to dance, using it as an excuse to touch her and fan the lust.

And yet...that's not what I want to do. Not with her.

"Do you want to go someplace quieter?" I ask, then instantly catch the first flash of hesitation in her eyes.

Shaking her head, she pulls back. "Um, I'm flattered, really, but I don't think—"

"That wasn't a line, as much as it sounded like one," I interrupt before she can get the wrong idea and move any farther away. Jerking my head toward the back, I explain, "There's a rooftop garden upstairs that no one knows about. You wouldn't even really have to leave your friends."

When she bites her lip with clear indecision, I add, "I meant what I said about wanting to talk to you."

Thankfully, she can tell I'm being genuine. Her expression softens once more, at ease as she nods.

"Let me just tell my friends where I'm going," she says, then quickly turns to the three girls behind her who are completely wrapped up in an animated, drunken discussion. They're only shocked out of it when Lily says something into one girl's ear, and her head snaps toward me.

I weather the once-over that can only come from the friend of the girl you're trying to hit on, letting her judge me and trying to look as non-threatening as possible. I must get the stamp of approval, because after a moment, she nods at Lily and says something back.

Lily kisses her on the cheek before turning toward me, a big smile on her face.

"Okay, let's go," she says sweetly.

And I can't help it. I need to touch her. So before I turn to lead us through the crowd, I reach for her hand.

# 3

## ROMAN

I take my time pulling us through the throng of people, toward the staff hallway, where I know the steps to the roof are located. We pass two employees on the three-floor trek upstairs, both nodding at me as they let us by. When we finally reach the top, I swing the door open and guide Lily onto the roof with a hand on her lower back.

"Wow," she breathes out, slowly walking toward the railing. "Roman, this is incredible."

I'm not sure if it's the sound of my name on her lips, or the beautiful sight of her wonder-struck gaze that makes my heart stutter. But it's enough to make me freeze in place and simply watch as she takes in the view of the Philly skyline.

I'm startled out of my reverie when she spins around and asks, "So is this another perk of the job? Getting VIP access to the most beautiful spots in the city?"

I grin sheepishly and shrug. "The owner is a big UFC fan," I say by way of explanation.

With a knowing smile, she turns back around and looks out at the skyline again. "What's it like being a celebrity, really? So far, I've seen you get free drinks and exclusive entrance into a literal garden paradise."

I walk over to stand beside her, leaning my forearms on the railing. "It's nice, right?" But when she only waits expectantly, I sigh. "Okay, in all honesty...it's pretty amazing. It's everything you're probably thinking it is. And more."

She hums thoughtfully, and I can see her mulling over my answer. Trying to decide if I'm just being a hotshot. And I don't say it out loud, but...I *am* telling the truth. The money, the connections, the respect—it's everything I've ever wanted.

Thankfully, she doesn't press me on it. Something about my tense posture must clue her into the fact that, despite answering her honestly, I don't exactly want to talk about what fame feels like. Instead, she turns to me and says simply, "Tell me something about yourself that most people wouldn't know."

I think for a moment, then answer, "I'm one fight away from becoming one of the greatest fighters in the entire history of the 205-pound division."

She takes that in, but she quickly moves past it. "That... doesn't tell me more about you." Her tone is flat as those pretty eyes look into mine. "I could've guessed you were a great fighter just by our interaction tonight. Give me something deeper."

I search for a different answer, I really do. But every fact I could give, every story I could tell...has to do with fighting. And all of them boil down to me being a great fighter.

"I think the fact that you can't think of anything else to say is the most telling answer you could give."

I frown at that, but before I can say anything else, she says, "Okay, how about this. You said you were sixteen when you started at the gym? Give me a memory from before that. What did you like?"

I say the first thing I can think of. "Girls."

She blinks, then sighs. "Honestly, I set myself up with that one."

Chuckling, I look out over the city. *What was my life like before fighting?*

"What is it?" Lily asks, sounding excited, seeing the answer on my face. She must also see my hesitance because she grins. "It's the opposite of girls, isn't it?"

I sigh. "Pretty much." When her grin grows, I let out an even heavier sigh. "School. I was a huge nerd in high school. Nobody knew because I hid it."

"That's exactly the kind of fact I was hoping for," Lily says with a content exhale. Then she becomes more serious. "Did you go to college before you went pro?"

"Only for a semester. Fighting professionally isn't super conducive to making a person want to do homework."

She nods, but before she can ask more about fighting, or my non-existent college career, or anything else that doesn't have anything to do with *her*... I quickly say, "Okay, your turn. Tell me something about yourself."

Turning innocent eyes toward me, she asks, "Like what?"

"I don't know. Anything that gives me a better idea of who Liliana is."

I watch her think for a moment. But for some reason, I'm not even a little bit surprised that it only takes her a second.

"When I was ten years old, I beat the crap out of a school bully for teasing a classmate who wore glasses."

My lip twitches as I fight back my laugh. "Did you pick that particular fact for my benefit?"

She shines a grin at me. "I figured you'd appreciate it."

Chuckling, I turn my body toward her, using the movement to shift that much closer. "I do."

We're once again close enough that I can see the blue of her eyes and the pink flush on her cheeks from the cool air.

I find myself saying gently, "It also tells me you're a kind, protective person who cares more about others than herself."

Part of me expects her to brush off the compliment. Instead, she holds my gaze and says, "You wouldn't think that if you saw the black eye I gave that bully."

I shake my head with a smile. "I would've loved to see baby Liliana square up with what I'm assuming was a bigger boy." Then an idea strikes. "Show me."

She blinks, caught off guard by my request. "What?"

I gesture at her hands. "Show me. Let me see how you'd fight me."

It takes her another moment to rise to the odd challenge. Taking a step back, she moves into a near-perfect stance as she raises her hands into two tight fists.

"Not bad." I cross my arms across my chest as I look her over, slowly circling her. "You have a brother, you said? Should I assume there was a lot of wrestling in your childhood? You look like you may have done this before."

"That's a safe assumption, especially because I have two brothers, and I'm the only girl. But in all honesty, I think I would be a naturally punchy person anyway."

We're both laughing as I stop beside her. And I playfully push against her shoulder to test her balance. When she doesn't budge, my eyebrows rise.

"Maybe you *are* a punchy person," I comment, continuing my walk around her, letting my gaze drop over ass and high-heeled legs.

"Well? What's the verdict?" she asks as I stop in front of

her again. She holds her pose as her eyes flash up to meet mine, a sexy smirk in place. "Any critiques, coach?"

I grin. *Fuck, I like this girl.*

"Only one." Taking one of her hands in mine, I brush a thumb over her fist. "We don't want you breaking any fingers, so I'd suggest curling your thumb around this way, instead of leaving it on the side." I move her finger where it needs to be, then guide her by the wrist to punch the palm of my opposite hand. "See? Way safer."

"Hmm, yeah, that makes way more sense," she mumbles as she lightly punches my hand again.

My lip twitches with a smile at the sight. "You're a natural."

That brings her focus back to me, her eyes darting up to mine right before dropping to my hands.

"Can I see you do it?" she asks, holding up her own palm for a target. "I'd like to see what this *best-in-the-world* fighter looks like in action."

Grinning, I step back into my stance and lift my hands into fists. "Yes, ma'am." Gently, I snap out a left, then right punch at her palm.

Her eyes narrow for a split second, then she shrugs. "Pretty good, I guess." But she quickly loses her playful teasing when she's distracted by something. Reaching for one of my fists, she pulls my hand toward her and brushes her other fingers over my knuckles.

"They're so rough," she says in awe. "I shouldn't be surprised, but..." Lips pursed, she glances up at me in question. "Why are your first two knuckles more calloused than the other fingers?"

I take a small step closer to her and curl my hand into a fist again. "Because when you punch, you want to punch with those two knuckles." I demonstrate a barely-there punch against her palm. "See? I'm twisting and driving them in."

"Wow," she murmurs, her hands cupping mine.

Her touch is warm, comforting, as her thumbs brush over my knuckles. I'm lost to the sensation of her touching *me*. Lost to anything that isn't her hand on me, holding me, feeling this connection between us. Because there *is* a connection.

My gaze drifts over her long eyelashes, her wind-chilled cheeks, her pink lips. And I wait for her to look up at me, for her to show me she feels it too.

After a moment, her face tilts up, and her eyes meet mine. I see exactly what I was hoping for.

Curling my hands around hers, I tug her closer to me, never taking my eyes off hers.

It isn't until she glances down at my lips that I grip her hips and lean in.

Her lips are soft and warm, perfectly welcoming. It takes me a second to do more than just melt into the feel of them, my whole body relaxing into the kiss.

But then she lets out the sweetest little sigh, and the heat spikes to a thousand.

Pulling her body flush against me, one hand lifts to sink into her hair and tilt her face up. With the new angle, I can pry her lips open with mine and deepen the kiss.

Lily's hands come up to fist in my shirt, her mouth moving eagerly against mine, matching my fervor.

And then she moans into my mouth. And I just about lose my mind.

"Fuck," I gasp, wrapping my arm around her lower back as I spin us toward the wall. Pressing her up against it, I take her mouth in a frenzy, tilting her head farther so I can slide my tongue against hers.

That just earns me another, more desperate moan. Her hips start to rock against mine, and I swear, I don't think I've ever been this hard in my life.

I move my hand from her waist, brushing it over her hip and down her thigh. Her dress is short enough that my fingertips reach skin, and I can't help the groan that rumbles through my chest at how soft she feels. I don't even question the urge; I simply hike her leg over my hip and grind into the warmth between her legs.

"Oh God," she says breathily, her hands coming up to cling to my shoulders. When her head drops back against the wall, I take advantage of the new position and move my lips to her neck, reveling in the softness there, too.

"You taste fucking delicious," I groan against her skin, kissing under her ear and down to her shoulder. I nip at the strap of her dress, tempted to slip it down and move even lower. But then she pulls me in for another, more eager, kiss, and I'm once again lost to her lips.

I can't get enough of her. I want more. More of her taste, more of her skin beneath my fingers, more—

The moment is shattered by the sound of a phone ringing.

Startled, I pull back. *Is that my ringtone? There's no way my manager already got me the title fight. That has to be—*

"Sorry," Lily gasps, her chest heaving. "It's on Do Not Disturb, but..." With an apologetic look, she gently pushes me back with a hand on my chest so she can reach down into her purse and pull out her phone.

Wincing, she says, "It's my friend downstairs." She lifts the phone to her ear and answers the call.

My head is still spinning, my heart beating out of my

chest. I can't bring myself to put any real space between us, so I just lean both hands on the wall behind Lily, caging her in.

I can hear the tinny sound of her friend frantically saying something on the other end of the line, the concern that fills Lily's eyes confirming my worst fears.

*Fuck.*

"Okay, I'm coming down." Lily's reluctance is obvious. When she hangs up the call and meets my gaze, there's guilt there. "I'm sorry," she says quietly. "I have to go. One of my friends is really sick."

When she begins to right herself, adjusting her clothes and straightening her hair, I begrudgingly take a step back to give her space. I have no idea what to say. I don't want her to leave. Don't want this moment to be over. "It was, umm, nice to meet you, though." She gestures out over the deck. "Thanks for showing me up here."

I'm still standing here like I've forgotten how to speak. It isn't until she makes a hesitant move for the door that I finally get my head on straight. It hits me that I'll probably never see her again after this.

"Wait," I blurt out. "Give me your number. I'll call you."

For some reason, my question snaps her out of her awkward goodbye. With one hand already on the doorknob, she studies me for a moment. Her voice is soft, but even, when she says, "I don't think that's a good idea."

That has me frowning, hoping I read this situation correctly. That she was into this as much as I've been. "Why not?"

She smiles, though there's a tinge of sadness in it. "Because if we're both honest with ourselves, you aren't even going to remember my name tomorrow."

I can only blink, stunned. And unfortunately, my silence seems to confirm her suspicions.

She pulls the door open and says, "Bye, Roman."

And then she's gone.

$$4$$

# ROMAN

The next morning, I'm stretching out on the mats when I come to the conclusion:

*Lily was wrong. I absolutely remember her.*

I grab a nearby tennis ball. With a groan, I begin rolling it under my tight back.

I slept like shit last night. I couldn't get Lily out of my mind, so I ended up tossing and turning until almost 5 a.m. I kept replaying my hour with her, the way she left, that *kiss*—

*Fuck*, that kiss.

But ultimately, it's not the mind-melting kiss that has me distracted this morning. It's the part that came after it.

Maybe I should've gone after her. I *wanted* to. But in a way...she was right. Not about me not remembering her—the crick in my neck is proof enough of that. But she was right about cutting things off last night.

My life is insane. Every hour of my day is scheduled, every ounce of my focus is taken; there's no room for anything, or any*one* else in it. Beyond a single fun night, I wouldn't be able to give Lily the time or energy that she deserves.

So then why am I still thinking about her this morning, frustrated by the truth that I'll never see her again?

"Roman."

At the sound of my manager's voice, I turn toward the gym office where he's standing in the doorway. I know what he's going to say before he even says it, the biggest grin I've ever seen on his face giving it away.

"You ready to win that title?"

My heart races at the news. I knew it was coming, but hearing it out loud...

"Born ready," I say firmly.

Instantly, every thought about Lily evaporates. I've been working toward this goal for over a decade, which means the title fight is the only thing I can afford to think about.

And just like that, I put everything that isn't that golden belt out of my mind.

*Four Months Later*

*"Ladies and gentlemen, this is your main event of the evening! Introducing first, fighting out of the red corner, your challenger, Roman Ward!"*

I bounce around on the balls of my feet, keeping my body warm and my excitement to a minimum. I've *never* felt this confident going into a fight. Not just because of this specific opponent, but also because of the *rightness* of this moment. I was born to do this, born to own the title of best in the world. I put a decade of work into getting to this point, weathered all the blood, bruises, and trying days. This is the easiest part.

"Alright, Roman, you know what to do," my striking coach says through the cage. I ignore the announcer's introduction of the champ and focus on my coach's voice instead. "Stay at your range and light him up with those punches. He's not going to know what to do at that distance."

I nod firmly in silent understanding. I've been visualizing how this fight is going to go for twelve weeks now. I know the game plan inside and out.

*"Fighters, are you ready?"*

I nod at the ref, though I never look away from my opponent. He signals with a nod, too.

But he breaks our eye contact as he does it. And then the bell rings. I'm grinning even before I've taken a single step forward.

Before he's even thrown out a single punch, I'm on him. Holding the center of the octagon, I impose my will within the first ten seconds of the fight, moving him where *I* want him to go and throwing out a three-count combo that he's forced to deflect immediately. I barely give him any room to breathe.

I snap out another combo, and this time, the left hook lands clean on his chin. The crowd *roars* at the contact.

"That's it, Roman, let those hands go!" my corner yells.

My opponent tries to return a punch of his own, but I slide away, staying at the perfect distance where I can touch him but he can't touch me. He quickly jumps back to regroup, frustration flaring in his eyes.

I throw out a jab, then another. When he retreats from my third one, he backs right into the cage. Which just puts him at the end of my kick range.

Grinning, I whip a vicious kick to his ribs.

Another wave of cheers from the crowd. When it dies

down, the sound of the ringside commentators reaches my ears.

*"Roman is really starting to light up the champ here early in the first round, Joe. I mean, we knew his striking was going to test Baker tonight, but wow. This is more impressive than I think anyone was expecting."*

Their praise only fuels the excitement in my veins. Biting down on my mouthpiece, I dart forward with another vicious combo.

*Double jab, cross to the body, left hook to the head.* Snaps his head to the right.

*"The champ is in trouble, Joe! Roman just landed a hard left hand, and Baker is clearly wobbly right now. Could this be the end already? We're only a minute thirty into the first round!"*

Another combo. Another shot landed.

*"This is the wildest championship fight we've seen all year! He's making the champ look like an absolute amateur!"*

I never stop attacking, never give him any space to breathe. I'm not searching for a knockout this early in the fight, but I'm damn sure going to pick him apart with my striking.

*"He's about to get desperate, Roman. Watch for that takedown!"*

My coach's instruction comes a second too late. By the time I read my opponent's body language, he's already ducking under my punch and shooting for my waist.

I drop my hips back, fighting the takedown. But he has too much space to drive me back, too much time to get me off balance. Before I can get my back against the cage, he's pulling my legs out from under me and taking me to the mat.

*"And the champ gets the takedown, just in time! What a turn of events, Joe."*

I manage to get my legs around my opponent's waist, controlling his posture and minimizing the amount of damage he can do. He still tries, though. Even with me pulling his head down, he tries to throw out some punches to my ribs, my head, anywhere he can reach.

I'm able to block most of them. When he starts to move more wildly, I decide to take the risk of unlocking my legs from around his waist.

But only so I can throw one leg over his shoulder and re-lock them around his head and arm.

*"Roman's going for the triangle! And he's got it locked! The champ is in trouble. This could be the end."*

Victory heats my chest when I feel how tight I have the submission locked. There's no space around his neck, and with my hand pulling his head down, I have no doubt I can put him to sleep in the next ten seconds.

"Hold it, Roman, *hold it!* He wants to tap!!"

My coach's scream only fuels my effort. Gritting my teeth, I squeeze my legs as hard as I possibly can.

I think I feel the champ's hand flutter against my leg, the sign that he's itching to tap out and end the fight. But before I feel the tell-tale pat, he somehow gathers his legs under his body and starts to stand.

*"The champ is trying to stand up! This is insane. He might not even be able to get to his feet before he passes out. Clearly, this is his last remaining effort to fight what's likely an imminent loss."*

I can hear him wheezing, looking for air he doesn't have. Impossibly, I squeeze the submission harder, even as I feel him stumble to his feet. The movement lifts my hips off the mat.

*"I think he's going for the slam! He's going to slam his way*

*out of it! Is it going to lock the submission up tighter, or will it make Roman let go?!"*

A sound like I've never heard before comes out of my opponent's mouth as he gathers every remaining ounce of energy he has left to lift my body into the air.

He gets me higher than I expect him to. But it isn't until I'm above his head that I start to question if I should let go and protect myself against the slam. Normally, I would just hold on, but—

It happens in slow motion. One second, I have a submission locked up that I'm convinced is going to win me the fight I've spent my whole career working for. The next, I'm dropping from a height I've never been dropped from, my confidence wavering and my concern spiking.

Then I'm hitting the mat, 230 pounds coming down on top of me with who knows how much force behind it. And I feel a *searing* pain in my lower back.

I don't know what happens after that. There's chaos, everyone's shouting, and suddenly, half a dozen people are crowded around me. I'm not even sure when I let go of my opponent.

My head is *throbbing*. There's a buzzing in my ears, and I can't tell which way is up. I'm frozen, both physically and mentally.

It isn't until my coach's face appears in front of me that I realize I'm lying on my back on the mat. His mouth is moving; he's saying something, but my brain can't make sense of what it is.

And then I'm being jostled, the ring doctor coming into my view. I watch his mouth move as he calls out to someone. The expression on his face—of shock, and fear, and downright panic—is the first thing that really filters into my consciousness.

My gaze jerks back to my coach. "What—" I have to clear my throat to try again. "What's happening?"

"Don't talk, Roman. The doctor's going to get you fixed up, don't worry," he says with false calm. I can tell he's faking it because his expression is morphing into the same one that the doctor was wearing.

Then I realize the doctor is no longer touching me. Which is weird, because *how is he supposed to fix me up without examining me?*

But when my gaze shoots back to the doctor, my blood turns to ice.

Because he *is* touching me.

I watch with growing horror as he inspects my legs, flexing my foot and then pushing my leg to bend at the knees.

"Dom," I say on a shaky breath.

Out of the corner of my eye, I see him move closer so he can hear me better. "What is it, Roman? What's wrong?"

Slowly, I turn my face toward him, shock and horror tensing everything inside me. I can feel myself starting to disassociate, can sense that this moment is going to change me forever.

My voice is devoid of emotion by the time the words make it to the tip of my tongue.

"I can't feel my legs."

# PART TWO

**5**

---

## LILIANA

*Two years later*

When I walk into my apartment at 7 a.m., the sweat from my spin class already cooled onto my body, I'm welcomed by the glorious smell of coffee.

I see my roommate and best friend, Tina, standing at the counter, her phone in one hand and a mug of coffee in the other.

"Morning," she greets when she spots me, her typical bubbly smile on her face. She nods at the other mug on the counter. "I know you're working a double today, so I made your cup a little stronger."

I make my way over to the kitchen but pause at the living room couch, where my fat orange cat is, predictably, sleeping. But when he notices me approaching, his purring rumbles to life instantly.

Leaning down, I give in to his silent demand for cuddles. "We really won the roommate lottery, didn't we," I muse.

"Freshly brewed coffee before work *and* she loves spoiling you."

As if to prove my point, Garfield answers with a huge yawn and a flip onto his back, exposing his treat-rounded belly for more scratches.

Smiling, I shake my head—while giving into the silent demand. "*Definitely* spoiled."

When I finally pull myself away to continue to the kitchen, I grab my coffee mug and take a sip, immediately sighing.

"I swear to God, Tina, you'd be my perfect woman if I was into women." I take another sip happily. "Thank you for this. I'm definitely going to need it today."

"Done at seven today, right?" she asks, glancing at the calendar we have posted on our fridge to keep track of our schedules. When I nod, she adds, "Do I need to feed Garfield?"

I think back to the conversation with my cat not twenty minutes ago and shake my head, amused. "No, he's good. He's got his automatic feeder." After a thought, I add, "By the way, we might have to limit the treats for a few weeks. He's looking a little *too* round lately."

Tina gives me a sheepish grin. "Sorry, that's my fault. I was teaching him a trick last week and may have given him too many fish sticks."

I wave her off with a smile. "It's okay. Teaching him to play dead at the sound of a gun was worth the extra pound." Glancing at the stove clock behind her, I realize I need to get going. "Thanks again for the coffee. I—" When she places a to go mug in front of me, I let out a heavy exhale. "See? Dream woman, I swear."

She chuckles. "Get out of here. You're going to be late."

By the time I get to the clinic, my coffee mug is empty,

and I'm vibrating with energy for the day. I absolutely *love* my job. Rehabbing patients and helping them better their lives is not only fulfilling, it's *exciting*. Even with a long day ahead of me, I'm stoked to tackle it all.

I'm mentally checking off the patients I have scheduled today as I walk through the front doors. Waving to our receptionist, I continue toward the break room to unload my jacket and bag.

When I find a gaggle of my colleagues huddled together, I freeze mid-step.

I pull off my jacket with a frown. "What's going on?"

Their heads snap up at the sound of my voice. They look downright gleeful.

"You didn't hear?" one of them says, basically bouncing on her feet. "We have a new patient."

That has my head tilting. "So? Why does that make you look like you've won the lottery?"

"Because it's *Roman Ward*."

At the sound of his name, my breath catches in my throat.

*It can't be...*

My colleague misinterprets my expression and says, "You know, the MMA fighter who was paralyzed two years ago in one of his fights? Don't tell me you don't know who he is."

*Fuck.*

Of course I know who he is. The night we met, as soon as I was done holding Tina's hair back while she puked in the toilet, the first thing I did was google 'Roman MMA fighter.'

I didn't let myself do a deep dive into his socials or biography, though. Despite regretting not giving him my phone number, I wasn't oblivious to the fact that we lived completely different lives. It was better that I tried to put him out of my mind.

But that doesn't mean I didn't hear about his injury when it happened. Or that my heart didn't shatter for him at the news.

And now...he's here. In my clinic. As a patient.

"Well, I see the gossip train has already left the station," comes my boss Fran's dry tone from the doorway. She plants her hands on her hips. "Is it out of everyone's system yet? Can we get back to being professionals now?"

The huddle looks properly chastised. "It's out of our system," one of them mumbles shamefully.

Fran nods. "Good. Because now I have to decide who his therapist is going to be."

My head is still spinning, but I somehow manage enough brain power to ask, "If it happened two years ago, why is he here now?"

She sighs, her expression turning sad. "It's a terrible story. The spinal injury is an incomplete one, so after two years of therapy, the doctors said he should technically be able to walk by now. But after the accident, he just...stopped caring. He's been through a dozen therapists at three different clinics, but none can get him to do any more than show up to his appointments. Sometimes, he doesn't even do that. Our clinic is just the next one to try to help him."

It's no longer shock I'm feeling, it's heartache. A spinal injury is bad in itself, but suffering an accident at the height of your career? For a man like Roman, whose entire life was based around that career? Even only knowing him for one night, I learned that much about him.

I can't even imagine how much pain he's in. No wonder he's not making progress.

"So based on that background," my boss continues,

looking around at the room full of therapists, "I need to decide who would be the best fit for him. Because he is *not* going to be an easy patient."

"I'll do it," one of my colleagues says. "I can help him."

"I appreciate the enthusiasm, but I don't think your soft heart would be able to handle this one," Fran says gently.

"I can do it," one of the men says. "I did some kickboxing in college; I could relate to the patient."

My boss assesses him, but after a moment, she says, "In that case, I'd like you to consult during treatment if necessary. For a primary therapist, I need someone..."

She trails off as she looks around the room, her eyes narrowing as she weighs each of our abilities.

And then her gaze stops on me.

"Lily," she says simply. Evenly.

I can only blink at her, right back to being frozen in shock.

"I'd like you to work with him," she says, either oblivious to my current state or, knowing her, ignoring it. "His introduction appointment is in an hour. I'll lead it, set the boundaries and expectations. Then I want you to take over."

"Why me?"

"Because he needs someone with a backbone, who also won't take his attitude and negativity personally," she explains. "I won't lie to you: he's in a bad place. Two years later, and he's still in a wheelchair. He's been passed around from tough love PTs to hippie wannabe therapists, and he hasn't responded to any of them. Whatever's keeping him from progressing, it's been working overtime for two years. I need you to figure out what it is and break it down."

My mouth opens, closes, opens again. But no words come out.

My boss nods. "Then it's settled. Here's his chart."

She presses the thickest folder I've ever seen into my hands. I'm functioning on autopilot as I take it and immediately open to page one, but there's a good bit of subconscious curiosity there, too.

My eyes scan over the document, taking in the key details.

*...Spinal Cord Injury (SCI) to the T11 vertebrae...*

*...diagnosed incomplete...*

*...demonstrates self-limiting behavior and fear avoidance tendencies which may affect his ongoing progress...*

*...patient shows no interest in speaking with a psychologist...*

With every word, my stomach drops more and more. I can't imagine having to deal with this kind of injury, and knowing it's *Roman* makes it even more incomprehensible. The last time I saw him, he was on top of the world. And now...

Thankfully, my first patient is no stranger to her therapy routine, because I'm only half-focused on her while we work through her exercises. I can't stop my mind from drifting back to Roman.

*Will he remember me? Will he even want me to work with him? Is this a conflict of interest I should be disclosing to my boss?*

Nerves have made me chew my bottom lip raw by the time I knock on my boss's office door. It's that last question that's stressed me the most, because I take my job very seriously, and I'm not even sure where the professional boundary is here. We're told not to treat family or friends, but I've seen colleagues treat random acquaintances from their past. Does my one night with Roman two years ago fall under the same category?

Fran waves me in. I open my mouth to say—I don't even know what. But before I get the chance, she says, "Perfect timing. I was just about to come grab you. We're going to meet Roman downstairs in the room closest to the back entrance. Apparently, he's uncomfortable with anyone who isn't staff seeing him."

And...that makes the decision for me. The thought of Roman not going out in public for *two years* because of his injury is something I'm determined to rectify.

"Sounds good," I choke out, clearing my throat when the words come out hoarse.

I follow silently behind her as we make our way downstairs, my pulse pounding faster and faster with every step. It's unlikely that this is going to go well.

But even still, a small part of me is looking forward to seeing him.

When we reach the room we use as a makeshift office downstairs, my boss swings the door open and says, "Ah, Mr. Ward. I see our receptionist has already shown you in. It's nice to see you again."

Then she steps aside, and I come face to face with Roman for the first time since the night we met.

Only, it's not the same Roman. The person in front of me is someone entirely different from the man I remember.

It's not that he's in a wheelchair. It's...everything else.

For one thing, he's covered in tattoos. The baggy t-shirt he's wearing exposes not only the massive amount of muscle he's lost, but also the black ink covering both of his arms, reaching all the way down to his hands. I can also see a few peeking out near his collar.

His hair's also different. It's buzzed, no longer the clean and styled haircut he had when I met him. Now, it's a low-maintenance, lazy style. Same with his facial hair, but with one key difference: it looks like he hasn't shaved in days. He's also got dark circles under his eyes, his exhaustion obvious.

As he lifts his head, and our eyes meet, two things hit me at once.

First, he's hungover.

And second, he has no idea who I am.

"Mr. Ward, I'd like to introduce you to Lily Davis. She's one of our best physical therapists here and the person I'd like to pair you with for the time being," my boss says, too focused on the file in her hand to notice my lack of breathing. "Were you able to fill out the new patient forms we talked about last time?"

It doesn't occur to me until this moment that Roman hasn't said a word. Not a hello, not an introduction with his name, nothing. He simply glanced my way and then turned an empty stare on my boss as she talked.

Now, he answers her question with a nod.

"Excellent," she says, clearly unfazed by Roman's demeanor. "In that case, I'll let Lily introduce herself and run you through what our usual approach is with an injury like yours. She's already reviewed your file and made herself familiar with what you have and haven't tried in your therapy."

I startle at the sudden handoff. "Oh. I—uh, hi, I'm Lily." I wave awkwardly, then want to smack myself in the head when Roman's dead stare meets mine. I'm rarely nervous, but this—Roman—is setting me off my game. "I've, um, been a physical therapist here for two years, and have helped multiple patients learn to walk again after surgeries and injuries. So I'm more than familiar with the rehab you're dealing with. And actually—" My voice grows stronger, less shaky, as I settle into the topic at hand. *This* I can do. "I worked on a lot with SCIs while I was in school. I learned about the spine from some of the best therapists in the area. Between consistent strength training and using exercises specific to your injury, I feel confident that I can help you."

I don't know how I expect Roman to respond, but he simply...doesn't. He merely continues staring at me, his expression blank and leaving me unable to read his thoughts.

I glance helplessly at my boss. "Um, okay. So, your file said you were seeing your previous therapists three times a week. Did you intend to stick with that routine?"

He nods, just once.

Flipping through his file, I try to busy myself with something so I can look away from Roman and give myself a brief reprieve from his intensity.

"What days work best for you? My schedule is fairly flexible; I'm here most days. Tuesday is the only day I'm not in at all. The clinic is open 8 a.m. to 7 p.m., so we can—"

"It has to be after-hours."

My head snaps up at the sound of Roman's voice. Even his voice sounds different. It's deeper, more...raspy.

Then his comment registers, and I frown in confusion. "Why's that?"

Something flares in his gaze. *Irritation, maybe?* "Personal preference," he answers simply.

I debate pushing him on it, but it doesn't take a genius to figure out Roman isn't going to budge on that request, and I'd rather pick my battles. Especially this early on. Besides, it's not like I have a life outside of here, anyway.

I turn to my boss, silently waiting for her confirmation that we can make this kind of exception for a new patient. She nods and says, "Of course, we can absolutely accommodate that. Whatever makes you feel comfortable."

Roman scoffs but doesn't comment.

I let out a weary breath. *I'm going to have my work cut out for me.*

"How about Mondays and Wednesdays at seven, and Saturdays at four?" I ask.

Once again, I only get a nod.

"Great." I snap the file closed. "Then I think we're done for today. Since I'm assuming you don't want to get started right now, during business hours?"

There's another flash of something in his eyes. And this time, it makes me wonder if maybe he *does* remember me...

"I'll see you on Wednesday, Miss Davis," he says in a hard voice, and my hope evaporates into thin air. He turns his attention to my boss. "If there's nothing else...?"

Without missing a beat, Fran stands to her feet, with me quickly following. "Nope, we have everything we need." She extends her hand, which, to my surprise, Roman actually shakes. "I'm looking forward to following your recovery, Mr. Ward."

Roman drops her hand and looks back at me. I feel like I need to follow my boss's lead, so I also extend my hand, albeit a little hesitantly.

Slowly, he slides his hand into mine, his gaze locked on me the entire time. His skin is warm, his touch a contrast to his abrasive personality.

"So am I," he rumbles, his voice so deep I swear I can feel the vibration of his words where our hands are still touching.

It takes me a second, but eventually, I pull my hand back with a tight smile. "I'll see you on Wednesday, Mr. Ward."

It isn't until I'm watching him wheel out of the room that I realize I'm going to be alone in the building with a man who gave me the hottest kiss of my life but who doesn't even remember my name.

**6**

———

# ROMAN

Of course, I remembered her.

I would've remembered her even if she wasn't the last woman I was interested in. She looks even better now than she did that night at the bar. Which shouldn't make sense, because a tiny dress should always beat out hospital scrubs. But it's not the outfit, it's...her energy.

The sound of the wheelchair ramp in my mom's van is a jarring reminder of how wildly different our lives are.

"How was it?" comes my mom's voice from the driver's seat. She knows better than to expect a real answer, but she's still a mom, which means she can't help asking.

I watch, impatient, as the ramp slowly folds out. "Just like all the others," I respond, wishing for the millionth time that *this* wasn't part of my injury. Needing my mother to drive me around like a child.

"When's your next appointment?" she asks as the ramp finally comes down and I can push myself up and into the van.

"Wednesday at seven," I answer, clicking my wheels into place in the passenger seat area. Pulling the seatbelt across

49

my chest, I add, "I can grab an Uber if you can't take me." Even though the only thing I hate more than having my mom drive me around is having a stranger witness me fumbling with my wheelchair.

She gives me a sad smile, and I know she sees through my façade. "I can take you."

I look out the window as she pulls out of the parking lot. "Thanks," I murmur.

She merely pats my arm once to let me know she heard me.

It's not that I'm an ungrateful bastard. I know exactly how lucky I am to have a mom who loves me enough to have changed her entire life around to orbit me. It's just that I hate having to ask for help.

"So did they assign you a therapist already, then?"

The reminder of Lily slams me back to reality.

*As if my life couldn't get any worse.*

"Yeah, some girl with stars still in her eyes," I force out. Hoping to shut the rest of the conversation down, I add, "She's nothing special."

My mom takes the hint, and we make the rest of the drive home in silence. Which is nice, except for the fact that I'm now stuck in my head.

Seeing Lily at the clinic was a shock. After two years of countless medical professionals and physical therapists, I'm not sure why I never expected to run into her.

And now, she's my fucking *therapist*.

I should've left as soon as I saw her. God knows there are enough clinics in the Philadelphia area; I could've easily found another one. The last person who needs to see me attempting a rehabilitation that's never going to work is the person I was trying to impress in another life.

I wince at the thought of what she's going to see *now*. It's not just the embarrassment of my current physique and physical capabilities, it's also what rehab brings out of me. Because nothing puts me in a worse mood, or makes me a worse person, than physical therapy.

And now, all of that is going to be aimed at Lily.

*Goddamnit.* I should've left that appointment. I have no idea why I didn't.

I'm just starting to mentally debate if I should call the clinic to cancel when we arrive back at my house. My mom pulls into the driveway, then shoots me a look that reads *need help?*

I shake my head, already working on unlocking my chair. "I'm good. Thanks for driving me. I'm just going to make some food and then call it a night."

"Alright, honey." She leans over to press a quick kiss to my cheek. "Goodnight. Call me if you need anything."

"Night, Mom," I say with a forced smile.

I watch her walk down the path to the detached in-law suite as I wait for the van's ramp to lower. As far as living with your parents goes, I don't have a bad gig here. It's my house, bought with my money, with complete separation from my mom. She has her own little cottage, and she doesn't come into the main house without calling first or in case of an emergency. I would consider this as independent as I can get with my type of disability.

A disability that's never far from mind. With a sigh, I direct my wheelchair down the van's ramp and click the button by the door that locks and closes everything up behind me. Then I make my way over to the side entrance and enter the code on the keypad that makes the door swing open.

I rarely notice the modifications around my house anymore, but on days like today, when my disability is front and center in my mind, I can't really help it. I move through the giant mudroom that has no shoes, down the wide hallway that can easily fit my wheelchair, into the kitchen that has low counters and where everything is stocked in the bottom cabinets. Everything in this rancher is set up to make my life easier.

It's also on days like today that I miss my old penthouse. But it became obvious pretty quickly after my accident that I couldn't keep it. Even if I would've customized a few things to make them wheelchair accessible, just the fact that it was a high-rise made it annoying to get to at best, and a serious safety concern at worst. I sold it for a good price, but I still hated letting it go.

Now, as I throw some leftover pizza in the countertop microwave and grab a beer from the mini fridge, I'm reminded of how different *this* place is compared to the condo.

At the ding of the microwave, I grab a paper plate and drag the greasy slice of pizza onto it. With dinner in my lap and beer in one hand, I struggle to get myself over to the living room. Once I'm there, I have to lift myself out of my wheelchair and onto the couch. By the time I'm situated and relatively comfortable, I regret not bringing the entire six-pack with me.

Some days, I try to remind myself how good I have it compared to other people in my situation. With the UFC's insurance covering everything on the medical side, and me being frugal enough to save most of the shit-ton of money I made while I was fighting, there are a lot of good things in my life that other SCI patients don't have. I'm not drowning in debt, I have a parent who retired early to take full-time care of me so I didn't have to hire a stranger as a nurse, and between disability and my savings, I don't need to work. I can structure my days the way *I* want to, the way that's "most conducive to my recovery," as my previous therapist said.

Whatever the fuck that means. I'm just glad I don't need to figure out what possible job I could work in this state.

With a huff, I reach for the TV remote, hoping to drown out my struggles with the sounds of an especially violent video game. I scarf down my dinner as the system powers up, putting all thoughts of jobs, accommodations, and physical limitations out of my mind. I'm going to spend the rest of my night playing a mind-numbing game until I pass out on this couch.

I'm just about to hit play when my phone vibrates with an incoming call.

Looking down at the screen, I'm not surprised to see it's Mikey. After two years of ignoring everyone's calls who might remind me of my old life, Mikey and my mom are the only two people who call me anymore.

"Hey," I grunt into the phone.

"Hey. You home?"

Another grunt, this time affirmative.

"Cool. I'm coming over."

I roll my eyes—I can't remember the last time Mikey *asked* if he could come over. Most of his phone calls are declaratory, just like this one.

Part of me wonders if I should be upset by it, if I need to draw a boundary.

But then I realize that that's never going to happen while I'm still relieved by Mikey's drop-ins. Because after everything, he's the only one still around.

Realizing he's already hung up the phone, I sigh and drop my phone on the cushion beside me. But before I can start my game up again, I hear the beep of a passcode being entered into the side door.

I frown at my middle school friend as he struts into my house and throws himself down on the couch, looking every bit as if he owns this place.

"Why even ask if I'm home if you're already standing outside my house?"

Reaching over, he steals the crust off my plate and pops it into his mouth. "I was trying to be polite," he says with a full mouth.

Shaking my head, I move the plate to the side table beside me. "Mikey, I don't think you even know the meaning of the word polite."

"Sure I do." Reaching over me once more, he grabs my beer from the side table. "I just don't waste it on you. I save it all for the ladies."

Irritation sparks, and I make a grab for the can. But he pulls it easily out of reach and moves to the other side of the massive couch.

"You *do* realize I'm fucking disabled, right?" I snap. "You're supposed to be getting *me* things, not stealing *my* fucking things."

He doesn't even look at me as he waves me off mid-swig. "You're fine," he says casually, then lets out an enormous belch. "It's not like you're incapacitated."

I gape at him and gesture at my immobile lower body. "Mikey, I am *literally* incapacitated."

"Nah, you just have to try a little harder than you're used to," he says with another nonchalant wave.

My exhale is heavy with frustration. I have no idea how I ended up with a best friend who is *this* unbothered by the idea of hurting my feelings. Although, if I'm honest with myself, it was refreshing to discover that Mikey's dark humor matched mine. I was beyond tired of people tiptoeing around me, saying only positive things because they had no idea how to talk to me otherwise.

Mikey has no such problem.

"You're an ass," I mutter, yanking my wheelchair closer to me so I can transfer into it. Then I go into the kitchen and grab another beer.

"See? Was that so hard?"

I send him a glare as I return to the couch. "Enjoy your first and last beer, because you're not getting any more of mine tonight."

Mikey shrugs and settles deeper into the couch cushions, pulling the video game controller into his lap. "That's okay. I have to work early anyway." He clicks something on the game. "Oooh, I haven't tried this level yet. Have you?"

Swallowing down my jealousy at Mikey having someplace to be tomorrow, I answer, "Not yet. I passed out right after I reached it last night."

Oblivious to my feelings—or, hell, knowing Mikey, he might just be ignoring them—he throws the second controller over to me. "Perfect. Fifty bucks says I kick your ass at it, first try."

After a moment's hesitation, I let out a heavy sigh, attempting with one breath to exhale every negative thought, feeling, and memory from the day.

"You're on."

7

———

**LILIANA**

"Hey, Lily. Whatcha working on?"

I close my laptop, wincing when I straighten my back for the first time in an hour. Apparently, I've been glued to my screen for my entire lunch break.

"Just reading over some case studies for Mr. Allen's concussion," I answer my coworker's question. "He's been struggling with the up and down motions since his fall, so I wanted to look up some other exercise options for him."

She shoots me a perplexed look as she reaches for a coffee cup. "Didn't you discharge Mr. Allen a month ago?"

I sniff. "Yeah. What's your point?"

She huffs a laugh and shakes her head. "I've never seen someone go so above and beyond for their patients." Quirking an eyebrow, she tacks on, "I bet he didn't even tell you that himself. You called him to see how he was doing, didn't you?"

I give her a flat stare in response.

Another chuckle, another shake of her head. "You are *such* an overachiever," she says as she hits the button on the Keurig machine.

"Whatever," I say with a sniff. "I like it when my patients make—and keep—their progress. Sue me."

"I'm pretty sure the only way a patient could sue you was if you *didn't* make them feel better," she muses to herself as she mixes cream into her cup. Frowning, she looks up at me before asking, "Have you ever had a patient you didn't successfully rehab? I know you've only had your license for two years, but proportionally, you've definitely had the most patients under your care."

Sighing, I trace the logo on my water bottle, thoughts of Roman flashing through my mind. "No, I haven't," I admit. "Not yet, at least. Fingers crossed."

She hums thoughtfully, studying me for another moment. Then she glances down at my computer.

"Guess I can't tease you for doing your homework, then," she comments as she turns back to her coffee. "Since it's clearly paying off."

My gaze also drops to my computer, my thoughts turning to the research I know I'll need to do for Roman's case. Something tells me the by-the-book tactics aren't going to be enough to help him.

"Let's just hope it continues to pay off," I say with a sigh. "In the meantime, I think a cup of coffee might do me more good than the article I just read. Mind tossing another pod in there for me?"

By the time Roman's appointment time rolls around, I've consumed two more coffees. I should've thought a little harder about taking on an extra patient at the end of my day —or at least bullied my boss a little for not giving me a heads-up about it before I said yes.

At 7 p.m., I walk into Roman's exercise room. He's early, and slightly less hungover, but he still looks just as unenthused as he did earlier this week.

I swallow the sigh that wants to escape. *I need another cup of coffee.*

With a smile pasted on my face, I greet him like I would any other patient. "Hi, Roman. It's nice to see you again. How are you today?"

Unsurprisingly, that earns me a blank stare.

I let out an awkward cough and try again. "Do you need anything before we get started? Can I get you some water?"

"Let's just get this over with," he growls.

Swallowing another sigh, I grab the folder with his pertinent medical history. "Your file says you worked with an orthopedic therapist and...a few PTs." I don't think either of us misses the way I stumble over the word *few*. "So, I'm not going to start with the basics. I just want to evaluate where you're at."

"Doesn't my chart already tell you that?"

Shrugging, I toss the folder onto a nearby chair. "We're going to forget the chart. *I* want to see where you're at."

His voice takes on an edge. "So you want to waste my time."

*Aaaand that's enough of that.*

I lean back against a treatment table and fix him with an even stare. "With all due respect, you're two years post-accident with an injury that your doctors said you could have rehabbed at least to the point of assisted walking. I don't think *I'm* the one wasting time here."

There's a flicker of surprise in his brown eyes. *Good. He's going to have to get used to some tough love.*

I gesture at the treatment table. "Should we get started?"

He aims a glare at me that's reminiscent of a teenager not getting their way, but moves toward the table anyway.

*Lily: 1 Roman: 0*

When I take up my stance beside the table, he only

appears confused for a second before he realizes I'm not going to offer to help him get up on it.

"You're seriously not going to ask if I need help?" he sneers. "What kind of physical therapist are you?"

For some reason, his question breaks through every barrier I have, reverting me back to the eighteen-year-old girl who decided on this career because she wanted to help people.

"The kind who's going to get you walking," I say softly.

I can't tell from his expression if he believes me, but at least he moves to climb out of his chair.

I'm watching him closely as he does it. He might think I'm being an asshole who's just trying to make him work, but this first session is critical for me. It's as much of an evaluation as he'll let me conduct without asking him a million questions that he's answered before. With Roman, I'll need to rely heavily on what his body is showing me he can do.

Sure enough, by the time he's lifted himself out of his chair and onto the table, I can already tell he favors his right side. Roman has an incomplete spinal cord injury, which means not every neural pathway between his brain and spine were damaged in his accident. For the ones that were spared, there's still a connection, and some sensation. It's those neural pathways that we need to retrain to recover the functions that he lost.

I just need to figure out where they are and which movements he's capable of.

"Can you flex the toes on your right foot?" I ask, ignoring Roman's still-intact glare.

After a moment, there's movement in his right toes.

"And your left?"

Less movement there.

"Can you contract your left quad and pull your leg up?"

No movement, but I also notice out of the corner of my eye that Roman's gaze has intensified.

"And your right?"

Some movement.

For the next ten minutes, I go through two dozen exercises with him, trying to identify where he has feeling and where he has nothing. By minute six, I'm feeling slightly frustrated.

The problem is, I can't tell if his muscles are actually weak or if he's just not trying. Or if his muscles are weak *because* he hasn't been trying.

For the most part, physical therapy comes down to simple exercises and repetition. There's no big secret to rehabbing an injury beyond identifying how best to do that, and most of my sessions with patients are spent in the gym doing countless reps of basic exercises that they've already heard of, just with lower weight or intensity.

For a man like Roman, I can only imagine what it feels like going from putting a hundred pounds on the leg extension machine to struggling to even lift your foot up. Part of me doesn't even blame him for losing motivation. I see every day how much of an ego-crush physical therapy can be. There's a reason we heavily suggest counseling for our patients.

Grabbing a thin resistance band, I wrap it around his socked foot and hand the other end to him. "We're going to use the bands for some strength training. Do you currently do any exercises at home?"

"Does exercising my thumbs on a video game controller count?"

This time, I release the sigh I've been holding back. "No, that does not count. Alright, we'll keep it simple today, then.

I'll write the exercises down so you can do them at home between appointments, too."

It doesn't take me long to confirm he's not going to do them at home. He's not even doing them *here.*

Roman doesn't technically defy my instructions, but he's clearly not trying. Even when he does an exercise correctly, and I expect it to boost his morale, all he does is double down on his non-reaction. I get more blank stares in one hour with him than I did with all six of my other patients today.

And that's not even taking into consideration the motions he can't do. I half-expect him to throw the resistance band across the room every time we discover one of those. When it happens, I see Roman grit his teeth and put even less effort in. It's like he feels more comfortable blaming the failure he is feeling on a lack of effort instead of on his body.

By the time our hour is up, I have no idea who's more exhausted: me or him. Honestly, it might be a tie.

"Alright, that's enough for today," I tell him, taking the band from his hands. "Do you have one of these at home?"

He nods, albeit reluctantly, so who knows if he's being honest.

"If I tell you to do the exercises we just did daily, will you do them?"

A muscle twitches in his jaw. "Sure, Doc."

I frown at that. I haven't had someone call me "Doc" since...

My eyes narrow as I study Roman, trying to see if he *does* remember me. But his face remains impassive, and after a moment, I decide it was just a coincidence.

"Do you need help getting back into your chair?" I ask instead.

Anger transforms his expression—*at me? Or something else?*

"No," he spits out. Then, with the practiced movements of someone desperate to be independent, he pulls himself up into his wheelchair.

"See you on Saturday at four?" I ask.

But he's already leaving.

*This might be harder than I thought it was going to be.*

8

———

**LILIANA**

I don't bother hitting the books that night, knowing I'm too tired to retain anything I might read about Roman's injury. But on Saturday morning, I wake up extra early for a spin class, then once my body and brain are wide awake, I curl up on my couch with Garfield and my laptop. And I get to work.

I already did a quick refresher on spinal cord injuries before taking Roman's case, so now I dive into case studies of SCIs that pertain specifically to T11 incomplete injuries. But even though there are thousands of documented cases with Roman's exact injury, it doesn't take long before I realize that reading about the science isn't going to help me very much. The physical aspect isn't the real blockade here.

Brushing my hand over Garfield, I nibble on my lower lip as I mull over my options. And then I click over to YouTube.

The accident is the first video that pops up when I type in Roman's name. And even though I know every detail about the injury I'm about to watch, my stomach still drops and my hands go clammy as I click play.

*"I think he's going for the slam! He's going to slam his way out of it! Is it going to lock the submission up tighter, or will it make Roman let go?"*

The commentator's voice is excited, at first. I can see the crowd on their feet in the background, the coaches screaming outside of the cage, and if I squint at my screen to look a little closer, I can even see the triumph on Roman's face as he tightens his legs around his opponent's head.

And then it's no longer exciting. In the blink of an eye, it's the opposite.

My focus stays on Roman as the ref stops the fight, a dozen people come streaming into the cage, and pandemonium erupts everywhere. His expression shifts from victory, to doubt, to confusion, to...nothing. By the time the doctor is waving the paramedics in with the stretcher, Roman's face is completely blank.

I didn't think it was possible for me to feel even more for him, but watching the injury that put him in my care does it.

For the next few minutes, I go through the articles that covered the accident, hoping one of them has a quote from Roman or the people around him. Anything to let me know where his head went after the fight. But there's nothing, and once he was transferred to outpatient care, the coverage pretty much died off.

So then I pivot my research, and instead of looking at the *after*, I look at the *before*.

I watch every fight of Roman's fights. All thirteen of them. Then I start watching the pre-fight interviews he gave for the marketing, and the post-fight interviews he gave directly after. And my understanding of Roman grows.

"Who is *that?*"

I startle at the sound of Tina's voice, my jump scaring Garfield off my lap with a grumpy meow.

"Sorry, bud," I call after him.

"You an MMA fan now?" Tina asks from her position draped over the couch, her gaze glued to my computer screen where Roman is currently shirtless and sweaty after one of his first fights.

I huff a forced laugh. "Not exactly. He's a new patient."

Tina straightens with an appreciative whistle. "Damn. That's a big change from your usual sixty-year-old patient."

"You can say that again," I murmur.

But then her brow furrows with a frown. "Wait...why does he look familiar?"

Twirling my coffee mug, I debate giving her the whole story, but it only takes her five seconds to put the puzzle pieces together.

Her eyes widen. "Oh my *God*." When her eyes lock on me, her mouth drops open in shock. "That's the guy who hit on you at the bar! The famous one who had you all gaga!"

Now it's my jaw that drops. I throw a pillow at her and exclaim, "I was not *gaga* over him!"

She tosses the pillow right back at my face. "Girl, I have *never* seen so many random smiles on your face as I did that week. Trust me: you were gaga."

I can feel my cheeks heat as I give away the truth. "He was hot and famous— I had no say in the matter."

"And a good kisser, if I remember correctly." Before I can toss the pillow again—harder this time—she's looking at me more seriously. "Wait, *he's* your patient? Isn't that an ethical violation?"

My head falls back against the couch with a heavy sigh. "It's a gray area. Technically, it's a judgment call. I was going to tell Fran, but it's been two years and Roman doesn't even remember me. And it's not like anything really happened, so..."

Tina snorts. "Maybe on his end."

I glare at my best friend. "Rude."

She blows me a kiss. "So, you're really just going to sweep everything under the rug and treat him anyway?"

I turn back to my computer screen, lips pursed in thought. "Yeah. He's been through a lot and...I think I can help him."

Tina sobers, sensing just how much I mean that. She's known me long enough to know if there's anything I take seriously, it's my job.

"Have you started with him yet?" she asks, and I nod. "How's it going?"

I nearly wince. "Let's just say, it's been a rocky start."

She nods in understanding. While Tina doesn't experience patients in the way that I do, as a nurse, she still understands the struggle of a difficult patient.

"I'm sure you'll figure it out," she says comfortingly. "I have faith in you both. I mean, look at you: braving the coffee machine on your own. If that's not dedication, I don't know what is."

I grunt in agreement before frowning down at my now-cold coffee. "Instead of faith, is there any way you could give me a decent latte instead? This one tastes like burnt dirt."

Tina lets out a loud laugh as she turns and strides into the kitchen. "Sure, babe."

"Thank you, love youuuu," I sing after her.

"So how late are you working tonight?" she calls over the sound of mugs clinking and cabinet doors closing. "I'm meeting some friends at Lucky's for dinner at five, if you want to join."

"I finish with Roman at five, so I can't tonight."

"You could always meet us for drinks after," Tina

suggests. When my nose crinkles in distaste, she laughs. "Stupid question, my bad. I forgot who I was talking to."

"I would've been down for dinner," I say, feeling a little bad for turning her down so quickly. I just really dislike bars. Usually, my weekends are spent hanging out with Tina at home, but on the rare occasion I go out to dinner with her and her friends, I always end the night when they switch from restaurants to bars. I think the last time I went out drinking was the night I met Roman.

Although the mocktail he introduced me to has been ordered a few times since then.

"I know, babe. You don't have to explain yourself," she reassures me as I hear the espresso machine turn on. "How about this: what if we do a movie tomorrow night? I'll order us dinner, and you can pick out the snacks."

I perk up instantly. My Sundays usually consist of a family barbecue at my dad's house—followed closely by an evening spent recuperating from my unruly brothers—but the idea of takeout and a movie sounds like the perfect weekend finisher.

"Sold. And that new bakery just opened that sells those incredible red velvet cupcakes. I could grab those tomorrow."

"There you go," she says with a chuckle. "It's a date."

Suddenly excited about my new weekend plans, I decide to push my luck. "I don't suppose I could convince you to watch Hugh Grant's new movie, could I?"

As she walks toward me with the steaming cup of coffee, she quirks an eyebrow. "That religious horror movie? Not a chance. Nice try, though."

I sigh. "Worth a shot. No chick flicks, this time, please. Let's watch a thriller or action movie or something."

"Deal." After she hands me the mug, she leans down to

drop a kiss to the top of my head. "I'm going to my parents', so I probably won't see you today if you're going into work soon. But we're on for tomorrow." She nods at my laptop. "Good luck with your research."

Settling deeper into the couch with my new cup of caffeine, I open my computer and murmur, "Thanks. I'm going to need it."

---

Later that day, I walk into my appointment with Roman committed to finding the method that's going to make Roman care about his recovery.

It takes less than fifteen minutes for that determination to fly out the window.

"Let's try the other leg now," I suggest.

Roman glares at me. "If I can't do it with *this* leg, what makes you think I can do it with the weaker one?"

So far, I've smothered every sound of exasperation. But this time, I fail.

Roman's eyes glitter with anger. "I'm sorry...am I *boring* you?"

I slump against the wall. "I'm sorry. That wasn't supposed to come out. I'm just frustrated."

"*You're* frustrated," he repeats in disbelief. "How do you think I feel?"

I cock my head. "I have no idea how you feel," I say, wondering if an honest conversation is what we need here. "I've never been paralyzed before."

Clenching his jaw, Roman goes back to the exercise.

Deciding to take the risk, I continue. "It must be even harder as a professional athlete. I'm sure you're not used to your body not doing what you tell it to."

"I'm not unfamiliar with failure," he says, almost as if he couldn't stop himself from engaging. He seems caught off guard by it.

I push a little harder. "But I'm assuming you followed that failure with pushing yourself until you achieved the victory, right?"

He doesn't respond, but the look on his face tells me I guessed correctly. This is a man who's not used to hard work not being the answer.

"You know, you could do that here, too," I suggest carefully. "It's just going to be different levels for success, and probably more failures than normal. But maybe if you look at PT the same way—"

"I've already talked to a dozen shrinks, Liliana, I don't need another one," he snaps.

My eyes widen. I introduce myself as Lily to all my patients, in the hopes of making things more casual. My dad is the only one who calls me Liliana. My dad and—

"Oh my God, you *do* remember me!"

His cheeks pinken. "I have no idea what you're talking about."

Suddenly overwhelmed—by emotions and familiarity— I lean forward and smack his arm. "Why on *earth* didn't you say something?"

He frowns down at the place I hit before turning his pointed gaze back to mine. "Clearly, I was worried it would ruin our professional relationship."

Now it's my turn to blush. "Sorry. I shouldn't have done that."

Roman glances toward the office I first met him in. "If you knew who I was, why didn't you tell your boss? Isn't this a conflict of interest or something?"

I also look toward the office, chewing on my bottom lip

with indecision. "I thought about it," I say after a moment. "But I figured...it was two years ago, and nothing really happened."

When I bring my attention back to Roman, I'm surprised to find an odd look in his eyes.

Even more surprisingly, I feel my body warm at the sight of it.

"Not *nothing*," he says in deep voice.

The same deep voice that had me following a total stranger up the steps to a roof deck.

The voice that now has a shiver running through my body at hearing it again.

"Do you want me to have her switch you to someone else?" I ask in an almost-whisper. I'm not sure if I'm more scared that he's going to say yes, or no.

He thinks about it, never once looking away from me. When his answer finally comes, relief flows through me.

"No, I don't want to work with someone else."

I swallow thickly, then paste a smile on my face and nod. "Okay then. But we agree that this needs to be professional from here on out. Which means we probably shouldn't talk about that night."

At that, a hardness enters Roman's eyes that cools every bit of heat from our conversation.

"I'm not too fond of talking about before, anyway. So that won't be a problem."

And *God*. His answer breaks my heart all over again.

But it also solidifies my desire to help him, so I tell myself the end decision is correct, no matter how we reached it.

I gesture toward the resistance band in his hand.

"Good. Then give me one more set on the right foot with this."

**9**

---

# ROMAN

Once our secret is out there, there's even more reason for me to ask for a new therapist.

I *should* want to work with someone else.

It's not just that I've spent the last two years avoiding anyone I know, or who knows who I was before the accident —though that by itself should be a reason to switch clinics. It's also that I don't relish *Liliana* seeing me in what has become the most vulnerable phase of my life. Therapy pushes me to levels of failure and frustration that I never reached even as a fighter. It also brings emotions and reactions out of me that I'm not proud of. To have Liliana be the one to witness those things...

And yet, I can't bring myself to walk away from her.

Maybe it's because I've reached the end of my rope, and it feels like I only have enough energy for one last try—the energy needed to give a fuck about shame and embarrassment is nonexistent.

But there's a big part of me that wonders if it's *Liliana* I don't want to walk away from. That maybe, even in my current state, I want to be around her.

And who knows...maybe she really can help me.

All that aside, however, it doesn't make entering the clinic a few days later any less awkward. Because where it was easy to ignore everything, including my previous and barely-existent relationship with her, now there's a slightly tense layer of *I know you, I know who you really are because I saw you before the accident, and—oh yeah—I know what you taste like.*

Maybe that last part is just me. I doubt Liliana is thinking about that kiss anymore when she looks at me.

"Hi, Roman," she says cheerfully as I push my wheelchair into the clinic's gym. "Did you have a good weekend?"

"Fantastic," I answer, my tone flat. "I was so busy; I barely had time to sleep."

She frowns when she catches my sarcasm. I wonder if she's going to tease me back, the way she did the night we first met. Or if she's going to stay with the professional hat she now wears during our interactions.

"You know sleep is one of the most important parts of your recovery," she says, matter-of-fact, as she walks over to the bins filled with therapy tools. *I guess that answers that question.*

"So I could be walking already if I'd just stop setting my alarm so early," I remark dryly. "Who knew."

That earns me a grin, but it disappears as quickly as it came, giving me only a glimpse of the Liliana from that night two years ago.

"Not exactly what I meant, but you knew that already," she responds as she digs through one of the bins. When she pulls out the resistance band we were working with during our last session, that now-familiar PT-mode smile is on her face. "You're going to need sleep *and* this band. Ready?"

My sigh is tired. "As ever."

We work in near silence. Besides Lily's instructions and occasional questions, plus my monosyllable responses, it's quiet in the room. To the point that Lily puts on some music halfway through.

*Weird. This album has my walkout song on it...*

Surprisingly, that makes me feel a little bit better. I try not to think about the workouts I put my body through when I listened to it in the past, but if I focus on the way I felt *mentally* when I was pushing myself, the motivation to do Lily's exercises becomes slightly easier to grasp.

"Your right side already looks stronger," she comments as she watches me push the band out with my foot. "Did you practice any of our exercises at home?"

I don't answer, guilt bubbling in my stomach.

But she reads it anyway. Brow furrowing, she says, "I obviously can't make you do anything outside of this building, but for the sake of verbally putting this into the world... doing these exercises twice a day for twenty minutes will make a huge difference in your recovery." Our eyes lock and she sniffs, adding, "Just saying."

My eyebrow quirks in disbelief at the underlying snark in her words. "Gee, thanks, Doc. No one's ever told me that."

An overly bright smile pinches her face. "Oh, good. I'm glad I mentioned it, then." She jerks her chin at the band in my hand. "See? I'm already adding value. I told you we'd make progress together."

*So much for my theory about the professional hat...*

And yet, I find myself fighting back a smile. For the rest of the session, there's less tension and more lightness in the air.

"Alright, I think that's it for today," Lily says as she straightens from the treatment table where we were finishing up with some exercises. "If you're sore tomorrow, don't do anything with the band, just work the motions. I want you fresh for our session on Wednesday." Her eyes twinkle with mischief. "You know, now that you know it's a good idea to do these exercises at home, too."

Amused, I say obediently, "Yes, Doc."

She snorts, the adorable sound making the leash on the smile disappear.

But just as quickly, everything sobers when she glances at the clock on the wall and asks, "Do you drive? Or are you getting picked up? I never got a chance to ask."

And just like that, embarrassment slithers through my veins.

Because I'm a twenty-eight-year-old grown fucking man and my mom has to drive me everywhere.

I thought about trading in my sports car for a truck and converting it to being hand operated. I could've eked out the money for it. But doing that felt...too final. Like I was accepting the idea that I'd never have use of my legs again.

I can't meet Lily's eyes as I answer with a gritted, "I have a ride."

She doesn't seem nearly as troubled by my transportation situation because she simply nods. "Same. I'll wait with you."

That makes me turn my focus back to her. "Wait, what? What do you mean?"

She's already moving toward the break room along the opposite wall as she calls over her shoulder, "Normally, I would stay later to finish up my patient notes for the day, but my friend Tina is picking me up today. I don't want to make her wait."

"Why is your friend picking you up?"

Lily appears with her coat and purse in hand. "My car's in the shop. I got in an accident the other day so they're fixing it up. Which means Tina gets to be my chauffeur this week."

She's grinning at the end of her explanation, oblivious to the fact that my heart has picked up speed. *She was in an accident? Was she hurt?*

It isn't until my eyes dart over her body, checking for injuries, that she catches on to my train of thought.

"Relax, Roman, I'm fine," she says, a little more gently. "It was just a fender bender."

"People can still get whiplash from fender benders," I respond gruffly.

Liliana grins and gestures around her. "Well, the good news is, I know some people who are really good at fixing those kinds of injuries. Not that I got whiplash." Her lip twitches. "Can I also add that I'm honored you didn't assume *I* caused the accident."

"That's more a reflection on the trust I put in the steady hands of my physical therapist," I say simply, trying to cover the worry I just revealed.

But that just makes her grin widen. "That's just as good of a compliment, so I'll take that too."

I let out a heavy sigh of defeat and leave the room.

It isn't until I reach the parking lot that I realize how awkward this is about to be. I never thought the vulnerability of rehab would be less embarrassing than waiting for my mom to come pick me up.

The discomfort makes me restless in my seat, the need to *do* something growing. Especially when I hear the door shut behind me and then Lily appears beside me.

She looks around the empty parking lot. "Looks like they're both late, huh?"

*The one time my mom isn't sitting in her car reading a book...*

Finally, the restlessness hits a point that has me reaching

into my pocket for my cigarettes. As soon as I light it up and take a big drag, everything inside of me calms.

And then I realize Lily's staring at me.

Frowning, I lower my hand. "What?"

"You smoke?"

I flick the ashes onto the pavement. "Clearly."

Her shock turns into a disappointed frown. "So much for only putting healthy things in your body, huh?"

I almost want to laugh.

"A lot of good that did me," I say, taking another drag.

"That doesn't mean you need to kill the *remaining* healthy parts," she says, her frustration evident.

Part of me wants to explain it to her—how it feels like nothing to tack on an unhealthy habit like this, because every part of my body already feels like it's reached the bottom of the pit.

But another part of me also dislikes that, out of everything she knows about me, everything she read in my medical history and everything I've revealed about my current state, *this* is what upsets her.

I take another drag before saying carefully, "I'll tell you what. If you get me on my feet, I'll quit."

When her eyes narrow in skepticism, I add, "There's no point before then, especially since it's my only form of stress relief, but I promise to dump the habit if you get me walking."

And as a gesture of good faith, I hold up the cigarette, then quickly lean down to scrape the lit end against the pavement.

After a moment, she sniffs and says, "You make it sound like I'm Jesus."

That pulls a chuckle out of me. The sound makes Lily's

eyes widen, and her tone is one of awe when she says, "That's the first time you've laughed."

And...*fuck*. She's right.

It might be the first time I've laughed in two years.

I look away, out over the parking lot, not knowing how to deal with that. Lily must sense my tension because she tries to lighten the mood. "And only four sessions in. I think I'll take *that* as an even bigger compliment than the comment about my steady hands."

Thankfully, I'm saved from having to respond because just then, a car pulls into the parking lot. And right behind her is my mom's van.

"Well, this has been fun." I unlock the brakes on my wheelchair as both cars stop in front of us. "Until next time, Doc."

The amusement is evident in Lily's voice. "Until next time, Roman." But just as she starts toward her friend's car, she pauses and turns back to me. "And by the way, you're on for that deal. When I get you walking, you quit smoking."

*When. Not if.*

Our eyes stay locked as I say, "You're on, Liliana."

**10**

---

# ROMAN

"Come on, Roman, give me one more set," Lily begs. "I can't get you walking if we don't strengthen your muscles."

I have an overwhelming urge to throw the resistance band across the room. I'm sick of therapy. I'm sick of being *weak*.

"I can't do another set," I spit.

Lily's look isn't pitying, it's just...sad. Which only makes my fury boil.

I was never this angry before my accident. I never felt so overwhelmed by rage that I wanted to hit things or react physically. I never got to the point where I *couldn't* calm myself down. But my injury changed all that. Now, my fuse is nonexistent.

My frustration only mounts as we keep working. Every time I can't move a muscle, or every time a muscle is too weak to move the band, my anger grows. There's a tidal wave inside me, one bigger than I've ever dealt with. I feel like screaming, or throwing something, just *exploding*—

"Let's try the other leg now," comes Lily's voice as she watches me fail at a move once again.

"If I can't do it with *this* leg, what makes you think I can do it with the weaker one?" I snarl at her without thinking.

And it feels *good* to aim some of this at her. After all, she's the one making me do this shit. She *knows* I can't do half of these exercises. Does she seriously think she's *helping* me? Maybe she just gets off on watching the big, bad fighter who didn't want her enough to go after her look like a complete and total weakling.

With my pulse beating harshly, I open my mouth to just *unleash* on her, but—

"God, it's like working with a toddler!" she snaps, throwing her hands in the air.

Shock douses me like a bucket of ice water.

"I... Did you seriously just...?"

Crossing her arms, she glares at me and doesn't take it back. "You're goddamn right I did. Do you know that you had me seriously debating this week if I should start offering you cigarettes as a reward? Maybe that'll help with your attitude problem. Might as well get your fill of them now, anyway, since you're gonna be giving them up as soon as you're on your feet."

I blink at her, properly chastised.

Something on my face makes Lily's eyes narrow, and her head tilt.

"*Would* you respond to a reward system?" she asks.

I quirk an eyebrow. "Sorry, Doc, cigarettes I can get any time, and I don't think sweets are going to do anything for me."

It isn't until I give the playful response that I realize her outburst has somehow driven all the anger from my body.

"Not sweets," she corrects. "Rewards."

That confuses me. "What kind of reward?"

Shrugging, she says, "Whatever you want. You name it."

"*Whatever* I want? I doubt that's a medically approved treatment."

She holds my gaze. "Humor me."

My eyes narrow. This feels like a trap, but I can't figure out how. "To be clear, you're saying if I go through your exercises—"

"And give me real effort," she interrupts.

"—you'll do, or give me, anything I want?"

"Within reason, yes. If it's something I can give you inside these four walls right now, I'll agree to it."

No part of me believes she's telling the truth. I know her well enough to know she takes immense pride in her professional persona—not to mention that she's kind of a goody two-shoes.

But the other part of me is intrigued. And I want to test her, to see how far I can push her.

"Fine," I concede. "I'll do the reps, if you...smoke a cigarette."

I almost smirk when she swallows thickly, already going green at the thought. But without any hesitation, she nods and says, "Deal."

My amusement disappears. "You're not going to smoke a fucking cigarette," I growl at her.

"Out of the two of us, I'm not the liar in this relationship," she sasses back. Then she takes a deep breath and calmly says, "Do one set of reps and find out. Kick the band out eight times."

I glare at her, realizing I now have to do the fucking exercise.

We've been working a lot on strengthening my leg muscles, using resistance to flex my foot up and also down, but also lifting my whole leg up and pushing back down. It's been depressing to see how weak my quads are, but that's one of the muscles that Lily has really been harping on. Before this ridiculous conversation started, she had me sitting on the table, pulling one leg up to a bent-knee position, and pushing against the resistance band wrapped around my foot while holding the other end.

Up until now, I had only been able to extend my leg completely twice.

"I need real effort, Roman," comes Lily's softened voice.

"I got it," I snap back, that fear of failure creeping back in. For some reason, this moment feels bigger. I can't *not* do eight reps.

Gritting my teeth, I adjust my position and my grip on the band. And I *will* my leg to move.

I get the first two extensions easy. Slowly, but easy. I've already done two, even on a shit day like today.

I get the next two as well. I've gotten four in the past a few times.

By five, my leg is quivering.

By six, I'm sweating, my stare locked onto my foot.

By seven, I can't tell if the fire in my leg is pain or something else.

By the eighth rep, my chest is heaving, my whole leg is shaking, and I swear it takes forever for my foot to push the band all the way out. With every inch, the resistance makes the movement harder. I don't think I'll make it.

But then...my knee locks out. My leg is straight. I did eight reps.

With a gasp, I let go of the band, watching it go flying across the mat. *Jesus.*

When I look up, Lily's expression is downright *giddy.* I mean, she's completely lit up.

"Shut up," I say, out of breath.

She grins. "I *told* you so."

I aim a glare at her. "Whatever. A bet's a bet."

Her wary gaze drops to my hand as I reach into the pockets of my shorts and pull out a pack of cigarettes.

I can't help grinning as I pull out my lighter and a cigarette. "Regretting your therapy strategy, doc?"

Her eyes snap up to lock with mine. "Gimme that," she grumbles.

It's amusing, watching her fumble with the lighter. But as she lifts the cigarette to her lips, I can't help asking, "Why are you doing this?"

There's nothing but honesty in her eyes as she says, "Because, apparently, it's the only way to get you to do your PT."

And then she lights the cigarette, inhales, and promptly coughs up a lung.

I snatch the cigarette from her. "Alright, just put it out. Jesus. I can't watch this."

As she sputters some more, I look for a place to put it out, since this isn't exactly a place loaded with ashtrays. In the end, I scratch it against the sole of my shoe before throwing it in the bag on my wheelchair that I use as a trash bin.

Leaning back on my hands, I watch Lily chug some of her water. When she has her breath back and collapses against the wall across from me, I still haven't figured out why she just did that.

"I really didn't think you would do it," I admit.

"I know," she says simply.

I study her for another moment. In the end, I just ask her outright.

"Why do you care if I do my PT?"

And again, there's nothing but honesty in her eyes as she says, "Because someone should."

My chest tightens as I drop my gaze to my hands in my lap. "I wasn't always like this, you know," I say roughly.

"An asshole?"

My head whips up in surprise. She's rolling her lips to keep from laughing.

"Just trying to lighten the mood," she says innocently.

Even as my eyes narrow, my lips twitch in amusement. "Bitch," I bite back playfully.

Somehow, her grin widens. "I love that title."

Shaking my head, I finally let my smile come through. "You are certifiable."

"And I *also* just got you to do eight reps of an exercise you've been pouting over for two weeks, so you can't say my methods don't work," she quips.

The reminder of my therapy is sobering. I drop my head back with a sigh.

In her spot across from me, Lily leans back against the wall and wraps her arms around her waist. Her grin has also disappeared when she asks hesitantly, "What were you like when you first started PT?"

*Right. My admission.*

I can't meet her eyes. It's easier to be honest this way.

"Determined. They told me the most recovery happens in the first year, so I went into it fully prepared to work my ass off. And I did—for a while. Even the hard days weren't enough to make me quit. It wasn't until—" I swallow thickly.

"Until what?" Lily asks gently.

I take a deep breath and admit the rest. "It wasn't until the UFC officially cut me from their roster and released me from my contract six months later that I realized none of it mattered. I don't know why it never occurred to me that I wouldn't fight again. God knows the doctors told me enough times. I just never heard it. But when that call came through..." I shake my head, clearing the memories. "I don't know. It just kind of hit me that none of it mattered. Why was I killing myself when my end goal was unreachable anyway?"

"And you didn't think changing your end goal to *walking* was worthwhile?"

I can hear the frown in Lily's voice before I even look at her. Sure enough, her expression is one of disbelief.

"I know it's not logical," I admit. "But that felt like changing my dream from shooting for the stars, to shooting for the top of the tree in the backyard. It felt meaningless and stupid. And then, by the time I realized *that* was stupid, a year had passed, and it had gotten harder to progress and...easier to fail."

Saying this out loud is...a relief. I've always held on to the anger and stayed quiet in rebellion. I've never felt the desire to unburden myself like this.

"You can, you know." When I give Lily a confused look, she explains, "You can still walk. Even though it's been two years. They say your spinal cord experiences a heightened state of neuroplasticity in the six months after an injury, but that doesn't mean you *can't* regain function. It's harder, sure, but it's still possible."

I want to tell her that it's been a long time since I've let myself believe that. That I've become so used to giving up, I don't remember what it's like to fight anymore.

*That I don't want to disappoint her.*

I don't know if she reads any of that in my face. But I watch as she straightens from her stance and picks up the resistance band, then walks over to stand before me.

"I know you don't want to let yourself hope for it," she says, eyes searching mine, "and that's okay. I'll carry the hope for a little while. I just need you to put your trust in me. Because I *swear to you*, Roman—" Determination blazes in her eyes. "I will get you on your feet."

I want to believe her. But she's right, I'm not ready to let that hope in.

So, I don't answer. I just reach for the band in her hand.

"Other leg now, right?"

## 11

—

## LILIANA

For the next two weeks, I watch Roman make progress.

It's not linear. And that doesn't mean he doesn't have bad days. But watching him rep until failure is a special kind of victory as a physical therapist. Not just that, but I can also tell he's doing his exercises at home. He's getting stronger and more fluid in his movements, and his confidence is growing. Even on the tougher days, he's pushing through and leaving with his head up high.

Today has been more of a rollercoaster, though. Since Roman still favors his right side over his left, we've been working the left side hard today, and his frustration has mounted. We're one failed rep away from the resistance band being thrown across the room.

"Come on, give me one more set," I beg. Half the time, the victory is just getting Roman to do the exercise after he's already failed. Once he can talk himself into trying again, the reps go a lot easier.

"Remember, even trying the exercise is helping to rewire your brain," I tell him. "As long as you're giving effort, you're getting better."

Roman releases a heavy breath. I know I'm pushing him to his limit.

"I'm going to burn this goddamn band one day," he growls. But he re-positions it and goes for the extra reps anyway.

I have to smother my smile so he doesn't see it in the mirror as he works to flex his foot up.

He does four reps easily. On the fifth, his leg starts to shake. Roman's jaw clenches in determination, and I internally cheer, since that's become the tell-tale sign that he's at the point of *I'll die before I give up.*

"Come on, two more," is all the encouragement I let myself vocalize as he finishes the sixth rep.

It feels like it takes forever, but he gets reps seven and eight. Relieved, I sigh happily, about to open my mouth to congratulate him on a hard session, when I see he's flexing against the band again.

He's going for a ninth rep.

And a tenth.

By the eleventh, my heart's nearly beating out of my chest. I can't breathe for the risk of disturbing this incredible moment.

He's shaking so badly, I'm worried the band is going to dislodge from his foot. "Come on, you son of a bitch," I hear him murmur through a strained breath of his own.

The moment his lift reaches full extension, he lets the band go with an explosive exhale. *Twelve.*

I plant my hands on my hips, not even attempting to keep the smile off my face. "Well, well, well, look who's an overachiever. I should've known."

Roman rests his hands behind him and leans back as he calms his breathing. "You should've seen me when I was fighting. I didn't know how to stop."

"As far as I'm concerned, that was the definition of a fight," I say, grabbing the band and putting it back in the bin. "Which you won, by the way. In overtime."

When I turn back to Roman, there's an amused smirk tugging at his lips. "There's no overtime in fighting, Doc."

I quirk an eyebrow, even as I battle a smile of my own. "Not anymore, there isn't, but Bellator used to do an extra round if the fight was scored evenly at the end." I force a mock-disappointed expression. "I would've expected you to know that."

Surprise lights in his eyes. *God, I love catching him off guard.* "Did you just...?"

I just stare at him, waiting expectantly.

He seems to finally pull himself together. "Why do you know that?" he asks bluntly.

I shrug. *I did a shit-ton of research into fighting so I could better understand you and hopefully figure out a way to help you. The fact that an organization's old round time rules stuck in my head was a total accident.*

"Everybody knows that," I say instead.

Roman's eyes narrow, but he doesn't push me on it, just studies me with a skeptical look on his face.

"Alright, that's it for today," I quip happily, clapping my hands together. "See you Saturday?"

Roman only nods in answer before pulling himself over to his wheelchair.

Just then, my phone dings with a text. It's set to DND when I'm with patients, which means it can only be from one of three people.

I sigh when I read the message.

"Everything okay?" Roman asks from where he's settled in his chair.

"Fine," I say with another sigh. "Just my boss."

Roman gives me an expectant look.

"One of our machines is broken, so a technician was scheduled to come out and repair it," I explain. "He was supposed to be here an hour ago. My boss just told me he's only now leaving his last job."

Roman frowns. "So he's still coming? Is there anyone else in the building right now?"

I shake my head. "Just me. Since your sessions are late, this place is empty by now. Which means I get to be the one that waits around to let him in."

"You shouldn't be in here by yourself. I'll wait with you."

My head snaps up, and now *I'm* the one frowning. "What? No, you don't have to do that."

"Fuck that. I'm not leaving you by yourself."

It takes one glance at Roman to realize he's made up his mind, and that nothing I can say is going to change it.

"Fine. But when I get bored and make you do more therapy, you only have yourself to blame."

He huffs a laugh. "Noted."

And just like that, it hits me that this means I'm about to be alone with Roman, for an undetermined amount of time, without physical therapy to keep us occupied.

Just two people alone in a room with time to kill.

Chewing on my lower lip, I look around the gym. "Should we...stay here? Or would the office be more comfortable?"

Roman glances toward the office, looking just as uncertain about it as I feel. Spending time together is one thing, but doing it completely outside of our usual environment feels...like a bigger deal.

"We should probably just stay out here, it's more—"

But he cuts off with a wince and reaches around to rub his lower back.

"Muscle or chair?" I ask.

"Chair," he responds. "I spent more time in it than usual today."

I look toward the break room. "Welp, I guess that answers our question about where we're spending the next hour. Come on."

I'm heading toward the break room before Roman can argue with me. I know he can see the giant couch from where he is, and that wince told me he's uncomfortable enough to want the relief.

Sure enough, he's made it into the room by the time I find the remote for the TV. Flopping down on one end of the couch, I ask, "So what should I put on?"

His uncertainty doesn't fade as he transfers from the chair to the couch. He still looks uncomfortable as he turns his attention to the TV.

I thought his tenseness was because we're in a weird situation, but if he's actually in pain, then that changes things. It's been a while since I've given a massage, but—

"I'm not watching some stupid reality TV show," Roman growls.

I roll my eyes to hide my relief as I turn on the TV. "If you think all reality TV shows are stupid, you haven't been watching the right ones. And our hour is up, which means I'm no longer obligated to be nice to you. There's the door."

I hear his huffed laughter from the other end of the couch. "If our sessions are an indication of you being 'nice,' then I'd hate to see what mean looks like."

Sending him a wink, I turn my attention back to the TV and the Netflix options that pop up. I'm scrolling through the Horror recommendations when Roman says, "*Midsommar* was fantastic."

My head whips toward him. "You're a horror buff?"

He nods.

"Wow," I breathe. "I think I like you way more now." Ignoring the way Roman's lip twitches, I add, "I normally lean toward the thriller side of things, but I'll take a horror movie with a good mystery any day of the week."

"I'll write you a list," Roman says with a chuckle.

I lift my eyebrows at him. "Bold of you to assume I haven't already seen everything on your list."

He tilts his head, smirking. "You sound pretty sure of yourself."

Bringing one leg up on the couch, I get more comfortable. "Try me."

He shifts his upper body to face me. "*The Conjuring*."

I roll my eyes. "What is this, amateur hour?"

"Just testing you," he says, eyes narrowing playfully. "Alright, how about *Seven*?"

"*So* good," I gush. "I think I stared at my TV with my mouth open for the last ten minutes."

"*Identity*?"

"No idea why that's considered horror, but I loved that one. The twist was brilliant."

"*Psycho*?"

"I once held a 24-hour Hitchcock watch party in college. I think I've seen every movie he's ever directed."

"Now *that* sounds like a party I would attend. *Saw*?"

I shudder. "Love the concept from a psychology perspective. Hate the movies."

Roman nods. "Ah, yes, I forgot. If you weren't a physical therapist, you'd be a psychologist."

I frown, confused by his comment. But when I realize he's remembering the conversation we had the first night we met, something in me warms.

"How about *The Shining*?" he asks.

"I think I'm scarred from trying to read Stephen King's books as a kid, but that movie deserves its spot as a classic. Stanley Kubrick is a brilliant director." I cock my head. "But I thought this was your list of lesser-known mystery horror movies?"

"Sorry, I got distracted," Roman says with another chuckle. "I wanted to hear your thoughts on the big ones. Okay, how about *Shutter Island*?"

"Okay," I gasp excitedly, crossing my legs so I can face Roman completely. He's watching me with an amused expression. "First of all, *love* a Scorsese movie. Second of all, that twist had me *fucked. up.* Did any part of you see that coming??"

"No," he admits. "I read the book before the movie came out and almost threw it against the wall when I got to the end. I love how it tied everything together, though. Have you ever gone back to watch it a second time knowing the ending?"

"No, but that's a good idea."

Now it's *Roman* whose excitement is mounting. Pulling one leg up onto the cushions, he shifts to face me slightly so he can drape one arm along the back of the couch. "Have you ever read the book?" he asks.

I shake my head, riveted. By the movie or Roman, I'm not sure.

"You should. Dennis Lehane's novels are incredible. But this one in particular is mind-blowing because he has one line at the very end of the book that completely changes the meaning of the ending."

I wrack my brain for the ending scene in the movie. "So the book ends differently?"

"It *implies* a different ending," Roman clarifies. "One sentence and it became the most incredible example of revisionism that I've ever seen between a book and a film. I've always wanted to know who came up with it, if it was Lehane or someone involved in the movie."

"Wow," I breathe out. "Guess I know what I'm reading this weekend."

"Have you ever read *Gone Girl*? That's another one that was adapted really well. Not horror, but the mystery story-line's breadcrumbs were exceptional in the book."

I stare at Roman, unable to hold back my smile. "Sounds like you read a lot."

His excitement fades to slight sheepishness as he shrugs. "I guess." Self-deprecation tinges his laugh. "It's not like I have anything else to do."

I'm not buying into his effort to diminish his interest. "*Shutter Island* came out over a decade ago."

He looks like he wants to brush me off again, but after a moment, he sighs. "Alright, fine. I like reading."

A slow grin stretches across my face. "If I'm remembering correctly, your exact words on the night we met were: *I was a huge nerd in high school.*"

He sniffs. "What's your point."

My grin grows. "Thrillers aren't your go-to reads, are they?"

*Bingo.*

He looks almost offended that I've figured him out. "So what if I like reading historical nonfiction?"

*History. Interesting.*

I raise my hands in surrender. "I don't know why you're getting defensive; I was the girl who liked going to the college library on Sundays for a ten-hour study day. I can probably out-nerd you by a thousand."

"Okay, yeah, you win. That's psycho behavior, Liliana."

*God, I love how he says my full name.*

The thought is a startling one. One I definitely shouldn't be having about my patient.

I mentally stumble over my thoughts as I try to return to an acceptable, *professional* question. "So…horror movies and historical nonfiction. Are there any historical horror movies?"

He's watching me in a way that makes me wonder if he can see my very *unprofessional* thoughts. After a moment, he answers, "Most people would call those war documentaries."

I laugh despite myself. "Touché."

"What do *you* like to watch?" Roman asks. "Or read, since we're on the topic. Those nerdy characteristics couldn't have disappeared after graduation." When something occurs to him, he makes a sour face. "Please don't tell me you still spend your Sundays reading clinical studies all day."

*Not until you came along.*

"God, no," I fib instead. "My job and my days are so insane that I usually need some kind of escapism by the time Sunday night rolls around."

He nods in understanding. "Guess that explains the thrillers. So, fiction then? What else do you like?"

Wrapping my arms around my knees, I debate my answer. "I go through phases, I guess. Right now, I'm in a fantasy phase. I'm either reading fantasy or watching it. Recently, I watched all seven seasons of *True Blood*."

Roman's eyes widen. "Jesus. That's a lot of vampires."

"And it's technically horror, too," I add with a grin. "You'd love it."

"Pass, but thanks," he says dryly. "I'll stick with my WWII documentaries."

Chuckling, I shrug. "Your loss."

"So...is that what your time outside of here looks like?" Roman asks curiously. "Or are you still jumping out of airplanes with your family in your free time?"

*Why does the fact that he remembers so much of our conversation two years ago make me giddy?*

But it's not just that. It's also that he cares enough to want to know more about me *now*.

"Not as much as I used to," I say with a smile I can't tame. "I was right about my job taking up most of my time and energy. Although I still go on crazy trips with my family." Then I have to ask, "How on *earth* do you remember that? It was *two years ago*."

Roman shrugs nonchalantly. I think that's going to be his whole answer, but then he says, "I liked you. I thought you were interesting."

My heart starts to pound. Because remembering our conversation is one thing, but admitting the *why*...

It's the first time I've gotten confirmation that I wasn't the only one invested that night.

Suddenly, a loud knock sounds on the back door of the clinic, interrupting my quickly spiraling thoughts.

My head whips toward the gym. "Who—?"

"The technician," Roman says stiffly, already pulling his wheelchair over to pull himself into it. "Make sure he confirms who he is before you open the door, though."

I glance at the TV, my brain still scattered from the interruption. It feels like we *just* sat down. I mean, we never even started watching anything.

I'm moving on autopilot as I stand up, round the couch, and near the back entrance. "Who is it?" I call out.

"Mark, from Humphrey's Repair," comes a gruff voice. When Roman nods, I open the door to an older man who looks more frazzled than I feel. "Sorry for the lateness.

One job got pushed and suddenly my whole day is screwed."

I stand aside to let him in. "I understand. Did my boss tell you which machine it is?"

He's already moving toward the treadmill in the corner as he nods. "Yup. I'll try to be quick so you can get out of here."

"Okay, thank you," I answer. "We'll just...hang out here in the meantime."

I close and lock the door, far too aware of Roman's presence behind me. Of the fact that when I turn back, I have no idea what to say to him.

Based on the clock on the wall, Roman and I talked for almost thirty minutes. We somehow went from being unsure we could even exist in a space where we weren't physical therapist and patient to chatting about our favorite movies.

"Out of curiosity," Roman starts, jolting me from my thoughts. "If you were alone in a room with a strange man, what would you use as a weapon in here?"

For a moment, I can only blink at him. "A weapon?"

He nods. "Something tells me you would pick an interesting one."

Frowning, I look around the room. "Um, I guess...maybe a dumbbell? Oooh wait, no, I'd grab one of the walkers. I've never checked, but I'm pretty sure Mrs. Wilson is whittling one of them down to a shank underneath the tennis ball at the end."

"See? I knew you'd have a good answer," Roman says with a light laugh.

I bite down on my smile, my uncertainty from a minute ago nowhere to be found. Now, the silence between us is a comfortable one. Roman's gaze stays locked on the technician as the man fiddles with the treadmill, while my attention moves back and forth between him and Roman. Once or twice, my smile gets away from me as I remember something Roman said tonight.

"Yup, I had a feeling it was going to be this pin causing the issue," Mark says, straightening from where he was crouched. "I don't have the part with me that I need to fix it, but I can come back tomorrow. During business hours, of course."

I nod. "I'll let my boss know."

He nods in return. "Alright then. I'll get out of your hair." He moves toward the back door, but pauses before he turns the handle. "By the way, as a technician, that was a terrifying conversation to overhear. But as a father, I'm proud of your answer."

My cheeks burn hot immediately. "Oh my gosh, I'm so sorry. I didn't know you could hear us."

With a hearty chuckle, he pulls the door open. "It's alright. Tell Mrs. Wilson I'm proud of her, too." And then he's gone, leaving me flaming with embarrassment.

I clap my hands to my scorching cheeks. "Oh my *God*."

As if he was waiting for the technician to leave, Roman suddenly lets out a full-bellied laugh. "That was amazing. Better than I could have hoped for."

I whip my head toward him. "What do you mean, *hoped* for?"

He's grinning shamelessly. "It means I wanted to make sure he knew not to fuck with you if you happened to be alone with him again."

I think I'm even more confused now. "Again? I wasn't alone with him *now*."

Roman sobers as he gestures toward his wheelchair. "I

mean, you basically were. It's not like I would've been able to do much."

I pinch the bridge of my nose. "I don't know if I should smack you for assuming I don't know how to protect myself from a strange man, or for assuming that you *can't*." When I prop my hands on my hips, Roman's surprised expression just makes me frown harder. "Let's not act like being in a wheelchair means you couldn't have broken that guy's limbs with fourteen different submissions. I saw the Santera fight. You basically choked him out with one arm."

A myriad of emotions flashes across Roman's face: more surprise, amusement, pride. But in the end, he settles on pure delight.

He's grinning like a fool when he says, "That tidbit of Bellator knowledge wasn't an accident, was it?"

I sniff. "I don't know what you're talking about."

"Liar. You did research on *me,* you little stalker. Admit it."

Crossing my arms, I aim a glare at him. "Only if *you* admit you're not nearly as helpless as you want me to think you are."

"Alright fine, I concede," he says, lifting his hands in surrender. "Last thing I want to do is make you angry enough to grab Mrs. Wilson's walker."

I glance toward the equipment room. "I should really figure out which leg she's whittling down."

Roman's smile has a giggle escaping my chest. This whole night has been unexpected, but I can't deny that I had a lot of fun. That *Roman* made it fun.

"You ready to close up?" he asks.

I nod. "I just have to grab my coat and purse."

Roman jerks his head toward the break room. "Go. I'll wait."

I don't know why I'm surprised to hear he's going to wait.

Clearly, there's a protective side of Roman I haven't seen before.

Once I have everything I need, I gesture for Roman to exit the back door while I set the clinic's alarm. Then before I know it, we're both in the parking lot, trying to figure out how to say goodbye. In the end, all I manage is, "See you on Saturday, I guess?"

He nods. "Sounds good."

"Don't forget to do your PT homework," I say with an awkward laugh.

That earns me a look that screams *really?* "I'll do mine if you do yours," he says with a lifted eyebrow.

I frown. "What's my homework?"

"Watching *Hereditary*. You're not allowed to call yourself a horror fan if you've never seen it."

A shudder runs through me at even the title. "I can't do paranormal horror by myself. I'll have nightmares for weeks."

Roman shrugs. "Didn't realize my homework was optional. Guess I won't do mine, either."

Now it's his turn to get a *really?* look. "Fine. I'll watch it. But if you get an email from my boss saying you've been traded to a new PT, you'll know why."

His chuckle floats behind him as he starts toward his ride. "Goodnight, Doc."

I'm still smiling as I walk toward my car. "Goodnight, Roman."

**12**

---

## ROMAN

"Come *on*, quit being such a pussy and play another game!"

Sighing, I pull my headphones off and place them beside me. I hit my limit of teenage boy insults twenty minutes ago, so that one pretty much did me in.

I drag a hand down my face as I lean back against the couch. I've been sitting here for almost three hours, killing time with video games while I wait for Mikey to get off work.

Debating getting a head start on the night, I look at the fridge where I put the beer earlier. It's become an unspoken tradition for our Fridays to consist of alcohol and video games. I already did my physical therapy for the day, made myself food, napped, and now I'm just bored.

Glancing at my phone, I have an errant thought wondering what Lily is doing right now. Is she working at the clinic tonight? Is she at home? Is she watching a movie? Maybe one that I recommended.

Part of me wishes I could text her. But even if I had her number, I'm not entirely sure I *could* text her, what with our professional relationship and everything.

*Or even if she'd be receptive to it.*

My sigh is heavier this time, knowing the likely answer to that question but not having the mental fortitude to acknowledge it. I should just stick to being her problem patient, horror movies aside.

I look at the time and calculate that I have another hour before Mikey shows up. I'm sick of playing video games with thirteen-year-old boys, so that's out. I also don't really feel like drinking, so that's out, too.

Glancing down the hallway, my attention zeroes in on the office-turned-gym. I already did my PT today, but...

I pull my wheelchair over without a second thought. I'm sick of slow progress. More exercising should mean quicker recovery, right?

And as I reach for the resistance band and start in on another workout, I ignore the little part of my brain that's imagining a certain blonde cheering me on.

---

The next day, my session with Lily starts the same way it always does. With me climbing onto the treatment table to complete the same exercises we always kick off with.

As Lily moves to the end of the table to flex my foot, I lean back on my hands and watch her. I don't know if I thought our late night at the clinic this week would make it weird between us, but I'm actually a little relieved to have things feeling more comfortable.

"So...since I don't have a new PT assigned to me, am I right in assuming you haven't watched *Hereditary* yet?" I ask her. Then, a slow grin stretches across my face. "Or did you watch it and actually *like* it?"

She sends me an exasperated look that only makes me grin harder. "You should make peace with the idea of me hating it because, I'll tell you right now, there's zero chance I'm going to like it." Ducking her head, she mumbles, "And no, I haven't watched it yet."

I tsk. "I'm disappointed. I thought we had a deal."

Lily huffs as she moves to my other foot. "Our only *deal* is your insurance paying me to be your drill sergeant."

"Ah. My mistake. I thought you were moral enough to honor a verbal contract."

She straightens and puts her hands on her hips so she can glare at me.

I shrug, unable to hide my smirk. "All I'm saying is, I kept up my end of the deal."

At that, Lily's gaze drops to my legs. "No kidding," she says distractedly. "I can see a difference in your range of motion. Have you been doing your exercises every day?"

When I don't answer, she cups my heel and calf and pushes my leg back toward my chest. I wince when it strains my hamstring.

"Did that hurt?" she demands.

"Just sore," I grumble.

A grin slowly stretches across Lily's face. "Because you've been working out a lot," she asks, though it doesn't sound like a question.

Once again, I don't answer.

"Who knew all I had to do to get you to do your homework is promise to watch a movie," she says with a chuckle, gently putting my leg down.

I drop my head with a sigh of defeat. "Believe me, I had no idea I was so easy."

I expect her to rip on me some more, but when she doesn't, my gaze moves back to her. She's watching me, her expression soft but unreadable.

"I'll watch whatever you want me to watch if it gets you

to do your PT," she says gently. Then she holds up two fingers with a warm smile. "Scouts honor this time. I promise to honor the verbal contract."

I quirk an eyebrow in mock-disbelief instead. "I'll believe it when I see it."

Lily returns her focus to my leg with a smile. "That's fair."

But then it fades, concentration appearing in its place. "Do you get massages?" she asks distractedly.

"Sometimes. When the aches and pains get bad."

She purses her lips. "You should get them regularly. They're great as preventative maintenance."

I open my mouth to tease her, to tell her I've heard that a million times, but I never get any words out. Because her thumb starts to massage my calf and every thought flies from my head.

I must be wearing a dumbstruck expression because she notices. "Can you feel that?" she asks, misinterpreting my surprise.

It's not that there *is* sensation that's stunned me. It's *her* touch.

She feels...warm.

Swallowing roughly, I nod. She puts her other hand on my calf, and I watch as she starts to massage the muscle.

I think I hold my breath the entire time. She drives her thumb into the meat of the muscle, kneading and pulling. Slowly working her way along my leg, it isn't until she reaches my ankle that the sensation changes.

Having an incomplete spinal cord injury means I lost some sensations but not all. The neural pathways that still connect to the brain are the areas where I can still feel—the other ones, it's either numbness and tingling or nothing at all.

"Have you ever done anything with sensory re-education?" Lily asks, her massage becoming more of a brush of her hand instead of a knead of the muscle as she glances up at me. "I lost you around the ankle, didn't I?"

Swallowing roughly, I nod. "I did *some* sensory stuff. But I was never..." I trail off. *I was never consistent with it.*

Lily hesitates for a moment before saying lightly, "We can add a few minutes of it onto our sessions, if you want."

My eyes drop down to her hand. I can barely feel her touch where she has it, and I kind of hate it. I *want* to feel it.

I want to feel *her*.

But I try to play off my mounting desperation anyway. My voice sounds rough as I say, "You don't have to do that. I know you're at the end of your shift by the time I come in."

She looks up from where she had her eyes trained on my foot, and locks onto my face instead. I can feel her studying me: my words, my intention behind them—my general fear around therapy. And I sense she can see through all of it.

Pulling in a small breath, she says quietly, "Touching you isn't exactly exhausting."

My eyes widen. There's no way to misinterpret her comment. It's the closest she's come to the professional boundary between us, and I'm at a loss for words as to how to respond to it.

Her gaze still locked with mine, she sees my speechlessness and seems to make the decision to just push right past the moment. Looking back down at my leg, she says, "You really *should* do some sensory re-education. With me or someone else. Neuroplasticity is the most heightened in the first year, but you can still do a lot with it right now."

The part that *I'm* going to push past is the idea of doing this with anyone else. "You're right, I should be adding that into my therapy." Clearing my throat with a cough, I add, "If you wouldn't mind taking the extra few minutes, I'd appreciate the help."

"Of course. How about this…" She looks around, then crosses the room to grab a towel. "I'll go over your legs with a towel first, then I'll follow with a massage. We'll try a different texture every session."

I nod, feeling weirdly nervous. "Okay."

The towel's texture is an odd one. Despite using one every day when I shower, the sensation of Lily dragging it over my skin, sometimes lightly and sometimes with a little more pressure, feels new. Especially when she reaches an area where I lost nerve sensation, the shift from feeling the rough texture to feeling only pressure is bizarre.

Lily takes her time moving the towel over my feet, my calves, and over the lower part of my thighs. After a few minutes, she sets the towel aside and says, "I'm going to wash my hands with cold water before I massage you. The temperature shock might help with things."

Once again, I nod automatically, trying to ignore the bubble of nerves in my stomach. *Why the fuck am I so nervous?*

When she lays her hand on the top of my foot, I suck in a startled breath.

"Shit, that's cold," I say through gritted teeth.

Chuckling, she moves to the other foot. Same jolt of surprise. When she moves to my ankle, her hands feel slightly warmer, but still cold.

I frown when I realize what just happened.

"You feel that, don't you?" Lily asks with a smug grin.

I don't respond, too stunned by the sensation of temperature on a part of my body that's been mostly useless for the past two years.

Slowly, Lily slides her hands around to my heel. And

then over my ankles, up my calves, and to my knees, tracing her hands over my skin and reacquainting my body with her touch. Before long, I'm lost in a haze of awe and sensation.

Her hands have warmed as she's moved up my leg, but it isn't until they register as *warm* on my quad that something occurs to me that makes me tense up.

I don't know how high on the leg she plans to go, but if she goes any higher, her hands are going to have an effect. And it's not an effect that either of us is ready for.

It's no secret that spinal cord injuries, even in the most minor of cases, affect sexual function. My injury affected everything below my hips, so obviously my dick is included in that picture. And even though I've been able to get somewhat reacquainted with it—and gain an understanding, if not always control, of it—in the two years since the accident, it's still an entirely unpredictable area of my lower body.

I have no idea what might happen when a hot woman is touching my leg.

I don't realize I'm holding my breath with anticipation until Lily stops her massage and straightens.

"Okay, that's enough procrastinating. Let's get you started on some strength exercises."

# 13

## LILIANA

When I walk into the clinic a few days later, I'm surprised to be pulled into my boss's office.

"So," Fran starts, taking a seat and gesturing for me to do the same. "How's the therapy going with Roman?"

Thank God, I don't blush easily because my first reaction to her question is sheer panic. Which is stupid because I haven't done anything to be panicked *about*.

"Good," I squeak out. I clear my throat and try again. "I mean, slow, but good. Why?"

Fran waves me off. "No reason. He's just a high-profile client—and a tough one, at that. This is more so me checking on you."

I frown, not liking that label for Roman. "He's not *tough*, he's just..." I search for the right word. "He can't find the right reason," I say after a moment.

Fran cocks her head, studying me. "What do you mean by that?"

I release a heavy breath. "I mean, a lot of our patients are just trying to rehab an injury. So their end goals are obvious. And the athletes...even if they won't *progress* their career, their goal is to get back to playing. At whatever capacity. But Roman... He'll never fight again. It might be a miracle if he even *walks* again. And..." I swallow roughly as I meet Fran's eyes, and I wonder if she can see the pain in my heart. "I think he thinks he's useless without those things."

Fran hums thoughtfully as she mulls over my assessment. "His file said he wasn't seeing a psychologist when he was admitted here. Do you know if he's started talking to someone since you started treatment?"

I shake my head, too nervous to admit that I think *I* might be the closest thing Roman has to a therapist.

"See if you can nudge him to see someone, if he isn't already," Fran says. "I'd be surprised if he wasn't, but you never know. If what you're saying is true, he, of all people, needs to be talking to someone." She glances at her watch. "Beyond that, how's the physical therapy going? Is he improving?"

I debate how to answer before saying honestly, "Slowly, but yes. Since he's seen so many therapists, I started a lot of things from scratch. But...yes, he's making progress."

Fran gives me a pleased nod. "Good. I had a feeling I made the right call putting him with you, but I'm glad to hear his progress is proving it. And he's been treating you okay? You know I won't tolerate him being disrespectful."

A memory of one of Roman's daily glares flashes through my thoughts. "He's been the perfect student."

Another nod at that. "Good. If that changes, just let me know. Say the word, and I'll transfer him to someone else."

I force down the flame of possessiveness that flickers through my chest at the thought. "Thank you, but I don't think that will be necessary," I say with a forced smile.

"Alright then," Fran says, standing from her chair and

opening the office door for me. "Keep up the good work, Lily."

When I leave her office and head downstairs for my appointment with Roman, my heart is still beating powerfully. I knew I had grown protective of Roman when he first started to let me in, and I knew I enjoyed his company even before that, but feeling the full weight of my emotions for him when confronted by it is a whole different story. I didn't realize how much I've started to care for him.

And as I walk into the gym to find Roman shirtless and sweaty, the kind of feelings I'm developing become that much harder to ignore.

My mouth immediately goes dry at the sight before me. Roman is still sitting in his wheelchair, but right now, he's using it as an exercise weight instead of a mobility tool. Because he's currently strapped in and working on pull-ups at the pull-up bar.

I watch in slack-jawed amazement as he pulls himself up once, twice, *five* times just in the time I'm standing here. His skin glistens with sweat, the shine making his muscles the only thing I can look at. Even the chain around his neck, the one I've been curious about ever since I realized Roman hides it under his shirts, isn't enough to pull my attention away.

I knew wheelchair users often have impressive upper body muscles from having to push themselves around all day, but I never could have pictured Roman's back and arms, even in my wildest fantasies. He's *shredded*. I don't know if he just has a naturally muscular build, or if he actually works them out, but either way, this vision of Roman is something that is going to stick with me for a long, *long* time.

When he finally maxes out his reps and instead hangs on the bar in a hold, I realize I need to make my presence known. I have to swallow twice—*twice*—before I can get my voice to work. "W-what are you doing?"

Roman lets go of the bar and lands on the carpet with a muffled crash. Spinning his wheelchair around, he faces me and says simply, "Pull-ups."

I feel a bead of sweat run down between my shoulder blades underneath my scrubs. "Um...why?" Then I shake my head to clear some of the haze from my brain. "And why are you shirtless?"

He's reaching for his shirt before my question is even finished. I feel a flash of disappointment as he pulls his t-shirt over his head, and I take that as a clear sign I need to get my shit together. Training my eyes on his face, I refuse to let them drift again.

"Sorry," he says—though he doesn't sound like he means it. "Ever since showers—and laundry—became a hassle, I try to limit how much I sweat. I just wanted to see how many I could do before we got started."

Curious, I can't help asking, "And how many did you do?"

Roman wipes his brow and says nonchalantly, "Ten. Not as many as I thought I could."

I gape at him. "*Ten* is not that many?"

"I used to be able to get thirty plus," he says with a shrug.

"I'm assuming that's without the forty-pound wheel-chair," I say dryly.

Another shrug. "I lost that much in muscle, so it evens out."

I throw my hands up in the air with a huff. "You are so *annoying* when you're negative, I swear."

Roman quirks an eyebrow, an arrogant smirk tugging at his lips. "Interesting. You didn't seem annoyed with me a minute ago." When I frown in confusion, he jerks his head sideways. "I could see you watching me in the mirror."

My cheeks *burn* when I catch his meaning. "I...I d-don't know what you're talking about."

"Is that how you want to play it?" Roman asks, his grin shameless. "That's fine; we can pretend like nothing happened."

I channel my embarrassment into a glare. "Let's just...get started with your session."

Roman's grin doesn't lose any wattage. "Sure, Doc. Whatever you want."

He rolls over to the treatment table, and as he pulls himself up onto it, I swear there's a pep to his movements.

It takes me busying myself with gathering some of our usual equipment to tamp down on my embarrassment over Roman catching me basically checking him out. But by the time I wrap the blood pressure cuff around his arm and realize he's still smug as hell, I manage a grumbled, "If I had known stroking your ego was going to put you in such a good mood, I would've done it weeks ago."

When I glance up at him, Roman's face is closer than I expect it to be. "You don't have to stroke my ego to put me in a good mood, Liliana," he says in a low voice. One that sends a shiver down my spine.

Swallowing roughly, I force myself to respond. "What else would put you in a good mood, Roman?"

Something flashes in his eyes, too quick for me to read. But then he plasters a clearly mocking grin on his face as he says, "Why, your charming personality, of course."

I blink, then let out a long-suffering—and dramatic—sigh as I take his wrist. "I'm going to remind you of that next time you complain about my methods. Now shush, I have to count."

It's impossible to ignore Roman's pleased expression as I finish checking his vitals, though Lord knows I try. I can't get the vision of him doing shirtless pull-ups out of my head. Because of the still-sweaty muscles, yes, but also because I'm now realizing he has way more tattoos than I thought. His usual t-shirt and shorts attire obviously revealed on day one that he has two full tattoo sleeves, but now I know most of his chest and back are covered, too.

By the time we start with our usual stretches, I'm too curious not to broach the subject. I keep my eyes on his legs as I say casually, "You've gotten a lot of tattoos since the night we met."

When Roman stiffens at my question, there's nothing flirtatious in the air between us anymore. I've touched on something sensitive.

But he gives me a stiff nod, which gives me enough of a green light to ask, "Did you have any two years ago? Or these are all new?"

A few seconds tick by. Then, "I had one back then."

I hum in thought as we move to the next stretch, debating how far I want to take my questions when so much of my job is keeping him comfortable. But something is telling me the tattoos are part of his post-injury psyche.

In the end, I ask the only question I want answered.

"So...what's the reason for all the ink?"

Again, he hesitates. But after a moment, he says simply, "I wanted to feel something."

My eyes shoot up to his face with a frown. "What do you mean?"

He shrugs. "After the accident, I got hyper fixated on sensation. I'd try to trick myself into believing I could feel my legs again. When that didn't work, I started to focus on sensations I *could* feel. Namely, in my upper body." His eyes meet mine. "The pain of a tattoo became addicting."

*Oh.* I never thought of it that way.

"I was fully intending to tattoo my legs in the spots I got sensation back, but..." He exhales, and it sounds dejected. "I don't know, I guess I started feeling guilty about the money. I spent way too much on the ink because even though I never had specific tattoos in mind, I realized I preferred the more detailed styles."

"No kidding," I murmur, my focus dropping down to the beautifully complex image on his arm. Roman's entire right arm has a Roman theme, everything from a gladiator to the statue of a god. The way the images are woven together in black and white...it's incredible.

Without thinking, my fingers trace over the sword on his forearm. "It's beautiful," I say quietly. "It must've taken forever."

When I'm met with silence, my gaze darts back to Roman's face. He's studying me, watching me admire the art on his skin.

"You have any tattoos, Doc?" he asks after a moment.

I let out an awkward laugh as I straighten. "Me? No. I'd be a total baby."

Roman's lip quirks. "So, you'll jump out of a plane, but a little tattoo is too scary?"

I shrug as I grab a resistance band for us. "That sounds completely logical to me."

Roman's chuckle has me relaxing, and I manage a small smile.

"Whatever you say, Doc."

# 14

# ROMAN

With a heavy groan, I slump down in the seat of the leg extension machine. *God, that was hard.*

I miss shit being hard. I *loved* when workouts were hard. There was a certain level of satisfaction that came from the training sessions that ended with me dead on the couch. It was a sign that I pushed my body as far as physically possible, and that always felt like a victory in itself.

Getting back into strength training these past few weeks has been incredible. It didn't take me long to realize after my injury that the *not feeling* was a much bigger mental roadblock than I anticipated—some days, I almost wished I felt pain instead of nothing, because at least pain used to be a sign of progress and strengthening. And when I started feeling fireworks in my body a few months after my injury, and I realized it was the sign I was about to recover sensation in that part of my leg, I thought I would have that sense of victory back. But it wasn't until I really committed to this strength training with Lily that it truly returned. I revel in the soreness these days. And if I'm not sore enough, I go home and do an ab or upper body workout to compensate.

Regardless of the muscle being affected, I feel *alive* for the first time in what seems like forever.

Lily peeks at the weight the pin is in and frowns. "When did you bump that to twenty pounds?"

I grin through the sweat dripping down my face. "I wanted to challenge myself."

She shakes her head, but there's a smile on her lips. "You're either an underachiever or an overachiever—you never know how to be right in the middle."

"I don't like being average," I muse, chest still heaving with exertion.

"Trust me, you're anything but average," Lily murmurs, her eyes still on the chart in her hand.

My grin widens. "Are you saying that as my therapist or as Liliana?"

My question makes her refocus her attention on me with a pinched brow, which then makes her quiet confession register and her cheeks to pinken.

*Fuck, I love making her blush.*

"So I was thinking..." she rushes to say, crossing her arms over the clipboard on her chest. "We should start doing some gait training exercises. They work best when they're done concurrently with strength training, so I think we're at a good spot for it. What do you think?"

I swallow thickly, all humor and playfulness disappearing as memories swarm me.

Sensing my mood shift, Lily's voice is gentle as she asks, "Have you done any gait training before?"

Another rough swallow, but this time, I nod. I don't want to tell her about how gait training was the trigger for my biggest meltdown last year, and the thing that made me lose all hope that I would ever walk again. It was what put me in the black hole that Lily found me in a few weeks ago.

Because when I failed as miserably as I did with *assisted* walking, I came face to face with the knowledge that I was never going to be able to walk again. I couldn't treat it as a *maybe one day* anymore.

And I'm terrified that it's going to happen again.

"I should probably focus a little more on lifting," I tell her, not making eye contact. "I'd feel better if I was stronger."

Lily studies me in my periphery, and I can sense she's about to push me.

My body tenses in preparation. I'm about to lash out at her, I know I am. I'm not *ready* for this shit.

"Okay. I understand. But I want to do some calves next time, instead."

My head snaps up. "What?"

She shrugs. "I said okay. You know your body better than I do. The last thing I want to do is tell you what you are or aren't ready for."

Eyes narrowing in her direction, my tone is skeptical as I ask, "Who are you and what have you done with my tough love PT."

Lily smiles, and I wonder if that was a flash of relief in her eyes just now. "She's on vacation today, but she'll be back next week." Her gaze slides down to my legs. "She'd probably tell you to do another two sets on the leg extension machine if she were here. But since she's not"—she throws a towel at me that I catch—"you're officially done for the day."

"I feel like this is a setup," I mutter, dragging the towel down my sweaty face. "I swear to God, if you make me do double the reps next week—"

Lily's laugh is a sweet, tinkling sound I can't get enough of. "It's not, I swear. I just know you're pretty sore and don't want to push you any harder. My old trainer told me it's better to be 90% trained than 101% overtrained."

"Remind me to introduce you to my old boxing coaches," I say with a snort as I transfer over to my wheelchair. "They'll dissuade you of that mentality real quick."

She shrugs, still smiling. "Maybe. But I'm coming from a place of health. In my experience, high-level pro athletes trample all over health as a priority when their goal is world domination."

I don't respond, too stuck on Lily's experience with high-level pro athletes. *Has she ever worked with a fighter? Is she currently working with a fighter? What if I know who he is? What if—*

"Case in point," Lily says, interrupting my train of thought as she steps closer to me. "You're sore everywhere, aren't you? You've been working out a lot. *Too* much."

She gets her answer when she squeezes my shoulder muscle, and I can't hide my wince.

"I knew it. Your movements have all been stiff today." Shifting to stand behind me, her other hand also drops to my shoulder. When she starts to knead the muscle, the deepest groan I've ever heard rumbles out of my chest.

"Jesus, you're tight," Lily murmurs, digging even harder into the muscle. "Is this all from pull-ups? How many did you do, a million?"

I don't know if she's actually waiting for an answer. Even if she was, I couldn't assemble one, lost to everything that isn't this massage.

*Fuck,* it hurts. Clearly, Lily knows what she's doing, because this is equal parts pain and relief.

"Holy shit, that feels good," I groan, my head dropping forward to give her more surface area to massage. "Fuck being a psychologist, you could be a masseuse."

"We had to take a massage course in school," Lily explains, but she sounds distracted. When she moves to the area between my shoulder blades and kneads twice as hard, I let out another groan of pain.

Her hands leave my body, and I lift my head to protest her stopping. But when I catch sight of her reflection in the mirror, I realize she's only pulling her sleeves up, a determined look on her face. Then she returns to punishing my muscles.

"Okay, note to self," she grunts after a few minutes of massaging—and several groans later. "Put limits on your strength training homework. These knots are *insane,* Roman."

I let out a half-assed sound of agreement, barely listening. In only a few minutes, her hands have rubbed out most of the knots, and now the massage has melted into that pleasant kind that people pay hundreds of dollars for as stress relief.

"Seriously. No more pull-ups for you," she grumbles. Shifting to the side of my wheelchair, she starts to work on my arms now, her thumbs digging into my tricep.

"Whatever you say, Doc," I slur, turning my head to watch her motions.

By the time she's massaging my forearms, I've become mesmerized by her hands. They're smooth and blemish-free, and her short nails are the cutest shade of pale pink. But it's the way they move that really draws my attention. She's so skilled, and the firm way in which she grips me makes me feel like putty beneath her touch. I've never felt like—

Suddenly, her movements stop. When she pulls her hands back, I look up at her in confusion, only to see she's avoiding my eyes and awkwardly rubbing her thighs.

"Well, um...hopefully, that helped," she rambles, still not meeting my eyes. "I can suggest a great massage therapist if you'd like to stay on top of those knots; she'll get you fixed up in no time..."

I frown, still lost about what just happened. Is a massage considered inappropriate? She just said she had to take a class—

It isn't until I glance down at my lap that I realize what happened.

And everything in me goes cold.

My dick is hard. And it's not like an *oh whoops, I saw a pretty girl and got a chub* erection, it's *hard*. Like a *I popped three Viagras, and I've never been harder* erection. And with the basketball shorts I'm wearing, there's no hiding it.

My cheeks heat, the embarrassment so thick it feels like tar as I try to take a breath. A buzzing starts in my head. I don't know what to say. How to react. What to *do*.

Logically, I know Lily is a professional. She's entirely aware of the things that can happen with this type of injury, and she'd handle it appropriately, regardless of if I wanted to ignore it or talk about it. Medically, there's nothing I should be embarrassed about.

Realistically, that couldn't be further from the truth.

My skin flaming hotter and hotter, I look in the opposite direction of Lily, searching for anything I can throw over my lap and attempt to hide my shame. But there's nothing. I don't even have the sweatshirt I came in here with since it's back on the treatment table.

One more second of indecision, another of sheer humiliation, and then I give up. I can't deal with this. Turning my wheelchair, I start toward the exit.

"Roman, no, wait—"

I ignore Lily's plea and simply leave the gym.

It takes my mom two unanswered questions to figure out that something's happened and I need to be left alone. She doesn't even ask me if I need help getting into the house like she normally does; she just gives me a sad smile as she gets out of the van.

I don't know why I rush into my house, because the second I'm in my kitchen, I'm at a complete loss with what to do with myself. Do I go to my home gym and workout until I pass out from exhaustion? Do I drink myself into a blackout? What's the quickest way to get me to unconsciousness so I don't need to think about what the *fuck* just happened?

It's been a long time since I've had an uncontrollable erection. I mostly figured it had to do with nothing turning me on mentally anymore. Some SCI patients get them from physical stimulation but don't feel pleasure from it, and some feel pleasure but need physical help to get it up. I thought I was one of the lucky ones who eventually gained enough sensation to have the best of both worlds—just with no one to experience it with. I never *dreamed* it would happen with Lily.

God*fucking*damnit, does she think I ran out of there because I was shocked to spring a boner? I'm sure my mortification was obvious, but if she thinks my dick doesn't work, I'm never fucking going back there again. A man can only take so many hits to the ego.

Looking down at my lap, I glare at my now-soft dick. *Fucking useless.*

I wrap a hand around it through my shorts, giving it one angry tug. *Nothing.*

But then I mentally drift back to the moment before

everything went wrong: the one where I was watching Lily massage my arms. It makes sense that the sight of her hands triggered what it did, what with the sight and feel of them. It doesn't take a big mental leap to picture them wrapped around my cock.

Instantly, I harden in my grip. A wave of pleasure nearly bowls me over at the thought of Lily using both hands on me, of her twisting and tugging and sliding them up and down my length. *Fuck*, I bet she'd feel good. Better than good. And if her hands are that good, I can't even imagine how great she'd feel if—

I yank back my hand with a snarl of disgust. I'm kidding myself if I think that would ever happen. She's young, and pretty, and has everything going for her. She deserves to have a guy who has everything going for *him*. Even if it's just the bedroom, she should have someone who can fuck her properly, not just lie there on his back like a useless sex doll. Even jerking off to the thought of it is a joke.

With frustration mounting in my chest, I grab my cigarettes off the kitchen counter and hope the smoke can drown out my self-hatred.

# 15

# LILIANA

Grad school doesn't prepare you for patients like Roman Ward.

I knew there were going to bumps in the road of his recovery. I may not have guessed that they would be *this* kind of bump, but the fact that his body reacted during a massage isn't really a big surprise. It's a common occurrence with SCI patients, both with the unexpected nature of it and the potential lack of sensation that lets them know it's happening.

The bumps in the road aren't the issue. It's Roman's reaction to them that I'm worried about.

Case in point...it's been a week since I've seen him.

And I've been stressed the whole time. Even my brothers noticed something was off when I showed up to family dinner last weekend. I almost called Roman that night, too worried to go another day without checking on him, but...I couldn't. Ethically, I probably could have, just as a simple check-in on a patient, but that's not why I'd be calling. And on top of that, I wanted to give Roman a chance to solve things on his own. To come back to physical therapy because he wants to.

I'm one missed session away from showing up at his house and banging on his door when he finally appears in the clinic.

I do a triple take when I spot him. He looks tired, with dark bags under his eyes and a general weariness to his demeanor.

"Roman. You're here."

He doesn't nod or respond with anything. I have a feeling today is going to be an appointment of few words.

For the first time, I'm flustered. I'm not sure the best way to handle this. It doesn't matter that I haven't been sleeping well with how much I've thought about what I'd say to Roman when he came back in, or that I've practiced a dozen different motivational speeches in the past week—right now, I'm terrified of doing or saying the wrong thing.

My hands are shaking as I hurry to put away my last patient's notes that I was finishing up. "Um... just give me a second. I can be ready in a minute."

He doesn't answer. He just turns and heads toward the stretching area.

After I finish cleaning up and move over to where Roman has started his exercises, it takes me a few minutes to work up the nerve to speak again.

In the end, what comes out in a too-high voice is, "Did you have a good week?"

I wince as soon as the words are out. "I mean...what did you do this week?"

Once again, he ignores me.

Another minute of silence. More of me frowning and biting my bottom lip.

"Did you think any more about starting gait training?" I ask, my voice gentler this time.

At that, Roman lets go of the retraction band he was working with, making it go flying across the room. Then he's pulling his wheelchair over so he can move to the weights area.

This is a quicker progression than we usually follow, but since I'm already paddling upstream with Roman, telling him what not to do probably won't win me any favors right now. So I let him go, while keeping a close eye on him.

Now he's on the leg extension machine working leg raises. I can see the way his jaw clenches after the first rep, and I know he's feeling the weight of it. I can also see how that fact makes him angrier than he already is.

Somehow, with shaky legs and gritted teeth, he gets to eight reps. Then he drops the weight with a loud clang and exhales a heavy breath.

My concern only mounts. "Maybe you should go a little easier—"

He locks his feet in for another set.

Six reps later, he drops the weight again, his chest heaving as he sucks in air. His legs are now shaking from the exertion, not just during the reps but after.

And yet, I still don't say anything. It isn't until he moves over to the free weights that I get seriously worried.

"I don't think that's a good idea, Roman."

"Well, you don't actually get a say," he spits back. Leaning down to grab one of the dumbbells, he settles back in his seat and places the weight on his thigh. One of the 'functional' exercises we had just started doing was first pressing up onto his toes to work his calves, and then lifting his knee completely to work his quads. But we hadn't gotten around to it yet, because working with free weights is a lot more dangerous than using the machines.

Roman sucks in a breath to prepare himself, then presses up on the ball of his right foot.

And then he does it again. And again, until his leg is shaking. On the fourth lift, I know he realizes that he's grabbed a weight that's too heavy.

*Goddamnit.* I want to snatch the weight out of his lap. I *should.* He's going to seriously hurt himself if he keeps up with this. But I'm still a little shocked that he's even here, and I'm so out of my element with his current emotional state. Plus, I know if I *do* grab it, he's going to absolutely lose his shit with me.

As all these thoughts flip through my head, Roman is moving the dumbbell over to his left leg. Which is even worse news, because his left leg is still weaker than his right. He's just setting himself up for failure.

He sucks in another determined breath, manages to press up on his foot one time, and then as I shoot forward to grab the weight—his pride be damned—I watch as his leg loses all strength in the muscles and goes crashing down, the dumbbell sliding out of his grip and onto his foot.

"Roman!" I shout, stomach sinking as I rush around to his front. "What the *hell!* Are you hurt?"

He's panting, looking stunned by the last few seconds. Too overwhelmed to react.

As I start to untie the shoe that the weight dropped on, that gets him talking.

"*Don't,*" he bites out.

My brow furrows as I glare up at him. "I have to check. You may have broken something."

"Wouldn't matter. It's not like I need the foot anyway."

With a growl of frustration, I straighten to stand before

him, planting my hands on my hips. "What is *wrong* with you today?"

He holds my eyes in challenge but doesn't answer.

But something in his defensive expression makes me soften, and I remind myself that he's struggling with a big hurdle in his recovery.

"Is this because of last week?" I ask, pushing through my hesitance around the subject. "Because you know that doesn't mean anything to me. I know with your injury—"

The reminder of our last session makes his face instantly blaze with visible humiliation. He spins away from me and starts to move in the opposite direction.

"Roman, come *on*, you can't let something like that stop your recovery." When I jump in front of him, and he brakes so he doesn't hit me.

"If you care about my recovery *at all*," he says with his jaw clenched, "you'll never mention last week ever again."

Swallowing thickly, I nod. "Okay. I understand... But only if you don't let it affect your sessions. You can't do what you just did, it's dangerous."

"You don't get to set my limits, Liliana," he spits, trying to get around me.

I hold my ground, determined to have this conversation.

"Isn't it against your physical therapist oath to hold your patients' disabilities against them?" He gestures to his wheelchair and lack of mobility.

"No," I snap without a second thought. "And even if it was, I'd still use whatever cheat method I could to get you to talk to me."

"I don't want to fucking talk to you," he barks.

"Too fucking bad," I bark back. "Clearly, it's affecting your therapy. We can't work on your recovery until we move past whatever this is."

He looks away, an angry scowl on his face. It's the first time in weeks that he's thrown what can only be called a temper tantrum.

"Did you honestly think this recovery process wouldn't come with hiccups?" I ask, holding firm in my stance and my confrontation. This feels like a make-or-break moment. "Did you think it was just a matter of lifting a bunch of weights, of committing to some walking exercises, and that was it?"

His frown deepening tells me I nailed it.

"It's hard work, Roman. There are *going* to be hiccups. But you know what? Hiccups mean progress. And you should know better than anyone that progress isn't linear."

His Adam's apple bobs, and it's the first time his expression softens. A little bit of that anger and embarrassment fade, to be replaced by pain.

But he's still scowling, still unable to let himself get past this particular hurdle. So I try the tactic that has been the only thing to work with him thus far: tough love.

I glare down at him, even though he's still not looking at me. "So, if you could kindly get the fuck *over* yourself, we could just treat this as one of those totally normal, part-of-the-process speed bumps, and get back to your recovery."

Roman finally looks at me again, a hundred emotions swirling in his eyes but with astonishment at the forefront. I just wait it out.

Finally, he murmurs, "Damn, Liliana. That was brutal, even for you."

I let out a huff and drop my hands to my sides, feeling suddenly exhausted. "Sorry," I grumble. "You had me at my wit's end."

"Apparently," he returns dryly.

Then I watch as my words *really* sink in, as he takes them to heart and finally accepts them.

"You're right," he sighs, looking uncharacteristically sheepish. "I'm sorry. I guess...I was riding the self-pity a little hard."

"A little?" I ask with a snort.

"Okay, fine. I've been an unbearable prick with it lately."

I sniff. "You said it, not me."

He shakes his head, the tiniest smile peeking out that might as well be bright enough to light up the entire room with the way it hits me in the chest.

"You should tell the board about your therapy strategies," he says. "I've never had a therapist talk to me the way you do, and yet I've made more progress in the past two months than anywhere else. Clearly, you've revolutionized patient care."

"Well, in that case, I'd like to continue that progress." I can't help glaring at him as I add, "So, can we get back to your therapy? Please?"

He nods, seemingly just as mentally exhausted as me, but at least he's here. At least he's willing to move on.

"Good. Before we do anything, I'm going to check your foot to make sure you didn't bruise or fracture anything—and FYI, you better *hope* you didn't." The more I go on, the more my tone hardens to one of taking no shit. "Then we're going to use the rest of the session for stretching and a massage so I can evaluate how much progress we've lost in the past week. And if you get an erection, we're both going to ignore it, *and* I'm going to see you right back here on Monday night. Capisce?"

"Jesus, Lily," Roman says with a wince, swiping a hand down his face. "Seriously? Could you not?"

But I'm not backing down from this. This last week can't happen again.

In a move I've never ever used before but that feels suddenly right to break the tension of this moment, I extend my pinky to Roman. "Pinky promise right now, or I'm transferring you to a different physical therapist."

His eyes widen before he smooths the expression. "I really hate you right now."

I keep my pinky extended. "I hate you back, so that's okay."

He glares for another moment, then quickly reaches forward to roughly entwine our pinkies together. "You are certifiable," he grumbles.

I hold on to his finger, ignoring the spark that shoots up my arm at the contact. "Whatever it takes to get you to your feet, Roman."

**16**

——

# LILIANA

To my surprise, Roman and I fall right back into our usual routine. He continues to progress, doing his PT homework on his own and showing up to every one of our sessions with a desire to get better. His consistent effort is really starting to pay off, and he's getting noticeably stronger.

Things feel easy between us, too. He still has grumpy days, and I still give him tough love, but things are friendly. Normal.

One month after I first brought it up, I decide to ask Roman about gait training again.

"So, are you waiting to hit your pre-injury leg press PR before learning to walk again?"

He pauses his movement of increasing the weight on the machine. "Sorry, Doc, I don't speak in code."

I nod at his legs. "We need to start your gait training."

Immediately, a wall shutters over his eyes. It happened the first time I brought it up, too. This part of his therapy is hard for him, which means I'll have to tread carefully.

He opens his mouth, then quickly closes it, his throat

130

bobbing on a swallow. I wait patiently for him to verbalize whatever is bothering him.

"This is where I gave up completely last time," he says after a moment.

I nod. I figured as much. Taking a seat on the floor in front of him, I take a deep breath and ask, "Was it one thing, specifically? Or what is it about this phase of your therapy?"

"Specifically? Specifically, it was failing at the act of walking."

I give him a look that says *really?*

Roman exhales a heavy breath and looks out into space. "I don't know, I guess the parts that came before gait training were just easier to deal with. They weren't *easy*, per se, but most days, I could think of regaining sensation as exciting, or strength training as familiar. But when I had to practice *standing* because my balance was off, and I got dizzy even being upright...it really punched me in the face how fucked up I was. I mean, I was literally working on the same skills as a *one*-year-old. And failing at it."

I nod my understanding as I pull my knees up and wrap my arms around them. Roman's admission doesn't surprise me, because it's a fairly normal reaction for SCI patients to have. There's something about learning to walk that humbles even the strongest patients.

But getting Roman to talk about this is a critical step in moving him along in his therapy. Unless I know where his head's at, he could very well give up on me like he has for every other PT he's worked with.

"Do you think being prepared for that feeling might make it easier this time around?"

He rubs his chest absentmindedly as he mulls over my question. "Maybe," he says finally. "It's possible that feeling like I was blind-sided by it last time made everything worse."

"Most likely." I hesitate for a moment before adding, "I think we should have a plan for how to deal with that feeling, though. Even if it's a plan of what *not* to do. Because it could very well happen this time around too."

Roman's gaze slides over to me, our eyes locking. "Is this where you tell me I should try therapy again?"

I shrug. "I think everyone could benefit from therapy. And yes, this is a perfect example of a situation where talking to a professional psychologist would be immeasurably helpful. But no, that's not what I was getting at."

Roman's eyes narrow in suspicion. "Then what are you getting at?"

Tightening my hold on my knees, I nervously chew on my bottom lip before finally admitting, "I'd feel better if we came up with some healthy coping strategies for you. Clearly, gait training is a stressor, and the last thing I want you to do is lose all your progress because you have a really bad day and go into a spiral."

Understanding dawns on his face. "Meaning, don't turn to my usual vices."

I wince. "It's just...you do so much better when you're not chain-smoking or hungover and actually doing your therapy between our sessions. Plus, you didn't show up for a *week* the last time things...went wrong."

*The time I made you hard with a massage and you got so freaked out that I thought I'd never see you again.*

I don't say that, but I can see by Roman's expression that he knows exactly what I'm referring to. What's worse is, it reinforces my point about him spiraling when things go wrong in his therapy.

Roman looks away from me, his throat bobbing. "Okay,

yes, I pick things that are bad for my health to deal with failure. What exactly would you like me to do instead? Take up knitting as a form of stress relief?"

Surprisingly, his sarcasm is a relief. Sarcasm is better than lashing out.

"I was thinking more along the lines of horror movies."

His eyes snap back to mine, his brow furrowed. "What is this, another reward system?"

I shake my head. "Not exactly. But you need to have something healthy to turn to when you inevitably have a bad therapy session, and escapism is a common stress relief tactic." My mouth curves into an amused grin. "Psychologists might argue that watching people get killed and mutilated shouldn't be classified as stress relief, but I was attempting to relate to my current audience."

Roman's own lip quirks with a reluctant smile. "There are *way* too many true crime junkies for that to be true."

I chuckle softly as I lean back and brace my hands on the floor. "Hey, I agree with you. Personally, I enjoy a little cannibal love story to wind down after a long day."

Roman's face twists with confusion. "What movie was *that*?"

"*Bones and All.* So good."

There's a pause before he responds with, "Okay, the psychologists might be right about this one."

I throw my head back with a laugh. "Fine, pick another coping strategy, then."

My word choice causes some of the levity to drain from our conversation, the mood between us sobering as Roman considers my request.

"I'll think about it," he says finally.

Which I'm actually thrilled to hear. It means he's taking this seriously.

"Deal," I say with a smile. "You think about it, and then next week, we'll start the next phase of your therapy. And we'll work through whatever comes. Together."

Something changes in his expression, something that's there and gone too fast for me to read.

But whatever it is, the sight of it makes my chest fill with a now-familiar warmth.

I can sense Roman's nerves the next time he comes into the clinic.

After our conversation the other day, I decided that the easiest assisted walking exercise for Roman to start with was going to be the parallel bars. His upper body strength is insane lately, so I'm not worried about any falls, and I figure since these bars are an actual Olympic sport, they're less likely to make him feel like a child learning to walk and more like a professional athlete practicing his skills.

That's what I'm crossing every one of my fingers and toes for, at least.

"Ready?" I ask Roman, plastering on as big of a smile as I can muster. Still not big enough to hide *my* nerves, though.

His posture is so tense, I wouldn't be surprised if he turned tail and left. But then a huge breath whooshes out of him, and he says in a voice like gravel, "As ever. Let's just get this shitshow over with."

I nod at Fran. With this being the first time, I couldn't in good conscience do it without some assistance. The fight with Roman to let someone else into our space just this once was worth the peace of mind that I got from knowing he'd be safe no matter how this session went.

And it *was* a fight. So much so that I thought we were

going to have to test his first coping strategy just because another human being was going to see him in a vulnerable position. Thankfully, it didn't come to that. And he's been amicable with Fran since she walked in here.

"Alright, come over to the bars here so Fran can get the harness around your chest," I instruct. "Let us know if anything hurts or feels uncomfortable and we'll adjust it."

"All this shit feels uncomfortable," he grumbles, rolling his wheelchair over to the parallel bars.

Fran's mouth twitches, but she doesn't comment. I made sure to remind her before she came in here that Roman was going to be extra crotchety today and in general doesn't do well with conversation, especially if it's motivational.

She holds the harness out for Roman to slide his arms through, fitting it around his chest and tightening everything so it can hold his weight. I mentally pat myself on the back for thinking to sleuth around for Roman's height and most recent weight before this. Moving around to stand between the parallel bars, I take up my place in front of him.

"You might feel dizzy at first when the machine pulls you up, so I need you to communicate with me about how things feel," I tell him. When he nods, I almost gesture for Fran to hit the switch that will lift Roman into the air.

But something makes me pause. Maybe it's the sheer terror in Roman's eyes, or maybe it's the fear beating in my chest. Whatever it is, it makes me sink into a moment where we're the only two people in this room.

I lower myself to my knees in front of Roman. His eyes stay locked on mine the entire time, enough trust flickering in his gaze that it makes some of the fear fade.

"Whether this takes one day, one week, a hundred weeks...we're going to get it. We'll figure out how to get you there. And not because you're no one if you can't walk, but because you're strong enough to make it happen."

Surprise alights in his expression. I hadn't intended to tell him that, and maybe I'm overstepping by saying it, but I'm glad I did anyway.

Straightening to a standing position, I add quietly, "I just needed you to know that."

I don't expect him to respond—the appreciation in his eyes is more than enough for me. Looking up at Fran, I nod for her to start the machine.

With a soft whirring sound, the line on the lift goes taut, then slowly starts to raise Roman into the air. I step forward and brace my hands on his hips.

"Harness okay? Anything cutting into you?" I ask hurriedly.

Roman shakes his head, though he's clenching his jaw so hard I can see every vein in his neck. He quickly reaches for the parallel bars.

"Okay? Are you dizzy? Do you need anything?"

"Doc...you're mother hen-ing," he says dryly, eyes sliding closed as he steadies himself.

A laugh bursts out of me. "Well, that's something I've never been called before."

"It's what I'm thinking every time you hover." He lets out a big exhale, then slowly opens his eyes. "Okay, I'm good."

*Thank God.* "Okay, then I'm going to sit in front of you and guide one leg at a time through a stepping motion. Slowly, so we hit every motion and muscle."

Roman nods, his jaw clenched once again. There's still dread in his expression, but I see determination, too.

Pulling over my rolling stool, I lower myself onto it so I'm at the perfect height to grab behind his knee with one hand and around his ankle with the other.

"I'm going to lift your leg and place it for the first step, but I want you to do as much of the lifting as you can. Ideally, I'm only guiding your leg." I send him a quick grin. "Time to finally put all that strength training to good use."

"One more of those and I might 'accidentally' kick you in the chest," he returns with a glare.

My focus is already back on his leg, my response unthinking as I mumble, "As your physical therapist, I mean it from the bottom of my heart when I say I would gladly eat a kick to the chest and consider it a roaring success."

I hear Roman's sigh above me. "I swear, your therapy methods need to be studied."

I give him an impatient poke in the thigh. "Yes, fine, I'll share my teachings with the Board. *After* you get walking. Chop chop."

Another sigh, but this time, I feel Roman's quad flex under my hand as he tries to lift his leg. It doesn't lift high enough for a safe step forward, but I'm pleased with the motion, regardless. Guiding his leg with the hand gripping his muscle above the knee, I adjust my grip around his foot that's now in the air and place it for a stepping motion: with the heel landing first, then rolling through the step to the ball of the foot.

"Nice. Feel okay?"

"Feels weird," he admits.

"We just have to build that muscle memory back up. Ten thousand kicks and all that."

"Did you just quote Bruce Lee to me?" he asks, the amusement obvious in his voice.

"Can't say I don't know my audience. Alright, other leg now."

We move through the same motion on his left side, guiding him through the lift, and then placing his foot for the heel-to-toe motion. He needs more assistance this time, his left side being weaker.

"Perfect. Give me another one. Let's keep going."

We work through a dozen more steps, moving slowly and emphasizing each one so his brain can start to log the muscle memory. It isn't until I catch two winces in a row on Roman's face that I call an end to our session.

"I think that's enough for today," I say, standing from my stool. "We don't want to stress your body too much. Fran's going to lower the lift, and I'm going to hold your chair behind you so you can drop right into it. Ready?"

At that, Roman's jaw clenches in a way that makes me wonder if me pulling a chair out for him is the part of our session that hit his ego. But even if it is, he follows my instructions without protest, which has me chalking up this entire thing as a victory.

He collapses into his chair with a grunt, relaxing into the space that's still the most comfortable for him.

*God. I'm so proud of him.*

It isn't until I catch myself looking at him from my place behind him, the urge to massage his sore shoulders becoming overwhelming, that I realize Fran is still here. She's standing by the lift, watching us curiously.

I mentally assure myself that she didn't see anything. *Fuck, was I staring at Roman like a starstruck girl?*

"Thanks for helping out today, Fran. I appreciate it," I tell her. "I'll let you know when I could use your help again."

She nods with a smile of her own. "Of course, it was my pleasure." She looks at Roman. "Great job today, Roman."

"Thanks," he says gruffly. "And I second Liliana's comment: thanks for your help today."

"Of course. Anything I can do, just let me know." She

turns her attention back to me. "I'm assuming you need me for a few more sessions in the harness, yes?"

I nod. "If you can fit some in, that would be great. We can schedule them on days that are best for you, since we're still mixing them in with strength training days, but if that's too hard, I can ask one of the other therapists. I just thought you might like to be involved."

Part of me hopes she says no, too worried about the possibility that she could pick up on my feelings for Roman.

But of course she says yes.

"Let's look at the calendar tomorrow and figure out how many and which days we want."

A tight smile pulls at my lips as I nod. "Great. I'll pop into your office tomorrow around lunch then."

It isn't until she leaves, and I'm left alone with Roman once again, that the enormity of what just happened hits me. Roman did a walking exercise. *Successfully.*

"Holy *shit*," I breathe, unable to stop the giddy grin that appears on my face. "Roman, you just *walked.*"

I don't know if it's because my energy is infectious, but the excitement is apparent on Roman's face, too. A small grin even peeks out.

"Let's not get ahead of ourselves," he says. Predictably. "I still needed two people and a ten-thousand-dollar piece of equipment to do it."

I throw my hands up. "You are such a *spoilsport.*"

A startled laugh bursts out of him. "I haven't been called that since elementary school. That's a nostalgic insult."

"I have to get creative if I want to stay professional while still getting my point across," I mumble, starting to put away the equipment we used during our session.

When that earns me another laugh, I soften, realizing

this is Roman in a good mood. He *does* feel good about his success today.

Relief floods me as I take the paper I slid into my pocket earlier and toss it in the trash.

"What was that?"

I startle when I realize Roman just watched me do that. And then immediately flush hot over my lack of stealth.

"Uh, nothing," I hurry to say, avoiding eye contact. "Just some trash."

"Then why are you blushing?" Roman presses. "You're the color of a tomato, Liliana."

I lift my head so I can glare at him. "That's a rude thing to say to a woman, Roman."

He grins. "Got you to look at me, though, didn't it?" When I only sigh, he jerks his chin toward the trash. "Seriously, what was that?"

Knowing I've been caught, I lean down to take the crumpled-up paper out of the bin. "It's my phone number," I mumble.

Roman's brow furrows. "Why did you write your phone number on a piece of paper and then throw it out?"

I hesitate for a moment, wondering if there's still a way I can get out of this. If I *should* get out of this.

"It was going to be for you," I admit before I can second-guess myself any more.

His eyes widen at that, but there's still a glimmer of confusion when they track back to the paper in my hand.

"So...why did you throw it out, then?" he asks.

I shrug. "Because gait training was a success."

His eyes pinch as he shakes his head. "Doc, you gotta give me a little more than that. I've been concussed enough times to need this spelled out a skosh more."

A whooshing exhale leaves my chest, then I'm admitting

in a ramble, "I was going to give you my phone number if today went badly, okay? I wanted to make sure you had someone to talk to if there was a chance of you losing all hope."

He blinks at me. Once, then again. Then, he pushes his wheelchair toward me and takes the paper out of my hand.

When he looks at me, there's a heat in his eyes that I've never seen before. And even when they flash with something I can't put a name to, the intensity there has my stomach flipping.

"Victory or not, I'm going to take this, Liliana," he says in a deliciously deep voice.

It takes minutes for my heart rate to return to normal after that.

**17**

---

## ROMAN

*I walked.*

*And I have Lily's number in my pocket.*

I must have a look of shell-shocked glee on my face, because the moment I load into my mom's van, she does a triple-take.

"Oh my God, what happened?" she demands. "You look…happy. You *never* look happy after therapy. What happened??"

I debate for a moment if I just want to deny everything to avoid the conversation but…*she* looks so happy that I can't do it to her.

I let out a heavy breath and make a half-admission. "I managed some assisted walking today."

Thank God, she hasn't pulled out of the parking lot yet, because her jaw-drop tells me it would've resulted in a brake-slam.

"Roman!" she squeals. And when nothing else comes out, she says it again. "*Roman!*"

I huff a laugh. "I know, I was pretty shocked, too."

"This is huge! Oh my gosh, we have to celebrate."

Victory aside, I'm still hesitant to truly hope. "I still have a long way to go. This just means the therapy is working."

"Apparently." Her eyes dart over to the clinic building. "Any idea what's different about this place?"

*Yeah. The therapist.*

"No idea," I lie instead. "I'm just glad it's working."

Her focus moves back to me, a warm smile on her face. "Me too, sweetheart," she says softly.

I return the smile, my chest warming at the sight of my mom being so giddy.

Her excitement is still palpable when she faces forward and grips the steering wheel. "Alright, well, even if you don't want to celebrate, I still want to do something special. Are we still on for dinner tonight?"

"Of course," I answer. "Always."

Once a week, Mom and I do a breakfast for dinner date night. It was recommended by an old therapist a year ago, and the idea stuck. Her theory was that with Mom being my sole caretaker and a huge crutch for me, I needed to remember that she was still my mother, too. That she loved me outside of my injury and would always be a mother over a nurse. She suggested we put a weekly date on the calendar to ensure we spend time together as a family. We've tried movie nights, brunch dates, and a dozen other ideas, but the one we keep coming back to a breakfast for dinner. I think because it reminds me of my childhood, and the nights that Mom gave in to my near-constant requests for pancakes. Now, we make the pancakes together, chatting about our week as we cook. It's easy, comforting.

When we reach the house, Mom is still chattering about the bonus breakfast foods she's going to make tonight, reciting her grocery list to herself and planning to make way too much food for two people.

"Anyway, honey, I'm going to run out to the grocery store real quick and grab what we need," she says. "Should we say dinner at eight?"

I nod. "Perfect. That gives me some time to clean myself and the house a little bit."

"You know I could do that for you," she says in the mothering tone she occasionally defaults to. Sure enough, when I give her a look that reads as my usual answer of *please don't baby me*, she reddens.

"Sorry, that just came out," she mumbles. "I promise that was a mom instinct, not a pity one."

I lean across the van to kiss her on the cheek. "I know, Mom. I appreciate you." I start to unhook my chair so I can unload from the van. "Eight o'clock, then. It's a date."

When I enter my house, I do a scan to see how much I need to clean up before Mom gets back. The cleanliness of my house has always been an obvious representation of my well-being, because in the past, usually during my deepest depressive episodes, the house would become disgusting. I couldn't summon the energy to do anything besides order takeout and play video games, and that always resulted in unswept floors, dishes in the sink and all over the counter, and rotten food in the fridge. That was the only time in my life when Mom *did* need to come in to clean, if for no other reason than to keep me from getting sick.

But lately, I've been keeping up with everything, for the most part. Looking around now, I decide there's not a lot I need to do besides unloading the dishwasher, wiping down the counters, and straightening a few things in the living room. I throw my couch blanket in the wash and turn the Roomba on for good measure, but beyond that, I don't have much on the to-do list.

I shower and change into fresh clothes, realizing I still

have an hour before Mom shows up. So I decide to kill time by starting in on the tasks I've been putting off.

When Mikey walks in a little before eight o'clock, I'm in the middle of unloading the books from my bookshelves and dusting.

Having heard the beep of the front door keypad, I finish wiping down the shelf I'm on before I turn around. When I do, I find Mikey staring slack-jawed at the sight in front of him.

"Did I just walk into Bizarro World?" he asks.

I roll my eyes and lean down to pick up the books I need to re-shelve. "Very funny. Come be useful and help me."

He must be *really* shocked because he follows directions without a single argument. He simply walks over and picks up a handful of books.

"So what prompted *this* freakish occurrence?" he asks. Suddenly, he frowns and looks at me, his eyes narrowing. "Are you on drugs?"

I toss a balled-up paper towel at his face. "You're an idiot."

He swats it away. "Hey, that's no crazier than walking in to see you *dusting*. What's going on?"

I shrug. "Had some time to kill. Felt like being productive."

His eyes widen. "Oh shit, it's your day with your mom. Fuck, I totally forgot. I'll leave."

"Don't even think about leaving, Michael," comes my mom's voice as she walks through the door. "I'm pretty sure I bought enough food to feed a dozen seventeen-and-going-through-his-first-growth-spurt Romans, so we're going to need you."

Mikey claps his hands together. "Don't have to ask me twice, Mama Dubs. How can I help?"

She lifts two gigantic fistfuls of grocery bags onto the counter. "Can you mix the pancake batter? I want to start on the stuffed French Toast."

"Yes, ma'am," he says, already walking into the kitchen.

I hear him rustling through the bags as I turn back to my bookshelves, and I already know what his next question is going to be. Sure enough, after a moment, he asks, "So...what's the occasion? Between the all-you-can-eat buffet that this is about to be and Roman's inexplicable cleaning, I'm assuming something happened."

I glance over my shoulder to meet Mom's eyes for a beat. She reads me easily.

"Roman had a good day at therapy, that's all," she says, giving in to my silent request to not make a big deal out of things. I send her a grateful smile. "Plus, you know me, I'll take any excuse to make a big brunch."

I think Mikey might sense that there's something more, but it's possible he also caught the look we just shared and realizes I'd prefer to move on to a different topic. So he does.

"Well, whatever the reason, my mouth is already watering. Damn, Mama Dubs, where did you find cinnamon rolls on a Saturday night?"

As I push myself into the kitchen, I catch my mom's proud smile. "I have my secrets." But then her smile straightens when Mikey tries to quickly swipe some icing off one of the rolls with his finger. Slapping his hand away, she says, "Good *Lord*, at least wait until I take it out of the box."

Properly scolded, Mikey hangs his head as she sends him into the cabinet for a plate. "Sorry," he mumbles.

I can't help shaking my head with a chuckle at their antics. Being my best friend in middle school, Mikey obviously knew my mom when we were kids, but it never ceases to amaze me that they've somehow managed to keep the same relationship as adults.

"What do you want me to do, Mom?" I peek into one of the bags. "Damn, you really did buy a whole buffet. How many courses are we having?"

"Four," she says cheerfully. And with the way she says it, I don't even think she's kidding.

When she pulls orange juice and a bottle and champagne out of the bags, I quirk an eyebrow at her. "What?" she asks innocently. *We're celebrating*, she mouths at me, which just makes me smile.

"Want me to make you one?" she asks.

I only consider it for a second before I shake my head. "No, thank you. Just orange juice is fine."

That only seems to make her *more* excited. Smacking a kiss on my cheek, she says, "You can get started on the eggs and bacon then. Growing boys need their protein."

At that, Mikey flexes his arm and makes a muscle. "Yes, we do. It's bulking season, baby."

I quirk an eyebrow at my best friend as I take the bowl offered by my mom. "Since when? You've never had an interest in lifting."

He shrugs as he starts to mix the pancake batter. "I don't know. Ever since I stopped playing in those basketball leagues, I've been thinking about picking something else up. I thought maybe it was time to choose something that didn't necessarily lead to having to compete."

I think carefully about my next words. This is the closest that Mikey and I have ever gotten to talking about sports or physical activities since my accident. But I also know him well enough that if he's talking about it, he's been thinking about it a lot.

"So then what's stopping you?" I finally ask. "If you want to do it…"

He shrugs again. "I just feel a little stupid. I don't know anything about lifting. It feels wrong to jump into it when I'm this clueless."

Later, I'll think about the relief that fills my body in this moment. About how good it feels to finally be able to give *Mikey* something when, for over a year, it's been him helping *me*.

About how it feels like the most natural thing in the world to say, "I can start you on a lifting program, if you want."

When both Mom and Mikey lift surprised gazes to me, I hurry to add, "Plus, I have my gym in the back room. I know it's not an LA Fitness, but there's enough equipment in there that I can give you the gist of the main exercises for the different muscle groups. I obviously can't demonstrate the lower body exercises, but I could at least write you a plan and—"

"I would love that," Mikey interrupts my nervous babbling. "Thanks, man. That would be a huge help."

A second wave of relief flows through me, and I nod before returning to cracking the eggs. "Cool," I say on a heavy exhale.

Mom also returns to her French Toast, but not before I see a sheen in her eyes. And her voice is oddly high-pitched when she says, "Well, on that note…we're going to need some *extra* eggs, Roman."

I don't bother trying to stop my smile. "You got it, Mom."

**18**

---

# ROMAN

By the time Mom says goodnight and retreats to her little cottage, Mikey is already snoring on my couch in a food coma.

I sigh and toss a blanket over him, but the sound is fond. I'm sure with everything that happened today that tonight would've been a fun night even if it was just Mom and me, but Mikey brought an extra dose of merriment. It's one of the best parts of having him around.

Glancing at my phone, I realize it's still relatively early. Early enough that I don't want to go to bed yet.

So, keeping the volume low and the subtitles on, I settle on the opposite couch and turn on the TV.

I scroll mindlessly through the streaming apps for a few minutes before eventually settling on a thriller I saw a few years ago. I watch the familiar gory opening scene before my thoughts start to wander.

Specifically, to Lily.

*I wonder if she's seen this one. She knew almost all the movies I had listed, so it's likely she has.*

*Then again, she admitted to missing a huge classic. So maybe not.*

*I wonder...*

It hits me for the first time that I *could* ask her. Because I have her number now. *She* gave me her number. To use for instances like this, if her stress relief suggestions were anything to go by.

Spinning the phone in my hands, I debate long and hard for a few minutes.

And then I pull up her contact.

> Roman: What's more important in a movie, the story or the cinematography?

I don't think I expected her to respond. Between my non-introduction and the fact that I don't get night owl vibes from Lily, I startle when my phone buzzes a minute later.

> Liliana: Story. Definitely.

Instantly, I'm smiling.

> Roman: Follow-up question: can impressive cinematography save a bad movie?

Bubbles appear immediately.

> Liliana: Not to the point that I could rate it a 10, but it could bump a movie a few points.

I'm in the middle of typing a response when I get a flurry of texts.

> Liliana: Here's my question though

Liliana: If a movie is shitty or uninteresting,
can a blow-your-mind ending still save it?

Liliana: Like if you hated 90% of it, but loved
the last 10, what's the likely rating?

Roman: Probably still a 9/10. The ending is
the part that sticks with you, so if the ending
is amazing, it's likely going to be your main
takeaway from the movie.

Roman: Fighting was like that too. We
always said to go hardest the last ten
seconds of every round, and then the last
round in its entirety, because that's what the
judges remember.

This time, it takes a minute for the bubbles to appear. Long enough to wonder if I somehow managed to turn her off of the conversation.

Liliana: That's valid, I guess

Liliana: I disagree, but it's valid

I huff a laugh to myself.

Roman: You'd still rate a movie low?

Liliana: Absolutely. A great ending can't
make me forget that I hated a large majority
of the movie. I'd still feel like I wasted two
hours of my life.

Roman: Have you ever walked out of a
movie theater because the movie was
so bad?

Liliana: No but one time I really, really wanted to

Roman: Why didn't you?

Liliana: It was one of my favorite directors and I absolutely refused to believe that it was as bad as it was. I was convinced there was going to be a twist at the end that explained everything.

Roman: Ah so you DO think a good ending can save a movie

Liliana: Nothing would have saved that movie. It just would've saved my best friend from the two-hour rant that followed.

Twisting on the couch to lay down into a more comfortable position, I quickly pick up my phone and find another text.

Liliana: By the way…who is this?

I quirk an eyebrow at the screen.

Roman: Are you telling me you'd entertain complete strangers with your movie theories?

Liliana: Of course. It's fun.

I shake my head, my smile still in place.

> Roman: No sense of stranger danger. See? This is why I stayed at the clinic when that repairman was coming.

> Liliana: I thought you said you didn't think you could protect me...

My heartrate picks up.

> Roman: I thought you said you didn't know who this is...

My phone stays silent for a minute, the weight of what's happening right now finally settling into the conversation. I'm texting Lily. And she's texting back. I don't need to ask to know this is against the rules, but at the same time, there wasn't a chance in hell I was going to let her throw that piece of paper away today.

Even if she had only intended it to be a lifeline for me.

But talking about movies isn't exactly a talk-me-off-the-ledge conversation piece, and now I'm wondering if I should feel guilty about chatting with her about non-PT things.

Just as that thought hits, my phone buzzes.

> Liliana: Are you a cat person?

I frown at the message.

> Roman: I'm more of a dog person, but I don't exactly hate cats.

> Roman: Why?

In response, I get a picture.

And immediately burst out laughing.

When Mikey stirs, I have to cover my mouth to smother

the sounds, but I'm still shaking with laughter as I look at the picture again.

It's of a giant orange cat, curled up in Lily's lap and glaring at the camera. Its expression fits every cat stereotype that's ever existed.

Roman: That is the fattest cat I've ever seen. What do you feed that thing?

Liliana: SHUT UP. He's not fat, he's fluffy.

Roman: I highly doubt that, Liliana. That cat looks like it sneaks double lunches and dinners.

Roman: And why is it glaring so hard? Does it hate you?

Liliana: HIS name is Garfield. And no, he does not hate me. This is how he expresses love.

Roman: I never thought I'd say that's the perfect name for a cat, but...

Liliana: I know, right? My brothers used to tease me that I only gave him the name because he was an orange kitten, but then he grew up and actually became Garfield. It was like a self-fulfilling prophecy.

Roman: That means you need an Odie, too

Liliana: Ugh I wish. Our apartment complex doesn't allow dogs.

Liliana: Do you have any pets?

Roman: Just Rocky

Liliana: And Rocky is a…?

Roman: My pet rock

Liliana: …

Liliana: I didn't think it was possible, but you're actually worse at naming pets than I was as a child

Roman: Well now I have to know

Liliana: For starters, my frog was Mr. Frog

Roman: That's not that bad. I feel like most kids give names like that.

Liliana: I was sixteen

I let out a snort at that.

Roman: Okay yeah, that's pretty bad

It takes another minute for another text to come through.

Liliana: Did you have pets when you were a kid?

I swallow roughly, my chest tightening the same way it always does when this aspect of my childhood is mentioned.

Roman: No. My dad's job had us moving around too much, it would've been hard to put any pets through that.

Liliana: Ah. I can see how that would make owning a pet difficult

Bubbles appear again, then disappear, then reappear. She's hesitating.

Liliana: You never talk about your dad

Another rough swallow.

Roman: He died when I was ten. It's just Mom and me.

Liliana: Oh Roman. I'm so sorry. I shouldn't have asked.

Roman: It's okay. It was a logical progression of the conversation. Plus, it was a long time ago.

Liliana: Even still, I'm sorry

Liliana: If you could have owned a pet, what would you have asked for?

The tightness in my chest loosens at the seamless way she makes things better.

Roman: A snake

Liliana: OH MY GOD

Liliana: I could NEVER

And I'm right back to smiling.

Roman: All caps, huh?

Liliana: YES

Liliana: A snake?? ROMAN

Liliana: YOU HAVE TO FEED THEM
LIVE MICE

Roman: So? Your pet kills mice for fun

Another picture comes through, and once again, I burst out laughing.

It's of her cat, of course. But he's no longer glaring. Instead, he's splayed on his back, legs sticking out every which way, with his eyes closed and mouth wide open.

Liliana: Garfield isn't killing anything,
trust me

Roman: Yikes. Fat and lazy, he really is
Garfield.

Liliana: Would you believe me if I said he's
so much like Garfield that he actually likes
pizza and coffee?

Liliana: I'm telling you, we must have
manifested his personality with the name or
something

Roman: The pizza I'm not surprised by. But the coffee is weird.

Liliana: Right?? I have to guard my morning coffee because he's slick about stealing it

Roman: And based on the way I've seen you clutch your coffee, I'm assuming the cat stealing it doesn't put you in a very good mood.

Liliana: Rude. I love coffee the same amount as the average American. I do not "clutch" it.

Roman: I saw you once steal your coworker's favorite pen because she took the last pod of your favorite Keurig flavor

There's a long pause before her response text comes through.

Liliana: Should I be flattered that you noticed that, or concerned?

Roman: You wear your emotions on your sleeve, Liliana

This pause is even longer.

Liliana: Yeah, I've heard that before…

I'm not sure what to say without making things too serious. I want to send another random question, something lighthearted, but I'm not entirely sure how to do that without making it obvious that I just want to keep talking. Which is odd in itself, because I've never been a big texter.

But I can't exactly talk to Lily like this during my sessions at the clinic, so—

In the end, she makes the decision for me.

Liliana: It's late, I should head to bed. This is already way past my bedtime.

Roman: Ah, sorry. I'm so used to my night owl hours that I didn't think about that.

Liliana: No, it's okay. I'm glad you texted me.

Roman: I'm glad I did too

Roman: Goodnight Liliana

## 19

## LILIANA

"Alright, babe, I'm out," Tina calls as she grabs her bag for her night shift. "Don't throw a rager while I'm gone!"

I roll my eyes at her from my spot on the couch, Garfield already planted in my lap. "I have no idea who you're talking to. My plans tonight consist of Chinese takeout, a laundry list of movies to watch, and Garfield as my snuggle buddy. I am *set.*"

At that, Tina sighs. "Okay, yeah, that does sound nice. Now I'm kind of jealous."

I grin and lift Garfield's paw to wave her off. "Say *bye, auntie!*"

"Bye, my beautiful fat nephew," Tina says, blowing a kiss. "See you in the morning!"

When the door shuts behind her, I start my scroll through Netflix, Prime, then Hulu, looking for the perfect movie to watch. And maybe it's because I was with Roman at the clinic a few hours ago and so he's still on my mind, but I find myself flipping over to the horror genre.

The buzzer for my takeout sounds just as I come across

the movie he recommended all those weeks ago. *Hereditary.* The one I said I've never seen.

In the time it takes me to collect my food, set it out on a tray, and settle back on the couch, Roman stays on my mind. Because of the movie, but also because of how things have been between us lately. He's slowly but steadily making progress with his recovery, even more than I could have hoped for. And during his sessions, our banter is still just as easy. We bicker, we tease, I give orders and he bites back. Easy and pleasant, and honestly, I have fun working with him.

We also text after-hours sometimes. Not a lot, but occasionally, when something reminds us of the other.

As I click play on the movie and dig into my food, I find myself wondering what Roman is doing tonight.

Ten minutes and an old woman jump scare later, I'm scrambling for my phone and typing out a text.

Liliana: I hate you

Bubbles form immediately.

Roman: I didn't think I was THAT bad today

It should be scarier how quickly Roman can make me smile.

Liliana: Not that. I'm watching Hereditary.

Liliana: I just started it and I'm already planning my revenge on you for making me watch this

Roman: Ah come on, it's not that bad

Liliana: Yes it is. Why are old ladies so scary?

Roman: Ok yea you're not wrong about that. They really are the most effective way to ratchet the fear factor.

Liliana: I'm going to have to picture sweet little Grandma Davis to get through this

Liliana: Also what is with the damn clicking?

Roman: Lol just keep watching

I still don't have an answer to my question, but twenty minutes later...

Liliana: ROMAN WHAT THE FUCK

Roman: Hahahaha I was waiting for the all caps

Roman: That movie is insane on so many levels

Liliana: ...I hate you.

Roman: Lmao now that text makes sense

I only make it another half hour before I throw all caution to the wind and click *Call*.

He picks up on the first ring, already laughing.

"How you doing, Doc?"

"This is no laughing matter, Roman Ward," I whisper-yell. "This movie has every single thing I'm the *most* scared of. I've been watching through my fingers for the past five minutes."

That only makes him laugh harder. It's a sound I've heard before, but not like this. This is a *belly* laugh. And it's the happiest I've ever heard him.

"It's the mom, isn't it?" he asks.

"*Yes!* How is it possible that everything she does makes me physically uncomfortable? And what the fuck is with the sleepwalking?"

"Yeah, she freaks me the fuck out, too," he says, chuckling. "I couldn't watch Toni Collette in anything else after this, because as soon as she popped up on the screen, a chill would run through me." I hear shuffling in the background. "Can you pause and tell me your minute maker?"

My eyebrows pinch. "Are you watching it right now?"

"Yeah. I put it on when you texted me. I kind of know where you are, but if we're both watching, we might as well sync up."

I grumble, reaching for the remote. "You just want to anticipate my screams."

I can hear his grin through the phone. "You know me too well."

"Just so you know, this counts as extra credit on my end of our deal. I'm going to put you through the workout of hell the next time I see you."

"Worth it," he says, chuckling.

Sighing, I tell him, "Alright, I'm at the one hour and ten-minute mark. Ready?"

There's a small pause as he finds the mark. "Ready. On three. Three, two, one, go."

I press play and watch as the movie starts again. But I'm distracted now, more interested in my phone than I am the movie.

"What's your movie snack of choice?" I ask.

He hums thoughtfully, then answers, "I'm a classic guy. So popcorn."

I let out a snort. "Classic would not be the word I would use to describe you."

"I don't think I want to hear the words you would use to describe me," Roman responds, his tone dry. "Alright, smartass. What's your movie snack?"

"*Obviously* Twizzlers. It's the best candy at the refreshment stand."

For a moment, Roman doesn't say anything. Then he sighs and says, "For someone who's as big of a health nut as you are, you also have the biggest sweet tooth I've ever seen."

"Excuse me, what am I *supposed* to eat at the movies? An apple? That would be blasphemous." Then I frown. "Wait, how do you know I'm a health nut?"

"Liliana, the first thing you did when Fran offered you a protein bar last week was check the ingredients list. Trust me. You're a health nut."

"You are *such* a know-it-all," I grumble, absentmindedly reaching over to pet Garfield as I shift my gaze back to the TV screen.

He snorts into the phone. "As if your job isn't to notice every little detail about my behavior and body."

Thank God, he can't see me, because my cheeks flame bright red. And now I'm picturing his body, and the way it looked during the workout I put him through today. His legs are getting noticeably more muscular, and I caught myself staring at the striations on his quads more than once.

I'm snapped from my thoughts when the scene on the TV screen finally registers.

"Wait...is that...?"

And then I'm tossing the phone in my hurry to slap my hands over my eyes.

"*Roman!*" I shriek, uncaring that I'm not holding my phone anymore. I'm still loud enough for him to hear. "What the *fuck* did you make me watch?!"

I can hear his tinny laughter from wherever I threw him. Making sure not to look at the TV, I scramble to the other end of the couch to grab my phone.

"This is *exactly* why I didn't want to watch this," I complain once I've lifted it to my ear. "There's just something about the paranormal stuff that messes with my head. I mean...what *was* that?!"

There's that full-bellied laugh again. "Just watch, Liliana."

"I *can't!*" I whine. "I can't do people crawling around on the ceiling." I peek through the quarter inch of space between my fingers and immediately look away with a shudder. "Roman, my limit has been reached. You're going to have to tell me what's happening. I can't watch it anymore."

"And you call yourself a horror fan," Roman says with a *tsk*.

"It's just this *one* sub-genre of horror. But fine. Take my fan card, I don't care. Nothing is worth this." With my hands still covering my eyes, my ears perk up. I hear a scream, then something banging against a door.

"What is that?" I ask despite myself.

Roman pauses, then asks, "Do you really want to know?"

Another groan, this time as I cover my ear that doesn't have the phone pressed against it. "This movie is taking away one sense at a time. First my eyesight, now my hearing."

"Alright, alright, just turn it off. Nothing is worth this."

"That's what I'm saying!" I scramble for the remote and quickly hit the Home button.

"Just so you know, you were five minutes from finishing the movie."

A shiver ripples down my spine. "I am 100% okay with that. I'm already going to have nightmares for the next three days."

"Will you really?" For the first time, Roman's voice is tinged with worry.

Sighing, I flip onto my back and stare up at the ceiling. "Probably. It's fine. I've been getting too much sleep lately, anyway."

"Shit, Liliana, I'm sorry." He sounds regretful. "I thought you were kidding. I didn't know it would be that bad for you. I'm a dick, I'm sorry."

His concern is sweet, and I smile to myself. "Roman, it's fine. I'm fine. I'm being *slightly* dramatic."

I think he's weighing my words. Finally, he says, "Are you just saying that for my benefit?"

My smile grows. "No, I'm not. Promise."

"In that case, I hate you back."

A laugh bubbles past my lips. "I deserve that."

"Yes, you do," Roman says, but I can hear the fondness in his voice. "So...what comedy are you turning on to counteract the paranormal horror effects?"

I roll onto my side and glance at the TV. I don't think I want to watch anything right now. I just want to keep talking to him.

"Probably *Friends*," I lie instead. "That's my usual feel-good show."

"Never seen it."

I gape at my phone before snapping it back to my ear. "Roman, I don't think we can be friends anymore."

When he doesn't respond, I glance at my phone with a frown, wondering if the call dropped. But then I hear the unmistakable sound of the *Friends* theme song.

"So, what episode is a good one to start with?"

Laughing, I shift into a more comfortable position and settle in to watch the show.

When we finally hang up six episodes later, I fall asleep with a smile on my face and the realization that this was the best Saturday night I've had in two years.

**20**

———

**LILIANA**

With every bit of progress Roman makes, he also grows more tense. I can see it in his eyes and his nervous drumming on his leg. I can see it every time we move from a strengthening exercise to a gait training exercise. His jaw clenches when he looks at the parallel bars.

It makes *me* nervous, too. It feels like we're both waiting for something to happen, maybe even for something to break, and only then can we deal with whatever is making him nervous. Which means with every session—every *successful* session—the tension just winds tighter and tighter.

And I think I've finally figured out the reason for it.

I'm sitting in the break room, mulling over the different ways I could approach this with Roman, when my phone buzzes.

*Dad calling.*

I'm smiling when I accept the call. "Hi, Dad. What's up?"

"Hi, sweetheart. How's your day going?"

I smother my sigh, because I know he'll know what it

means. "It's good. Same old. I only have two more patients before I'm done for the day. How are you doing?"

"Same old," he replies with a chuckle. "Retired life doesn't change much."

"Uh, didn't you just come back from a three-week motorcycle tour along the East Coast?"

"Yeah, and?"

"Hate to break it to you, Dad, but that's not same old. That's the definition of *different new*."

I can visualize him waving me off even through the phone. "That was just a random idea. It wasn't anything special."

I roll my eyes to myself. Only my sixty-five-year-old father would think a drive like that *wasn't anything special*.

"But on a similar note, that's actually the reason I called you," he says. "I wanted to talk to you about our annual trip."

I glance at the clock on the wall. "I only have a few minutes before my next patient. Should I call you on my way home instead?"

"Sure, honey, you can call me after. I just wanted to see if you'd thought any more about where you wanted to go for our family trip this year."

For as long as I can remember, our family has gone on a trip to a different destination every year, chosen by someone different. It's always an active trip, ranging from snowboarding in Colorado to riding ATVs in the Vegas desert, but we try to plan things none of us have ever done before. Last year, my brother picked Mexico, where we spent five days visiting Mayan temples, diving into cenotes, and getting our scuba diving certification. The year before that, my other brother picked skiing in Vermont. This year is my turn.

I chew on my bottom lip for a moment before saying, "I

was actually thinking about Utah. We could go canyoneering."

"That's a new idea," Dad comments. "Where'd that come from?"

"I heard one of the clinic's patients talking about it. I thought it sounded fun."

"I love it. Let's do it."

"Yeah?" I say, feeling giddy. "Okay, cool. I'll run it by Sean and Colin during our next family Trivia Night."

Movement catches my eye, and I turn to see Roman enter the gym. He gives me the barest smile when he sees me looking, which is Roman for *ecstatic*. I have to bite down on a smile that would undoubtedly look too excited, and wave to him instead.

I'm just about to say goodbye to my dad, when he suddenly exclaims, "Oh, speaking of Trivia Night, don't forget we had to push it to next week since neither of your brothers could make this week. Which is unfortunate because I think this week is history week and the Knowing Stones would have crushed the competition."

I shake my head, smiling, at the reminder of the team name my brothers came up with over a decade ago. Somehow, it stuck all the way to our monthly family catch-up dates at the local restaurant, where we played musical bingo, themed Trivia Nights, and dominated dart tournaments. It became a tradition that came second only to our annual family trip.

"I didn't forget, Dad, don't worry," I respond, never taking my eyes off Roman. "I'll be there next week." But then something occurs to me and I shift my full focus back to my phone. "Oh, and since I'm not seeing Sean this week, you have to be the one to bug him about doing his PT on his wrist. You know as well as I do that he needs a regular kick in the ass if he wants to get his full range of motion back."

My dad's chuckle floats down the line. "Okay, okay, I'll remind him. Have a good rest of your day, Liliana, I love you."

"Bye, Dad. Love you."

As soon as I hang up, my attention shifts back to where Roman is already starting his warmup exercises.

Twenty minutes later, I'm placing my hands on my hips and announcing, "Alright, today, we're going to do some cycling."

Roman quirks an eyebrow at me from where he's sitting on the treatment table, having just finished stretching. "As in, biking? Did you forget I can barely move my legs, Doc?"

I drop my hands to my sides with an exasperated sigh. "Why, yes, that did slip my mind. My apologies, I thought we were dealing with an ingrown toenail." I lift my chin in the direction of the machine in the corner. "You're going to try the cycle machine. But combined with FES."

*That* triggers the reaction from Roman that I expected. Any time we try something new with gait training, his body locks up and a wall drops over his eyes. So far, I haven't had to fight him to try an exercise, but I think that might be because I've stuck with what he's familiar with. I've been waiting for one to elicit an even bigger reaction.

Which, judging by the expression on Roman's face, I just found.

"Have you ever tried FES?" I ask gently.

His headshake is stiff. "Never got as far as we've gotten."

My eyebrows shoot up. "How far did you get before?"

His jaw clenches as he looks over toward the parallel bars. "I quit as soon as they put me in the harness last time."

I blink. *He...what?*

When he sees my expression, Roman huffs a laugh that has no humor. "I told you, your therapy style was working."

*Holy shit.*

That means he never really got on his feet. He may have regained some sensation through range of motion exercises and strength training, but he hasn't done any functional training with walking motions.

No wonder he gets so nervous.

I glance at the cycle machine in the corner, chewing on my lip and second-guessing my plans for today.

But to my surprise, Roman asks, "FES is the electrode thing, right?"

My gaze jerks back to him. He's not looking at me, though; he's sizing up the cycle machine.

"Yes. Functional Electrical Stimulation." I step over to one of the cabinets and pull out the electrode pads. "I'm going to put them on your leg while you pedal the bike."

Roman's eyes narrow at the pads in my hand. "Is this just an excuse to electrocute me, Doc?"

I bark a laugh, but shake my head. "I'm not *that* mean. No, it's like a TENS machine. I'm sure you used those when you were fighting, right?" He nods. "It's kind of like that. It's an electrical pulse meant to cause a muscular contraction and stimulate movement. We just want to trick your body into moving."

I wait patiently while Roman stares at the pads before giving me a barely perceptible nod.

"Let's give it a try," I say, gesturing toward the bike.

He pulls in a deep breath, then slides out of his chair and transfers into the bike seat. The machine isn't a stationary bike, it's more like a deep seat closer to the ground that has pedals in front of it. Like a pedal boat.

Once he's settled, I look over his leg and decide where

I'm going to put the electrode pads. On any other day, I might be nervous to move his shorts out of the way, but today, the borderline-fear on his face as he stares at the pedals makes any overthinking evaporate. All I want to do is hug him and tell him everything is going to be okay.

"I'm going to stick four pads on your right leg," I explain, making sure I talk him through every detail so that he knows what to expect. "Two on your quad, and two on different areas of your calf. We're going to try it with one leg first."

He nods, his eyes shooting to the first pad in my hand. He watches me like a hawk as I place the four pads, and as I strap his foot into the pedal. I settle his left foot, too, even though I want him to try with his stronger leg first.

"Before I ask you to pedal, I'm going to send a pulse to the pad on your quad so you know what it feels like. Let me know when you're ready."

I can see his pulse going haywire in his neck, but he still manages to give me a gruff, "Ready."

When I trigger the pulse from the remote in my hand, we can both *see* when it hits Roman's thigh. The muscle twitches, and his leg jerks.

Roman gapes at his leg. "Holy shit."

"Does it hurt?

He shakes his head. "It's just...weird."

"Can I try the one on your calf?"

When he nods, I send a pulse to the muscle. Once again, it twitches, and Roman's leg jerks.

"Technology is fucking wild," Roman mutters, staring at his leg.

Chuckling, I ask, "Can I put the pads on your left leg, too? Then we can try pedaling."

When I get the okay, I place the pads and stand back.

"Alright, same drill with your left leg. I'll stimulate your quad first, and then your calf."

By the time he's ready to try the bike, I'm relieved he looks less skeptical about the training exercise. And when I ask him to start pedaling, there's no hesitation in his movements.

His brow furrows in concentration as he pushes his right leg forward. The motion is slow, but once the leg is extended, he shifts his focus to his left leg.

On that side, he needs help. So, I send an electronic pulse to the pad on his left quad.

Roman's entire leg jerks forward, his eyes going wide in shock.

"Keep going," I urge gently.

He presses against the right pedal again, then the left. Again, I send a pulse to his leg when he wavers.

"So fucking weird," he breathes out, continuing to pedal. But now, he's staring at the bike in amazement.

I'm absolutely giddy by the time I call an end to our session. Roman did so much better than I let myself hope for, and he did it with barely any motivation from me. He made an insane amount of progress today physically, and *he* did it.

I'm mulling over the pros and cons of telling Roman I'm proud of him when I finally notice the shift in him. Because in the time it took me to take the pads off his legs, he's somehow gone from awed, to that same numb demeanor he started with.

I'm still kneeling on the floor beside the bike, so I settle back on my heels and ask, "What's wrong?"

His frozen gaze slides to meet mine. "Nothing's wrong."

I hum thoughtfully and start to wrap up the cords. "If

you don't want to talk about it, I'd rather you say you don't want to talk about it. Lying doesn't help either of us."

"I don't want to talk about it," he says instantly.

My hands slow for a moment, and I think he expects me to push back on him, because I can feel his suspicious gaze on me. But I just shrug and stand up.

"Okay, then. Same time Wednesday? It'll be a strength day."

His eyebrows rise. "I— Uh, yeah. Sounds good."

He pulls his wheelchair over, fidgeting with the seat and with his positioning on the bike. But then he collapses against the backrest with a sigh.

"Are you a hypnotist now, too? What is this, reverse psychology?"

I stop what I'm doing and face him with a grin. "I have no idea what you're talking about."

"Yeah, yeah," he says with an eye roll. "I call bullshit. What are you really asking me?"

Immediately, I sit on the floor in front of him. "What are you so scared of?"

"Who says I'm scared of anything?" he asks, eyes narrowing.

Now I'm the one rolling my eyes. "Roman, we've been working together for months. At this point, assume I can read your facial expressions."

He opens his mouth to argue with me, then thinks better of it. Letting out a sigh of defeat, he says, "In that case, I'm assuming you've already guessed the answer to your question."

I shrug. "Maybe. But I want to hear your answer."

He chews on his bottom lip, contemplating how much he wants to reveal.

"This part is...hard for me," he finally admits. I nod for

him to continue. "I told you this was when I quit. Because it hurt too much to fail at something as basic as walking. And when you made me start gait training again, I only did it because I trusted you. I still *wanted* to quit again. Just as much as last time. But...you made me want to try it anyway."

*Fuck. I think I'm gonna cry now.*

Sure enough, my eyes fill with tears. It's not just that the sentiment is what every physical therapist wants to hear, it's that it's *Roman* saying it. Because I know how trying this whole process has been for him. The fact that I'm the reason he's working through it is...everything.

I try to be inconspicuous about my sniffle, but Roman sees it anyway. His cheeks pinken the tiniest bit in embarrassment, so to cover it up, he rolls his eyes and murmurs, "Jesus, get it together, Doc."

I let out a wet laugh. "I can't help it. That was beautiful."

He awkwardly rubs at his neck. "Yeah, well, don't be flattered just yet. I could very well quit again."

The unthinking confession sobers the mood instantly. I clear my throat, collecting myself as I ask, "Is that what you're scared of? Coming all this way and then quitting anyway?"

Roman lets out a humorless laugh as he drops his hand back to his lap. "That would be the logical answer, wouldn't it? I *should* be scared of that."

"Nothing about this has to be logical," I tell him. "You went through something life changing. Your path to recovery isn't going to be linear."

He watches me for a moment. "I've said it before, but you really would make a great psychologist," he says eventually.

I try to hide my smile but fail. "I'll add it to the resume as a special skill."

"You should. None of the therapists I ever talked to got any of this out of me."

Warmth fills my chest. "Side effect of my bullying therapy style," I try to joke.

He doesn't laugh. He just looks at me in a way I can't read.

My smile fades as our eyes connect. I wait for him to say something else, but when he doesn't, I ask gently, "So then what are you scared of if not quitting?"

The reminder of the true target of this conversation makes him exhale heavily. He looks away from me to stare at nothing on the wall.

"Succeeding, I guess."

*Bingo.*

"Why does that scare you?" I coax.

"Because I don't know what happens after."

That has me frowning. "After...what? After you walk again?"

His gaze slides back to mine. And he nods.

"I mean...you can shoot for running after that. And working out. There's always another goal to reach."

"The goal I want to reach is unachievable," Roman deadpans. "I can work as hard as I can for as long as I can, Liliana, but I'll never get back in the cage again."

Even knowing that fact doesn't stop my heart from hurting for this man. I wish for every one of my patients to reach 100%, but that's never been as true as it is for Roman.

"And I don't know who I am if I'm not a fighter." He continues, his voice taking on a slightly panicked edge. "I don't know what to do with my time, I don't know how to make money. *Everything* in my life revolved around fighting. I don't know who I *am* if I'm not a fighter."

Head spinning, I pull in a deep breath as I organize my

thoughts. "Okay, let's ignore the problematic pieces of that and assume for argument's sake that that's true. You're done fighting. Is that usually the end of the world for fighters? What do they do after they retire?"

"Teach. Open a gym. Train the next generation of fighters."

I should've known he'd be stubborn enough to have an answer for anything.

"So *no* fighters ever enter another line of work? Or retire into a different hobby?"

"It's not a *hobby*, Liliana. That's exactly my point."

"Okay, that was a poor choice of words—"

He leans forward onto his thighs, begging me with his eyes to understand.

"The people who make it into the top 10 in an organization like the UFC don't just stop being a fighter. Those qualities and habits and memories that got them to the highest level? That stays with them. And when they're too old or injured to stay at the top, they *choose* retirement. They prepare for a life without fighting." Sadness shines in his eyes. "I didn't get to do that."

I nod in understanding, my eyes searching his. "Okay, I get that. And I hate that you didn't get to do things at your own time. But Roman...those guys still have a whole other life after fighting. They don't just *stop* living."

Roman slumps back into the seat with a defeated sigh. Raising my eyebrow, I give him a look that screams, *well?*

He throws his hands up in exasperation. "I don't know what to do with myself, alright? I don't have anything outside of MMA."

My thoughts flash back to our very first conversation that night on the roof. We had a similar conversation then, him asking me about my hobbies and me realizing he had none. The only interest he mentioned was—

"What about school?" I blurt out. "Have you thought about going back?"

Roman blinks at me, clearly shell-shocked by the turn in conversation. "Have I...what?"

"School. You had said you were really good at it but that you didn't go to college because that's when you started taking fighting seriously. You could always go back, find new interests."

I can *see* his head spinning as he tries to catch up to the current topic. "So just...go back to school," he says in a disbelieving voice. "As if I'm an eighteen-year-old."

"Why not? Plenty of people go back to school later in life. And don't act like you're not still in your twenties."

He turns an angry glare on me, finally giving me a real reaction. "I'm not twenty-*one*," he spits out. "I'd stand out, no matter what. Plus, it wouldn't take long for someone to recognize me and spread it all over campus that the former contender-turned-nobody is now spending his Saturday nights in the library studying the Civil War."

*Civil War. That's right; he likes history.*

But instead of latching on to that fact and driving my point home, I quirk an eyebrow and say, "So now you're too good for school *and* too arrogant. Nice."

"That's not—" Roman exhales his exasperation. "Of course, I'm not too good for school. It's just...not a good idea for me."

I push a little harder. "Why not? You said it yourself, it's not like you're doing anything else right now. You could do an online undergrad program and get your degree. Figure out what you like and go from there. Find a new career the same way twenty-year-olds find their first one."

I know I'm getting through to him when he doesn't answer, he just glares at me in annoyance.

"I think you'd do great as a history major," I comment casually.

His eyes might actually bug out of his head. "A *what?* Where did that come from?"

I shrug. "You just seem to like history."

His baffled expression doesn't fade an ounce. "So... because I can appreciate a good history documentary, obviously I need to go to college to make a whole new career out of it. Makes sense."

I sigh, knowing I've reached the end of this argument and that there's no way I'm winning it. Today, at least.

Which is okay, because I'm suddenly hit with an idea so perfect, I have to actively fight against wiggling in excitement.

Instead, I stand and wipe my pants down. "Alright, fine, forget I said anything. It was just a stupid idea."

He relaxes at that, but only slightly. There's still a flicker of suspicion in his gaze.

"So...Saturday then?" he asks. "Are we doing strength or gait training?"

"Strength," I answer, restarting my cleanup of the FES pads. But then I snap my fingers and turn to look at Roman again, as if something just occurred to me. "Oh, before I forget. Wanna grab dinner with me this week?"

He blinks at me. Then again.

"Are you on drugs?" he finally asks.

A huge grin splits my face. "Nope. Just using my patented physical therapy method. What do you say?"

"You're serious," he says. Not a question.

"I told you, I've never lied to you," I answer.

His eyes narrow slightly. "I don't understand what's happening right now."

"Nothing's happening. We'll just hang out for a little, have a conversation that doesn't revolve around muscles or sensation. That's it. It'll be fun."

I can *see* that he wants to say yes. But beside the suspicion, there's also a little bit of nervousness, which he confirms when he says, "Going out in public isn't exactly my idea of a fun time."

My heart softens for him, and I'm about to assure him that *it's okay, it was just a stupid idea*, when he sighs, and all those feelings fade. Or at the very least, don't stop him from saying yes.

"Alright. I'll go. I still don't know what you have up your sleeve, but I'll go. And I reserve the right to leave at any time, for any reason."

I grin and just barely stop myself from excitedly clapping my hands together. "You'll love it, I promise."

After a moment, Roman looks up at me and asks, "Is this a bad idea? I mean, I'm assuming it's not normal for physical therapists to hang out with their patients outside of the clinic. Are you even allowed to do this?"

I meet his eyes and answer honestly. "No, I'm not."

But somehow, my brain never takes that thought one step farther to the idea of consequences. Because there isn't a sliver of doubt in my mind that this is the right thing to do for Roman.

**21**

---

**ROMAN**

Approximately zero percent of my confusion has faded by the time I get to the restaurant on Thursday night.

I have no idea what I'm doing here. I thought for sure Lily would text me after our session this week and say *just kidding*. I didn't understand what she was thinking when she first asked, and I still don't now.

I don't think it's a date, because there was nothing romantic about the way she asked me. If she had brought it up after a lingering touch, I might think otherwise, but no, she asked after a passionate argument about what I should be doing with my life. It doesn't make sense.

And yet, there wasn't a chance I was saying no. The only reason I didn't say yes immediately is because I was startled and confused by the question. But more time with Lily? And outside of the place that I hate the most? Yeah, she didn't have to twist my arm. Confusion be damned.

But that doesn't mean I'm not embarrassed when my Uber drops me off at the bar. I haven't been to a bar since my injury, or really any public place, because it's both annoying to do research on whether a place is wheelchair accessible, and frustrating to have to orient myself in a new place once I'm there. It's easier to just stay home, where I'm at least comfortable.

Lily must have sensed my trepidation because she assured me more than once that she wouldn't let it be stressful for me. I can admit to myself that her promise was enough, but having her pick a non-weekend evening and seeing on Google Maps that it's wheelchair accessible definitely helped.

The moment I enter the bar and spot Lily at a table in the back, all of my nerves disappear. I'd fumble my way through any new environment for her.

I try not to move toward her as quickly as my chair will allow. But then she sees me, and a blinding smile appears on her face, and that becomes immediately impossible.

"Hi," she says excitedly when I reach her.

"Hey," I return gruffly.

She gestures to the place across from her, where she's already cleared out the restaurant chair for me. "Perfect timing. I think that's our waitress is coming with our drinks."

I settle my chair just as her comment registers. Frowning, I say, "Bold choice, ordering for someone you don't know."

She huffs a laugh as she leans back in her seat and crosses her legs, every bit the picture of a self-assured woman.

"Roman, I could put your observation about my coffee preferences to shame. Trust me, I know your drink order."

I lean back in my own chair as I study her, letting myself accept the truth of her statement, but not letting myself believe that it's for any reason besides those observations being necessary to do her job.

I spot a waitress approaching our table with a smile and two glasses on her tray. "I guess we're about to find out," I muse in a low voice.

The waitress stops next to our table with two red cocktails, the same one for both of us. I squint at it, trying to figure out what Lily ordered.

"Hi, folks, how's everyone doing?" the waitress says cheerily. "Are we planning on some food tonight, or are we just here for the vibes?"

Lily glances at me, then quickly looks back at our server. "We might get some food in a little bit, but we're good with just drinks now, thank you."

"Sounds good, I'll check back in a little bit then. Just wave me down if you need me."

Once she's gone, Lily turns her attention back to me. "*Are* you hungry? I guess I just assumed we'd chat over a drink first, but this place has great burgers if you want food."

"What is this?" I ask, gesturing at the drink and ignoring her question.

Her lips twitch. "Try it."

When I realize she's not going to answer my question, I sigh and lift the glass to my lips. Immediately, berries and mint explode on my tongue.

And with that comes a memory from two years ago.

I huff a laugh as I set the drink down. "I forgot about this. I don't think I've had a mocktail since that night."

Lily quirks an eyebrow. "Seriously? But you were selling mocktails so hard that night."

I shrug. "I could tell you weren't a drinker. It was the perfect way to flirt with you."

She twirls her own glass in front of her, clearly hesitating. "You could've come over with any line and I would have flirted right back."

The air between us heats at that quiet admission. I hold her gaze for long enough to see her pupils dilate and her breath catch, until she quickly looks back down at her drink. Which gives me free rein to look at *her.*

It's the first time I'm seeing her in street clothes. Normally, she's in scrubs, and that first night she was in a sexy dress. Now, she's wearing a simple white long-sleeve shirt with jeans and a pair of tennis shoes. Her hair is down, and I think she's wearing makeup because her eyes look brighter than they normally do and her lips are pink in a way that makes her look freshly kissed.

*Fuck, now I'm thinking about kissing her. Would she taste like berries again?*

I cough to clear my throat. When she finally looks back up at me, I gesture between us.

"What is this, Lily?" I ask, my voice sounding rough even to my own ears. "Why are we here?"

She chews nervously on her bottom lip. *Fuck, I'm thinking about kissing her again.* What did I ask her?

I look down at the drinks and remember. "Are we reliving the night we met or something?"

She shakes her head. "No, of course not. This has nothing to do with our history."

"Then what? Even with your twisted therapy methods, I doubt a field trip to a restaurant is going to help my recovery."

*Tell me it's a date. Tell me this night has nothing to do with my recovery.*

But no matter how badly I want those to be the words that come out of her mouth, I'm also not surprised when she says, "I just thought it would be good for us if we spent some time outside of the clinic. Is that so bad?"

Thinking back to the moment she asked me out, I

try to remember what we were talking about. "You asked me out after our conversation about me going back to school. How does your brain jump from that to dinner?"

She gives me an innocent look that I'm not buying at all. She's up to something.

"So, what is it? Why are we—?"

"Hey there, folks, happy Thursday and welcome to Trivia Night!"

I'm interrupted by a voice coming over the loudspeaker. Frowning, I turn toward the sound to find a curly-haired guy sitting in a high-top chair with a mic in one hand and tablet in the other.

"My name is Ted, and I'll be your host for tonight," he says into the mic, an excited grin on his face. "In just a moment, our lovely waiters and waitresses will be coming around to offer you a pen and paper if you'd like to participate. Just fill out a team name at the top, and we'll get started once everyone's ready!"

I turn back to Lily, my confusion only tripling when I realize she doesn't seem surprised by this turn of events.

"You brought me to Trivia Night?" I ask incredulously. "Why?"

"Our prize tonight is a little different than our usual." The host continues. "The team that answers the most questions correctly will win *two* tickets to the Movie Tavern! So, strap on your trivia caps, and get ready for Trivia Night – History edition!"

My eyes widen as a lightbulb goes off in my head. And my suspicions are confirmed when Lily's expression turns sheepish.

"Okay, before you get annoyed," she hurries to say, "I'll preface this by saying, we can leave if you want to. Or we can stay and not play. The trivia thing was secondary to wanting to hang out with you."

I sigh. "So, what was the plan, enter me into a competition against my will and revive my love for history?"

Her lip twitches, relief shining in her eyes. "Something like that, yeah."

I take the pen and paper that our waitress offers us. "The only reason I'm doing this is because I'm incapable of walking away from a sure-fire victory." Scribbling a few words on the paper, I add, "And when I win those movie tickets, I'm going to make you watch whatever paranormal horror movie is playing in theaters."

She shudders at the idea. But then she realizes what I was writing and angles her head to look closer.

"*The Agony of De Feet?*" She gives me an exasperated look. "Really?"

I lean back in my chair, feeling entirely too pleased with myself. "Take it or leave it."

Huffing a laugh, she slides her drink closer to her and finally takes a sip. "If you end up losing, that's going to be a really embarrassing choice."

It only takes her five questions to realize...that's not going to happen.

"How on earth do you know the answer to *that?*" she asks, gaping at me as I'm, yet again, writing on our paper as soon as the host finishes reading the question.

"Probably remember it from some documentary," I say with a shrug.

She shakes her head as if to clear the haze. "Okay, I can understand knowing World War Two facts, but what documentary could you have possibly been watching to know that the construction of the Great Wall of China began in the 7th century?"

"Probably a documentary on the Great Wall of China."

For a moment, she only blinks at me. Then she sighs. "You're annoyingly smart, aren't you?"

I wink. "One of my good qualities."

"Which two city-states fought in the Peloponnesian War?" comes the next question. I scribble down *Athens and Sparta*, feeling Lily's gaze on me as I do it.

"So, why don't you want to go back to school again?" she finally asks. "Clearly, you've got the brain for it. It probably wouldn't even be very hard for you."

I tense slightly at the question, despite having a feeling this was coming.

My shrug is stiff. "I just don't see what it would accomplish."

She hums thoughtfully, and I suck down half my drink to busy myself.

"Who was the president during the Cuban Missile Crisis?"

I scribble down *John F. Kennedy.*

"I heard you spent a lot of time teaching classes, even when you were fighting," she says it nonchalantly, swirling the straw around her drink.

I, on the other hand, am immediately suspicious. "You *heard* that? Where?"

She waves me off. "Okay, fine, I read it. But is it true?"

I consider the risk of answering, but eventually nod.

"Interesting," she muses. I open my mouth to ask her *what* is so interesting, but I don't get a chance to get any words out.

"You know, when I was training to become a scuba diving instructor, I had to go through an Instructor Development Course," she says, staring out at nothing as she speaks. "I thought for sure it was going to be a bunch of practice exams, so I studied like crazy during the weeks leading up to it. And then I walk in on day one and realize: we're not doing anything with academics. It's all about teaching. They spent two whole weeks teaching us *how* to teach. Nothing to do with diving. Somehow, it had never occurred to me, that was a skill in itself. Arguably the most important skill. One that not everyone mastered, because some people flunked the exam."

She gives me a pointed look, but all I can manage is a bewildered, "You're a scuba diving instructor?"

Groaning, she drops her head in her hands. "*That's* all you got out of that?"

"Uh, yeah, pretty much. That's one of the coolest things I've ever heard."

Lifting her head, she sighs and begrudgingly acknowledges, "Okay, yeah, it's pretty cool. But that's not my point."

"Then what's your point? That because I like documentaries and I've taught a couple kids how to throw a punch, that I should be a history teacher now?"

"I mean...yeah, kinda."

The disbelief likely written on my face just makes her sigh.

"I'm just saying, you have more options than you think. That's all."

I don't respond, I just write down the answer to the next question that's called out.

"Because when you inevitably get back to your feet and you stop having an excuse to put off living your life, you're going to need something to turn to. And I think you'd be a great teacher."

The breath I let out is rife with frustration. I don't want to deal with this part of my injury right now; the physical aspect of it is hard enough.

"If I promise to think about my future career possibilities, will you let this go?" I ask. "Or is this going to become a career fair?"

She hides her smile by taking a sip of her drink. "No, I'll stop."

And maybe I'm still grumpy about the intervention, because I'm still frowning as I ask her, "So, are you going to leave now that you've accomplished your mission? Is that the only reason we're here?"

Slowly, she puts her glass back down. "No, I'm not going to leave," she says quietly. "We can just relax and hang out now." When her gaze meets mine, I see everything she's not saying.

Before I realize it, I'm lost in thoughts of *what if this was a date?*

I wonder what it would've been like to call her after the night we met, to set a time and place for dinner. To pick her up in my nice car, and to open the door for her when I did. To spend the night talking and laughing, knowing I could offer to walk her to her door at the end of the night.

And then I think about what it would be like *now*.

Because even if she wasn't my physical therapist and we were just two people on a date, I still wouldn't be able to do any of those things.

Before I can drown in an inevitable spiral of self-pity, the host's voice rings out over the speakers.

## 22

# ROMAN

"Alright, folks, that's the end of our first round! We'll take a quick break while I check through each team's answers and then reconvene to announce the winners in about twenty minutes. So go ahead and order another round of drinks for the table or grab some food while you wait. I highly recommend the burger of the day if you're hungry."

As if on cue, my stomach grumbles loud enough to be heard over the bar chatter.

"Hungry?" she asks innocently, smiling into her drink.

I look around for our waitress. "Just a little. I somehow forgot how many calories my body needs when I'm actually working out hard."

Locking eyes with our waitress, I send the universal gesture for *when you get a minute*. When I turn my attention back to Lily, it's just in time to catch her eyes snapping from my chest to my face.

Realizing she was checking me out, a smirk lifts the corner of my lips. I wore a simple black t-shirt tonight with jeans, but I realized when I was getting ready earlier that I'm probably going to have to buy some new clothes soon. With the way I've been working out lately, my muscles, especially my upper body, have filled out to the point of stretching my clothes at the seams.

Which Lily has noticed. And if the way her cheeks go pink is any indication, she's not having very pure thoughts about it.

"What do you want to order?" she asks. But one of the words comes out as a squeak, making Lily wince in embarrassment.

"The cheesesteak hoagie," I answer easily. "A full one. I'll probably get some fries and mozzarella sticks with it, too. What are you getting?"

Her eyes widen at the amount of food I plan to order. "Uh, I guess I'll get a cheesesteak hoagie, too. But just a half."

I nod my approval just as the waitress stops by our table. We order our food, then settle back into a comfortable silence after she leaves. But I'm terrified of lapsing into any discomfort now that we've decided to treat the rest of the night as an ordinary hangout, so I speak first.

"So...what would you normally be doing on a Thursday night?"

She seems amused by my question. "Rotting at home on the couch with Garfield."

I chuckle. "Alright, what if we were doing this on a Saturday night?"

She hums. "Saturday *night?* Probably nothing. Not much has changed from when you met me two years ago. I'm still not a big partier. Possibly going out to dinner with my friend Tina, but that's about it." I'm about to ask a follow-up question when she adds, "Now if we're talking weekends in general...that's a different story."

My eyebrow quirks in curiosity. "Do tell."

She shrugs, smiling. "Tina always teases me for it, but I really only have two modes: homebody or adrenaline junkie. I'm either sitting at home, bingeing five seasons of Breaking Bad, or diving a shipwreck with my brothers. I have no in between."

"I feel like those things would appeal for different reasons," I say with interest. "Although, even before my injury, I don't think you would have gotten me into a shipwreck. Swimming with turtles, absolutely, but going *inside* a shipwreck? That sounds terrifying, Liliana."

"You say that now, but I bet I could change your mind," she says. "It's a surreal and incredible experience to be swimming between the tables of an old dining hall."

I try to picture it, which is why it takes me a second to notice that Lily is looking at me funny, her eyes slightly glassy.

And then I realize...it's the first time I've talked casually about the before and after of my injury.

The thought is a shocking one. So much so that I need to steer the conversation back to Lily before I can dwell on it.

"So...brothers? Plural?"

She nods. "Two. Sean is older, Colin is younger."

"What about your parents?"

I watch her throat move on a rough swallow. "It's just my dad. My mom passed away when I was young."

My chest tightens, knowing the loss of a parent all too well. "Shit, I'm sorry, Liliana," I say quietly.

She gives me a shaky, but genuine, smile. "It's okay. It was a long time ago."

I take a sip of my drink, giving her an opening. After my dad died, I shut down any conversation about him when people tried to talk to me. But on the other hand, I could see that it helped my mom to talk. I want to give Lily the opportunity to take this conversation whichever way she needs, and I'll be supportive regardless.

I think she might know what I'm doing because she gives me a grateful smile. "Do you have any siblings? And if you don't, would you like to borrow any or all of mine?"

I let out a relieved chuckle. "No and no. Sorry, I've already got a friend who acts like an annoying little brother. I don't think I could handle any extras."

She seems to perk up at that tidbit. "Oh yeah? Who's that?"

"His name's Mikey. We were best friends in middle school. We...lost touch after high school for a few years, but one day, he just showed up on my doorstep like a stray." Huffing a laugh, I add, "At any given point, he might walk into my house and raid my fridge. The guy has zero boundaries."

When Lily's smile grows, I study her for a moment. "He would absolutely love you," I tell her. "If he were here, I guarantee you two would become instant best friends, and I'd be left third wheeling in the cold, suddenly the butt of every joke."

"Well, now I have to meet him," she says with a laugh. "I'll take all the help I can get with making you the butt of every joke."

I shoot her a glare, but there's a playful undertone in it. We've come a long way from the grumbles and glares of day one.

We're interrupted briefly when the waitress appears with our orders, and the food smells so good that our conversation stops for a few minutes as we both tear into our cheesesteaks.

Lily lets out a groan of appreciation, then covers her

still-full mouth with her napkin and says, "This is the ideal pub cheesesteak."

I nod my agreement, too busy taking another giant bite to answer with words.

"What would you say your favorite food is?" she asks.

"Right now? This cheesesteak."

She laughs. "No, seriously."

I take my time chewing as I think over my answer. Then I swallow and say, "Steak. Doesn't matter how many times I've eaten it, somehow, it's always going to be my favorite." Gesturing at my cheesesteak, I add, "It's probably why I was only half-kidding about this cheesesteak."

She's smiling as she shakes her head. "For some reason, I expected you to go in the opposite direction and say some kind of greasy, super unhealthy fast food."

My nose scrunches in distaste. "Definitely not. I won't argue that some of them taste really good, but I don't think any exist that don't make me feel like total shit immediately afterwards."

I'm too busy taking another giant bite of my cheesesteak to notice Lily's hesitation.

"So...then what's the excuse for smoking?"

My eyebrows rise as I look up and meet her gaze. She's clearly calling me out.

After a moment, I sigh and drop the sandwich on my plate. "Touché. It's a filthy habit."

She snorts, which might be the cutest fucking sound I've ever heard, especially with the added sight of her chowing *down* on that cheesesteak. "No shit. But that doesn't answer my question."

Another sigh, this one heavier. I figured she would ask me eventually. It's too-obviously a side effect of my injury.

"It started as a 'fuck it' moment where I just wanted to

destroy my body," I admit. "And then it kind of grew on me. It became this weird form of stress relief, and after that, it was just a habit." I shrug. "So bottom line is, I don't really have an answer for you."

She cocks her head. "I guess it doesn't really matter at this point. You'll probably walk any day now, and then you'll have to quit because of our deal."

"I basically already have," I murmur, more to myself than to her.

She frowns. "What?"

I shrug again, trying to play it off. "I haven't really been smoking lately. Only time I do is when I light one out of habit or when I'm stressed."

Her mouth drops open. I want to tease her about the lettuce stuck between her teeth, but instead, something very different comes out of my mouth. Somehow, acknowledging the fact that I'm smoking less feels...freeing. This disgusting habit that I only picked up as a way to self-destruct feels way less needed than it used to.

"You know what I hate about it?" I ask, suddenly animated. "It kills my taste buds. Food tastes different when I smoke. It makes everything bland."

Lily's nose scrunches adorably. "That sounds horrible."

"It's the fucking worst. Between that and not being able to work out the way I want to, I feel like I haven't been able to enjoy food in two years." Absentmindedly, my gaze drops to my plate. "Or not until recently, I guess," I muse.

When I look up, that same glassy look from earlier is back in Lily's eyes. But this time, I don't run from it, I just accept it with a smile and say, "You have lettuce in your teeth. By the way, what's *your* favorite food?"

She goes bright red and fumbles for her phone so she can pull up her camera app. I chuckle at the way she demurely picks the lettuce out, turning so that I can't see her do it.

I'm finishing off the last bite of my sandwich by the time she turns back. Her eyes widen at my plate as I go for the mozzarella sticks, but she still answers my question.

"Um, probably Hungarian food. It's my comfort food."

I pop an entire mozzarella stick in my mouth. "That's meat and potato dishes, right? Would I know any specific ones?"

"Goulash, maybe. It's a beef stew."

"I didn't know people even made stew still."

"Somewhere, my poor grandmother is turning over in her grave," she mutters. When I give her a confused look, she explains, "My dad's mom was Hungarian. She's one of the reasons it's a comfort food—the other is that I *love* a good meat and potato dish. But a lot of the famous ones are stews." Her eyes light up with excitement. "Their food is *incredible*. You would love it." And then she hesitates in a way that has my focus zeroing in on her next words. "Maybe I'll make you some after you're discharged from the clinic."

The air becomes suddenly thinner. Because that's not a casual comment.

That's a future comment.

I don't get a chance to respond to it—if I even could—because static suddenly crackles through the speakers and the MC's voice sounds out.

"Alright, folks, we have our winners! And it looks like it's by a *landslide*. Wow. This is incredible. Congratulations to our winners... *The Agony of De Feet!*"

A cocky grin slowly slides across my face.

"Where are our winners sitting?" the MC calls out, looking around. "I've got your prizes right here!"

When I raise my hand, he makes a beeline over to us,

microphone still in his grip as he drops an envelope on the table.

"Congratulations to *The Agony of De Feet!* Not only have you won two tickets to the local movie theater, but you've also set a History Night record here at King's Cross. Out of the thirty questions asked, you got *twenty-nine* of them correct!"

There's a smattering of applause around the restaurant, but I barely notice, because all I can think about is that I'm annoyed I got one question wrong.

When the MC finally walks away and calls an official end to Trivia Night, I wipe my hands and reach for the envelope.

"Movie Tavern. Nice." I slide the tickets back inside, then meet Lily's gaze with a grin. "So, what horror movie are we going to go see?"

---

I don't think either of us is ready to leave when the waitress finally brings us our bill.

We've been here for almost two hours. After Lily finished her cheesesteak, she ordered another drink, pulled her leg up on her chair for a more comfortable position, and promptly asked me for my top three movies.

After that, we snowballed from one random question to another. We talked about our likes and dislikes, shared memories, told meaningless stories. It was comfortable and...refreshing. Because God knows our entire relationship has been centered around the most serious part of both of our lives, so being with her in this kind of setting has been a relief.

It didn't help that my affection for Lily grew when a

dessert menu was dropped at our table and her eyes grew adorably large at the idea of cheesecake. She tried to get me to eat some, but I lied and said I'm not a fan of that particular dessert. In reality, I just wanted to watch her as she ate it, dancing excitedly in her seat.

But it's our waitress's second pass by the table to ask if we need anything else, so it's obvious that the night needs to end.

"We'll take the check," I tell her with an apologetic smile. It turns into a sigh when she has the check immediately ready to whip onto our table, but I just reach for my wallet and pull out my card.

"Here, we can split it," Lily argues.

I quirk an eyebrow at her. "Not a chance, Liliana."

Her lips purse. "But tonight was my idea. Honestly, I should be the one paying."

"Not a chance," I repeat. Then I drop my card on the tray and hold it out toward our waitress, who hurries off. It earns me a glare from Lily, but I merely wink at her in return.

The gesture is something of a mask, though. I always would have paid, but the real reason I wanted to is because it's the only semblance of masculinity I can gather tonight. If I can't pick her up in my car, or hold a door open for her, or even call this a true date, the least I could do is pay.

Once we've settled the bill, we silently gather our things and head toward the door. It isn't until we're outside and I pull out my phone that I realize, *fuck, I should've called an Uber while we were still at the table.*

I'm trying to figure out how to convince Lily to leave me here to wait alone when she notices the open app on my phone. And it all becomes a moot point because she doesn't even hesitate before asking, "Do you need a ride?"

And every attempt at feeling like a normal guy on a normal date with a normal girl goes right out the window.

I wave her off, trying to hide my discomfort. "Nah, don't worry about it, I'm just going to call an Uber. You don't need to wait for me."

With the way she's gesturing for me to follow her before I'm even done talking, I don't think she was really asking. "That's silly. I have my car here and nothing else to do tonight. I'll drive you home."

I suck in a breath, still undecided, and watch her walk toward her car. It's only twenty feet from the restaurant entrance, so when she reaches it and turns back to lift her eyebrows at me in question, I let out a shaky exhale and direct my wheelchair her way.

She drives an SUV, so finding space for my chair isn't a problem. It's the awkward process of getting in and out that makes me nervous.

I eye the passenger door, mentally calculating if I can get in without needing her help. But I realize quickly that I would need to take the wheels off if I wanted to do that, and this chair is a bitch for that kind of thing.

Lily must notice—and translate—the muttered curse under my breath, because she looks at her car, then back at me. "If you get into the passenger seat, I'll just put your chair in the trunk. Easy."

A huff of frustration escapes me. "We're not at the clinic, Liliana. You don't need to be my PT."

She cocks her head, wearing that same familiar look of patience that she wears during our sessions. When she speaks, her voice is gentle, but firm.

"Roman, I'm not being your PT. I'm being a human who cares about you and wants to help."

When I meet her eyes and see the truth in them, I swallow thickly and nod. I should know by now that any offer from Lily is genuine. That knowledge is what makes me move to the passenger side of her car and transfer into the seat.

# 23

# LILIANA

Roman is tense. I can feel it in the air, can see it in the stiff way he transfers into the passenger seat, even though I've seen him do the move a million times and know it's as natural for him as breathing by now.

So once I've loaded his wheelchair into the back of my car, I focus all my effort on making him feel as comfortable as possible.

I'm already humming to myself as I settle in the driver's seat and start scrolling through the music on my phone. Based on Roman's walkout song, I think I know what kind of music he likes, but that's not the vibe I'm going for.

After a 2000s punk rock station starts playing through the speakers, I turn to Roman.

His mouth quirks with amusement. "Reliving our teenage years, are we? Should I be picturing you looking like Avril Lavigne in high school?"

I only press my lips together in answer. Which only makes a loud laugh burst out of him.

"Oh my God, you're serious. I was totally kidding. Did you do the pink hair and everything?"

I press my lips harder, and his laugh becomes louder.

"Well, what did *you* look like?" I demand with a glare and shove at his shoulder. "What was your weird teenage phase? Because we all had one, so don't you dare lie that you didn't."

He's still chuckling as he responds. "I was a six-foot string bean the first half of high school. My eyesight's also really bad, so until I got Lasik as a fighter, I had to wear glasses. I wasn't exactly popular."

I smile at the image that conjures in my mind. But then I latch on to one part of his answer and say, "Wait, you said first half of high school. What did you look like in the second half?"

His grin drips with arrogance. "That's when I started training, remember, Liliana? By junior year, I was tall *and* jacked, contacts instead of glasses, and I had finally stood up to the guy who had bullied me since freshman year. Took his place as the most popular guy in school."

For a moment, I only stare at him. Then I let out a heavy breath and grumble, "You are *so* annoying." I shove my phone into his hands. "Put your address in before I channel my teenage hatred of the popular guys and leave you on the side of the road."

He's still laughing when we pull out of the parking lot.

The ride is just as easy as dinner was. Between surprising him with Trivia Night—something I had no idea how he would react to—and sitting down in a place where there were zero expectations or responsibilities for either of us, I wasn't 100% sure how tonight would go. I could only *hope* I would get this version of Roman.

The version that's relaxed, that makes jokes and lets himself be the witty, playful man that he naturally is.

The person he is *outside* of being a fighter.

By the time we near his neighborhood, my face muscles hurt from laughing at Roman's out-of-tune rendition of whatever songs have come up on my playlist. I have to lower the volume to be able to focus on the houses we're passing.

"This neighborhood is so cute," I comment, looking around. "I've never been around here."

"What kind of place do you live in?" he asks curiously.

"Two-bedroom apartment with Garfield and my best friend. It's tiny, but I like the coziness."

It's at that moment that my GPS signals our arrival, and when I turn into the driveway, a cottage appears in my line of sight.

I frown as I lean over the steering wheel. "Is that part of your property?"

He nods and unbuckles his seatbelt as I put the car in park. "It's my mom's house." He hesitates before adding, "Since she's my only family, I obviously needed her help after my accident. But I didn't want to completely blow up her life, so when I went house hunting, I only looked at houses with a pool house or in-law suite."

My chest warms. "That's so sweet," I say softly. "I bet she really appreciated that."

He hums a non-answer as he continues looking out at the cottage, clearly lost in his own thoughts.

I don't think Roman knows *how* sweet that actually is. That even during the hardest, most painful time in his life, a time when anyone would understand him being selfish, he still put the needs of the people he cares about before his own.

I suddenly wish a mirror existed that I could put in front of Roman to show him *see? This is the person you are. This observant, strong, caring, smart man. You may have been an incredible fighter, but you're also so much more than that.*

When I cover Roman's hand with mine, he startles and turns his attention back to me. I give him a smile that hopefully doesn't look as emotional as I feel and whisper, "Do you even realize how thoughtful you are? How good you are to the people you care about?"

His throat works on a rough swallow, and I wonder if maybe he doesn't believe me.

I smile again, squeezing his hand before letting go. "I just thought someone should tell you that.," I say softly.

When I lean back in my seat, he suddenly blurts out, "I lied at the restaurant."

My eyes widen and my heart nervously skips a beat. "You lied? About what?"

I can't read his face as he says, "About why I know so much about history."

My surprise fades into confusion. "Okay…"

He pulls in a big breath. "I told you my dad passed away when I was a kid. What I didn't tell you was that he was in the military." Reaching up, he pulls a chain out from under his shirt. The chain I've noticed before and wondered about.

A chain with dog tags on it.

"He's the reason I'm good at history," he explains, looking down at the tags. "It was what we bonded over. And when he died…it became the only way I could hold on to him."

My eyes prickle with tears, and I place my hand back on his. "I'm so sorry, Roman," I whisper.

"I don't want to make things sad or anything," he rushes to explain. I feel his hand turn over on his thigh so he can grasp mine, and I wonder if he's searching for comfort despite his words. "I just wanted to tell you, I guess. And to say…thank you. Because he would have loved tonight. *I* loved tonight." He lets out a laugh, the sound cracking slightly. "He wouldn't have missed whatever question I got wrong."

Laughing lightly, I sniffle before saying, "I should have asked the guy what it was and then lorded it over you."

An affectionate smile lifts his lips. "I'm a little surprised you didn't, honestly."

"A misstep on my part, for sure," I say with a smile of my own.

A comfortable silence settles between us. He's still holding my hand, clearly not in a rush to break our connection. And despite the tiny buzzing in the back of my head telling me this moment isn't as perfect as it feels because I shouldn't even *be* here, I make no move to take my hand back.

"It was nice being able to spend time with you outside of the clinic, too," Roman says quietly.

Just like that, the air in the car stretches like a taut, just-plucked string. And that tiny buzzing becomes an even drone.

I'm not blind to the fact that we've been pushing boundaries at my job. Physical therapy is a unique healthcare profession in that it relies on building a relationship with clients. It's not like a doctor/patient relationship, where it's a short period of time, with an occasional checkup once or twice down the line. As a physical therapist, I spend hours with my patients, weeks and months, and I need to make them comfortable with me to build the trust that's necessary for me to do my job. It's not uncommon to develop friendships with patients, to joke and tease the way Roman and I do. To support them as a human, not just a professional. It's how I gave him my phone number. Everything I've done with Roman has felt natural—maybe to the point of being oblivious to the implications.

This moment, right here, is the first time I've felt aware of them.

I know Roman feels it, too. Not just because of his comment that was clearly an opening, but also because his pupils have dilated, and his breaths are coming quicker.

He's waiting for me to either acknowledge the dangerous territory we're in or move us back to safer ground.

And in the end...

"I enjoyed that, too," I whisper.

Because right now, being with him in a space like this, I feel a little crazed. Not quite out of body, but definitely beyond reality. Like I'm in a dream. And the world doesn't exist outside of this car.

His gaze drops to my lips, which only makes my heart rate speed up. When he meets my eyes again, his pupils have blown black. And I'm powerless to everything else.

"Can you do me a favor?" he asks. Quietly. Maybe trying not to disturb the moment.

"Anything," I breathe out.

My instant answer seems to have an effect on him. He swallows roughly, the movement calling attention to the pulse point in his neck that's going wild.

"I've been thinking about the night we met..." he starts, shifting his body slightly. "About...how it ended." The memory only makes the air thinner, and my breaths come quicker. "And regardless of what...*could* have happened, my biggest regret is that we weren't allowed to finish that kiss." Once more, his gaze drops to my lips, and his voice, impossibly, deepens, setting off flutters in my stomach. "Can we— just for a minute...pretend it's the night we met and redo the ending?"

I don't think I'm even breathing anymore. "You want to...pretend?"

He nods and leans closer, our faces now barely a breath apart. "Just pretend, Liliana." With only a small moment of hesitation, he slowly reaches up to tuck a strand of hair behind my ear, then lets his hand come to rest on the side of my neck in the lightest caress.

I'm already leaning in, eyes on his mouth, moving like my heart is in charge of my body. "Okay," I breathe, so close now that my lips brush his with that one word. "Just for a second..."

The moment he kisses me, every warning bell in my head winks out, leaving a blissful silence.

I release a breathy sigh as his tongue slides along my bottom lip, opening my mouth to him without hesitation.

When his tongue finally touches mine, the kiss takes on a whole new level of urgency. Going from soft and tentative to desperate.

I *moan,* twisting so I can fist my hands in his shirt and his chain to pull him closer. I must not be the only one eager for less space, because Roman immediately tightens his grip in my hair and angles my head to deepen the kiss, consuming me in a way that tingles all the way down to my toes.

The taste of mint and berries on his tongue has flames dancing along my skin. I want to be closer, I want to touch him all over, I want... I want *more.*

But the center console and weird positioning makes it impossible. The only thing I can do is try to memorize every taste, every breath. I want to bottle this moment forever.

In the end, my only option is to either climb into his lap or stop the kiss. When I do finally pull back, we're both breathing heavily, still holding tightly onto each other. Neither of us speaks, we just sit in the moment.

And I think maybe a little bit of reality slipped into the space between our lips, because I suddenly have enough self-awareness to know this bubble is going to pop as soon as I step out of the car to get Roman's wheelchair for him.

But...I don't care. Because just for a few blissful minutes, we weren't patient and physical therapist.

We were Roman and Liliana, just two people who shared an earth-shattering kiss.

# 24

# ROMAN

There's a lightness in my movements today.

I feel good. *Really* good. At this point, it's been weeks since the last hiccup in my therapy, and since then, I've been on top of everything: diet, sleep, working out but not over-doing it, all of it. And despite the fear of success that Lily pulled out of me this week, gait training has also been going well.

Somehow, our conversation during Trivia Night made it disappear.

As I enter the clinic for the first time since that night, I tell myself that those are the reasons I'm excited to be here today.

But I don't think it works very well, because the moment I set eyes on Lily, happiness warms my chest like the morning sunrise.

*God,* she's so fucking beautiful. It's not just her physical appearance, with the shiny blonde hair and easy smile and sparkling blue eyes, it's...*her*. It's the heart she wears on her sleeve.

Not for the first time, it registers that she's one of the few people to never give up on me. She dealt with all my self-hatred, my constant apathy, and she took my angry barbs on the chin like they were nothing. She withstood all of it and never stopped caring. Never stopped pushing me toward a better life.

She's the closest thing to an angel on earth I've ever seen.

That happiness expands, tangling with such an immense wave of gratitude that my breath catches. And when Lily locks eyes with me, and the brightest smile appears on her face, the tsunami inside of me is overtaken by an entirely new emotion.

"Hey," she greets cheerfully when she meets me in the middle of the gym. Her smile hasn't dimmed a watt.

I don't have a shot in hell of containing mine, either. "Hi, Doc."

She presses her lips together, trying not to make her delight over the nickname obvious. And I try not to think any more about those lips, and how they felt on mine.

"Feeling okay?" she asks in that sweet tone of hers, eyes dropping over my body. "Anything hurting?"

I shake my head, my gaze never leaving hers. "I feel great, Liliana."

I watch her shoulders drop the tiniest bit, losing the tension she always carries before she asks me that question.

And that inexplicable feeling in my chest grows.

"Okay good, that's good," she muses, her eyes still traveling over my body. She doesn't see my amused smirk until she asks, "Ready to get started then? Why are you smiling?"

I shrug. "Just happy, I guess."

Affection floods her expression. "Oh," she breathes out, trying to hide her own smile. "I...guess that's acceptable."

I bark out a laugh. "Well, thank God, it's *acceptable*."

She shoves at my shoulder, but she's grinning. "Shut up. You know what I mean." Letting out a mock exasperated breath, she braces her hands on her hips. "Well, since you're feeling so *great* today...let's see if we can hit some PRs with the weights."

I grin, excited to tackle the challenge. "Sounds good to me, Doc."

She shakes her head as I make my way over to the treatment table, where we start with our usual exercises. We don't speak for the next ten minutes, but the silence is a comfortable one. I catch her with a random smile on her face a few times—not that I'm much better today. It isn't until she hits a sore spot on my calf, and I wince, that we speak.

"That hurt?" she asks, immediately concerned.

Chuckling, I respond, "Relax, Liliana. I'm just sore."

"That's because you're working too hard again," she grumbles to herself, already starting to knead the sore muscle.

I have to wait until her massage goes from painful to helpful before I can respond. "Well, what about you?" I tease. "What's your workout regimen? I can't believe I haven't asked you that yet with all this torture you put me through." When she doesn't answer, just leans even harder into the massage, my eyes narrow. "Oh God. You're a 5 a.m. workout girlie, aren't you?"

She shoots me a grin. "Guilty."

Shaking my head, I ask, "How on *earth* do you wake up that early when you're here until 9 p.m.?" When she merely shrugs in answer, clearly trying to tamp down on her grin, I sigh. "Even as a professional athlete, I was always amazed by you people. Earliest I could ever get up for a workout was 6. And that was just wakeup time."

"I don't know, I kinda like being up before the world," she says thoughtfully. "It's quiet. Gives me a chance to catch my breath before the chaos of my day seeps in."

I quirk an eyebrow at her. "You calling me chaotic, Doc?"

When she pinches me, I yelp and jerk away from her. Which only earns me a pleased grin as she straightens.

"Roman Ward, you are the definition of chaos in my life."

I don't know if the underlying meaning is good or bad. I can't read her right now, even though I'm suddenly desperate to. Especially after—

"Come on, let's get started," she says, gesturing over at the weights. "Enough yapping."

Swallowing roughly, I nod and reach for my wheelchair. It isn't until I'm seated and making my way over to the leg extension machine that I have myself composed enough to continue our conversation.

"So...what's the 5 a.m. workout of choice?"

"Spin," she answers excitedly.

I let out a thoughtful hum. "You like biking?"

Lily nods as she sets the height and weight on the machine. "Yeah. My family's mountain biking trips are always my favorite. Sometimes on weekends, I'll bike down Kelly Drive along the river."

"It's a nice view down there," I say absentmindedly as I transfer into the machine's seat. "I used to like running that path."

I feel her gaze on me, can feel her hesitating as she mulls over something. I turn my head to look at her curiously.

"In full transparency, I'm thinking about putting a freeze on my spin class membership," she blurts out. Which only makes my eyebrows pinch. She pulls in a shaky breath and explains, "I kind of want to switch to kickboxing classes."

At that, my eyes widen and my stomach flips. I have to clear my throat before I can ask, "Oh yeah? Why's that?"

But with our gazes locked, I don't even need her to answer. I can see every bit of her heart in her eyes.

And now I'm thinking back to the MMA factoids she dropped when we first started working together, and the day she played my walkout song when I was having a hard day. And I wonder if she goes above and beyond for every patient, or if, maybe, impossibly, I'm just a lucky one.

My chest squeezes at the possibility. I open my mouth to ask *some* version of that question—

"There she is. I *told* you she has a client on Saturdays."

Mine and Lily's attention snaps to the doorway, where two men are entering the gym. The older man has graying hair and a big smile on his face, while the younger man adopts a casual hands-in-his-pockets stance as he looks curiously around the clinic. It looks like there might be a familial resemblance. And actually...

"Dad," I hear Lily say from beside me. "What are you doing here? Is everything okay?"

Lily's dad waves off her concern before walking over and pressing a kiss to her cheek. "Everything's fine. We were in the neighborhood, so we wanted to stop by."

The guy behind him—who I'm assuming is Lily's brother—rolls his eyes and says, "I tried to talk him out of it, but you know he loves his pop-ins." He jerks his head toward me and adds, "She's with a client. You can ask her later, Dad."

"Ask me what?" Lily asks with a frown.

"It's about our trip at the end of the month," her dad explains. "I figured it'd be easier to ask in person, but you're right, I shouldn't be interrupting. I thought you were done at four."

"No, I'm with Roman until five."

"Ah, okay. I'm sorry, I shouldn't have assumed. I'll just call you afterwards, then."

But Lily still looks thrown off by the visit and confused about its purpose, so I tell her, "I don't mind if you take a few minutes. I can wait."

Sure enough, Lily sends me a grateful look before asking her dad, "Can you be quick?" When he nods, she reaches for his arm to pull him aside. "I'll be right back," she assures me.

Once they move to the other side of the room, I'm left alone with her brother. Based on the descriptions Lily has given me, I decide to take a guess.

"It's...Sean, right?"

His eyebrows shoot up in surprise, before a big grin appears on his face. "Yeah. She talks about me, huh?" He chuckles. "Probably because I'm the family's agent of mayhem."

I huff a laugh. "She's never put it like that, but...yeah, that fits the description she's painted."

He shakes his head with a smile. "She's always been the sweet child, that one."

I think about the hell she's put me through with PT and murmur, "I don't know about that."

Sean catches on to my meaning and lets out a loud laugh. "Okay, I can see how a patient of hers wouldn't agree with that. I can only imagine how much of a hardass she is in here."

I snort. "That's putting it lightly. Your sister's kind of a terrorist."

Another booming laugh. "Oh God, I can't wait to put that in the family group chat. The cousins will love that."

Eventually, his laughter fades, and his gaze drops to the

machine I'm working on. Which makes *my* mirth dissolve as well. "Hopefully, the terror she's instilling is working, though," he comments.

I fidget awkwardly in my seat. "Yeah, she's been great."

But then Sean's brow furrows, his eyes moving over me again.

And then they go wide, and his mouth drops open in shock.

"Holy shit, I *know* you!" he yells. "You're Roman Ward!"

*Ah, fuck.*

I clear my throat with a cough. "Yeah."

"Oh my God, I saw you fight at the Garden in 2021! Your fights were *insane*, dude. I swear, you made it look like your opponents were working in slow motion."

Another awkward throat clear. "Thanks, man."

Finally, fucking *finally*, reality hits Sean in the face like I've punched him. His gaze lowers to my legs, and then flicks to my wheelchair.

"Oh... Oh shit. *Shit.* I completely forgot about the accident. I'm so sorry. I feel like an asshole."

"All good, don't worry about it." But my voice is like sandpaper.

Which Sean hears, because he rushes to fix his fuckup. Gesturing toward Lily, he says, "But you said she's been helping, yeah? That's good!"

I don't respond this time. And Sean can't seem to help himself because he still follows that up with, "Do you think you'll fight again?"

That familiar feeling of dread starts to slowly drip down my spine.

I give him a half-answer. "Not at the UFC level, no."

"Ah. Okay. But I bet they have tons of coaching jobs, right?"

I force a smile this time. "Yeah, probably."

And because I don't think I can handle any more of his questions, I quickly steer the conversation in a different direction, not caring how sudden it is. "So...what's the reason for the visit?"

Thankfully, Sean accepts the topic switch. Looking over at his dad and sister, he says, "We've got a family trip coming up, and Dad just wanted to pick Lily's brain for some of the planning. We were finishing up a late lunch when he got the idea in his head."

"Ah, okay. Where's the trip?"

"Moab out in Utah. We're going canyoneering."

I rack my brain for what that might be, but the only thing I can think of people traveling to Utah for is the national parks. "Is that...hiking?"

Sean's face lights up. "More like extreme hiking. They take you to these awesome canyons, but to get to and through them you have to hike, rock climb, rappel, swim, everything. The package I found also includes white water rafting in the tour. It's awesome."

"And Lily's going with you?" I ask.

"It was her idea. For every family trip, a different person picks the destination and activity. I picked last time when we went shark diving. My brother picked skiing in the Alps the year before. This year was Lily's turn."

*Shark diving? Skiing? Extreme hiking?*

*I can't even fathom going for a walk along the river.*

The discomfort inside me grows, slowly morphing into an entirely different animal. This is...a lifestyle I can't access. I'm not sure why it's only sinking in now, considering I've known how much she enjoys adventurous activities, but hearing her brother talk about how often she does them and how excited they make her... It's finally hitting me just how different our lives are.

I swallow roughly, then again, trying desperately to swallow my unease.

At the same time, Lily starts walking back toward me, her father in tow. She must see something on my face because her steps stutter.

I will my face to become blank, hoping she couldn't read much from it just now. Then I force a smile.

"So, you've got a trip coming up?" I ask, attempting a light tone.

She turns toward Sean, her brow furrowing. But almost immediately, she's turning back to me, her confusion morphing into worry. "Yeah..." she starts, sounding hesitant. "I'm sorry, I was planning on telling you, I just hadn't gotten around to it yet. We're doing a long weekend, so I'll miss your Saturday session." She twists her hands, and I wonder who she's nervous for—her or me. "I always schedule a replacement PT for my patients when I travel, so you'll still get your session in. If...that's what you're worried about."

I wave her off with an attempt at nonchalance. "I wasn't worried. I knew you'd take care of me."

I'm more worried that I can't take care of *you*.

*Not that I'll have the chance.*

Lily seems to want to say something else, but her gaze cuts to her family, then back to me.

"Okay, well, we've clearly interrupted *and* overstayed our welcome, so we'll get out of your hair," Lily's dad says, looking between the two of us. "I appreciate you giving us a few minutes. Hopefully, she goes easy on you after this."

Despite myself, I snort and look at Lily. "I don't think she even knows the meaning of that word, Mr. Davis."

"Apparently, Lily is quite the ball buster," Sean excitedly

explains to his dad. "I believe the exact word used was 'terrorist.'"

Lily's jaw drops as her head snaps to me. "You *didn't*." When I only hold my hands up in a gesture of surrender, she plants her hands on her hips and orders, "Take it back."

I quirk an eyebrow at her and say dryly, "Liliana, I've had Philly boxing coaches that didn't push me as hard as you do."

She rolls her eyes. "Oh, I'm sorry, were you expecting me to grab some pom-poms and make up cheers?"

"Honestly, it might be nice to feel supported for a change."

At that, her eyes narrow.

And then she slaps me across my shoulder.

"You're a dick," she grumbles. Which just makes me chuckle.

It takes us both a second to remember that it's not just us in the clinic, that her family is quite literally standing beside us, watching this entire exchange. When I turn my attention toward them, her dad's eyes are wide, and her brother is blatantly gawking.

"Oh, umm...as you can see, Roman is one of my tough love patients," says Lily, stumbling over her words.

Her brother is still staring, but her dad gives us a polite smile and says, "Well, some of us need that, don't we? Whatever helps the recovery." Then he gestures toward his son. "We'll let you two get back to your session. I'm sorry again for interrupting. It was nice to meet you."

I nod at him and reply, "It was nice to meet you too, sir."

"I'll walk you guys out," Lily says hurriedly. Then she looks at me. "Light weights until I get back, yeah?"

I roll my eyes and make a scene about putting the machine's pin in a lighter weight. "Yes, Doc."

It earns me a smile, even as she's already ushering her family toward the exit.

And all my worries about Lily and I living vastly different lives outside of the clinic are forgotten.

For now.

# 25

## LILIANA

Finding out a previous elderly patient passed away shouldn't hit me as hard as it does. It's been months since I've seen Mr. Allen, and even then, he was only my patient for a few weeks. He also passed away in his sleep, in the natural way that older people do. No pain or reason. I shouldn't be fighting back tears when Fran pulls me aside to tell me.

I feel silly about it, so I assure her that I'm fine. And I go back to my day, trying not to let the sadness creep in, trying not to feel as much as I do.

I think I manage because no one says anything. Not even Fran or any of my other coworkers.

When it's time for Roman's session, it becomes apparent that I'm not the only one having a hard day.

He's off, both mentally and physically. It's clear to me that he's having a bad day with nerve pain. I've seen him wince and flinch away from contact a few times, and with the dark circles under his eyes, I can tell he probably hasn't been sleeping well.

Once we finish our warmup and a very light strength

training session, I'm prepared to suggest switching our session to more of a stretching one, instead of the gait training we had originally planned. But Roman surprises me by gritting his teeth and moving over to the parallel bars.

Thank God, I already asked Fran to help today, because I can already tell we're going to need her. Determination or not, Roman's body is struggling.

When I call an early finish, I don't know who's more exhausted, me or Roman. I give Fran a grateful smile behind his back before she leaves us to finish her own work.

"How you doing?" I ask Roman once he's settled back in his wheelchair.

He lets out a heavy exhale. "Fine."

I hand him a cup of water. "I know you're a little touch-sensitive today, but if something hurts that I can fix with a massage, we can always finish with that."

He shakes his head and downs the small cup in two gulps. "I'm okay. But thanks." Once he tosses the plastic in the trash, he glances toward the hallway and adds, "I'm going to go use the bathroom."

Knowing we both need to call it, I wave him off. "Go. We're done for today. I'm going to finish up my notes, so just yell when you're ready to leave."

He hurries out of the room quicker than I expect him to. But I'm too tired to speculate, so I pull my laptop over and start in on my session notes right there in the middle of the gym.

"I'm leaving," Roman calls out ten minutes later. I didn't even hear him come back into the gym. "See you Saturday?"

I nod my confirmation as I close my laptop. "Yup. But wait up, I'm going to walk out with you."

It distantly registers that Roman stiffens at that. I don't realize why until I make my way into the break room to grab my jacket and bag and notice something on the table that wasn't there before.

It's a small pastry box. I can see the extra-large cookie inside it even from here. And on top of it is a Post-it note with a rough scribble of my name.

Surprise freezes me in place, but curiosity moves me forward. The box's design looks familiar. But there's no way—

"Roman." In awe, I lift the box and spin back toward the gym. "Did you... Did you do this?"

He doesn't answer, doesn't meet my eyes. He's embarrassed. He didn't want to be caught with his gift; that's why he was trying to rush out of here.

"How did you do this?" I breathe out.

He gives me a stiff shrug. "I had it delivered. It's not a big deal."

"Yes, but...when? *Why?*"

He still won't meet my eyes. "You seemed like you needed it. Like I said, it's just a cookie, Liliana. All I did was click a few buttons on my phone."

Maybe, but...he noticed. He *cared*. On a day when he's clearly struggling himself, he cared enough to see someone else's pain—and do something about it. And he would've done it silently if I hadn't called him out on it.

"It's from my favorite bakery," I whisper as I open the box. When the heavenly smell of it hits my nostrils, my head jerks up to find Roman's eyes. "How did you know?"

Thank God, he doesn't look away. "I remembered," he says simply.

Emotions crash over me, ones that I try to shove down when it comes to Roman. The main one being affection.

My eyes fill with tears. I want to hug him. I want to return the favor. I want...*something.*

"Liliana," Roman growls, his deep voice bringing me back to this moment. "No crying. It's not a big deal."

I can't help it: his comment makes everything bubble over, and I let out a wet laugh.

"You're so delusional," I tell him lovingly. "You have no idea how thoughtful you are. I mean, no one else even noticed I was having a bad day. And you not only noticed, you took the time and money to do something that you knew would make me feel better."

His eyes soften, and he says quietly, "Of course I noticed."

There's zero hesitation in his words. Combined with the intense way our eyes have locked, suddenly I'm sucking in a sharp breath.

But then he asks, "*Do* you need to talk about it?"

Another laugh bursts out of me, this one easier, and less tear-filled, helping to jolt me from my thoughts. "See? *And* you're good with crying women."

He doesn't laugh with me. He just waits expectantly.

I shake my head, feeling lighter. "No, not really. A patient I worked with a few months ago—an older patient—passed of a heart attack, and it's just...hitting a little harder than I would've expected. I know it's a part of life and has nothing to do with me, but...I don't know, it still makes me sad."

Roman nods. "It speaks to your heart," he says.

It's my turn to shrug awkwardly. "I guess I just feel things more than I should."

"Which is one of your best qualities, Liliana," he says firmly, never looking away from me. "It's what makes you a great physical therapist. And I should know: as a trouble patient, I've benefited greatly from that quality."

Fondness for Roman hits me so hard, it almost bowls me over. *This sweet, incredible, deserving man.*

"I've never thought of you that way, Roman," I whisper, scared to say it any louder. "Not once."

Whatever's passing between us feels...big. Too big for either of us to understand. But it's no less powerful because of it.

Forcing a smile onto my face, I nod at the box in my hands. "And anyway, there's no way you could qualify for that title after this. Surprising me with my favorite dessert on a bad day? You might even earn favorite patient with this."

A playful smile tugs at his lips. "Who knew all I needed to impress you was some sugar. I should've guessed."

I let out a laugh and try to subtly blink the wetness from my eyes. "Well, either way, you're going to need to help me eat this. Blueprint cookies are too much for one person."

Roman glances at the cookie in my hands and lifts an eyebrow. "I could eat three of those in one sitting, Liliana."

I roll my eyes before quickly walking into the break room to grab two forks. "Okay, well, you can get your own cookies then. I'm only offering you half."

His amusement is right back on the forefront. "I ordered that cookie for *you*. If you don't finish it, give it to your roommate or something. Or Garfield."

"He wishes he could have a cookie like this," I murmur, taking a seat on the treatment table beside him. "No, I want to share this with you." I hold one of the forks out to him and add, "Please?"

Shaking his head with a smile, he takes the fork and moves closer to the table. "As if I could say no to you. But you take the first bite. I was pretty sure I got the right flavor, but..."

I stab the fork into the cookie and pop the bite into my mouth. "Definitely the right flavor," I moan, my mouth still full. I cut off another bite. "Double chocolate cookie is a win by itself, but add in a Ferrero Rocher cheesecake filling? *Hellooo, heaven.*"

Laughing, he takes a bite for himself and lifts it to his mouth. Then his head rears back as he points at the cookie with his fork. "Okay, that might even be good enough to fix *my* day. Holy shit. How have I never tried Blueprint before?"

"I think they only opened in Philly recently. They're technically a franchise." I take another bite. "You have a sweet tooth all of the sudden, huh?"

"I think I just grew one," Roman mutters to himself.

*Why can't I stop smiling?* "So, I shouldn't be surprised if you acquire a muffin top? Noted."

With a snort, he takes another bite. "Do you have any idea how much ab work is required to wield a wheelchair? *And* that goddamn harness?" He jerks his chin toward the harness we used today at the parallel bars.

"I have *some* idea," I mumble. My head snaps up, my cheeks heating as I realize what I just let slip. And that Roman is grinning shamelessly at me. I seriously cannot keep my mouth shut around this man.

"Checking me out again, Doc?" he teases. "It's alright, I do the same thing. And personally"—his gaze drops down my body, and my cheeks heat for an entirely different reason—"I think the sweets you eat go to all the right places."

*When did the air thin out? There's not enough oxygen in here.*

This is how it's been for the past two weeks. Ever since that "pretend" kiss turned my world upside down. Our sessions consist of the usual exercises, and our banter is the same as it's always been, but...there's an energy in the air that wasn't there before. It's in the way I know when he's looking at me, and the way his skin always feels warm under my touch. The way my breath hitches sometimes when we make eye contact.

"Roman," I chastise on a breath.

He chuckles as he takes another bite. "You started it."

I start to stutter over a response, but I have none. Instead, I let out a defeated exhale and scoop up the last bit of the cookie.

"So much for keeping things professional..." I roll my eyes at myself.

Another rumble of laughter from Roman, and this time, he puts his fork down. "I don't think we've ever been truly professional, Liliana," he says. When his eyes meet mine, an electric charge zips over my skin.

Reaching up to slowly brush his thumb over my mouth, his hand comes away with a little bit of frosting, and my lips tingle from his touch. It becomes hard to breathe all over again, even before he sucks his thumb into his mouth to lick the frosting off.

His eyes never look away from mine. "All I know is, I'm better with you in my life. Professional or not." There's a beat of hesitation, and something flashes in his eyes. "I just...want you to know that."

My heart rate accelerates even more. After that kiss, it's become an unspoken thing that we don't talk about...whatever *this* is. That because that outside moment didn't technically exist, we weren't going to speak it into existence by acknowledging it.

This is the closest we've ever come.

And despite the risk, knowing that Roman thinks his life is better with me in it...

It's everything.

I have no hope of responding to Roman's declaration. He knows it, too, as he wordlessly takes the empty box from my hands and throws it out. We leave the clinic together, but we're both uncharacteristically quiet as we do it, speaking only when we separate in the parking lot.

"Roman..."

He pauses to look at me.

"Just...thank you," I say simply. "For the cookie. For... tonight." *For noticing. For caring. For...being you.*

He only nods, the smile on his lips so imperceptible, I wonder who would even be able to catch it. "Anytime, Doc."

And just like every other night for the past two weeks, I don't fall sleep for a very, very long time.

**26**

---

# ROMAN

Liliana: Are you a 'blend-in color' swimsuit kinda guy or a 'this is the only time I'll wear crazy colors' kinda guy

I stare at my phone, blinking.

Roman: It's weird that this is the second time I have to ask my physical therapist if she's on drugs

Liliana: It's weird that your first ever sentence to me was offering a mocktail and you still think you need to ask that

Liliana: Now focus and answer the question

I'm unable to tamp down on my smile.

Roman: Hate to disappoint, but I am not a pink flamingos on my swim trunks kinda guy

Liliana: Roman, that just makes me think you DO have shorts with pink flamingos on them

Liliana: Wear them tonight

I frown at my phone.

Roman: Am I to read this as fashion is now part of my therapy? Because I know your methods are insane, but...

Liliana: Hmm. An interesting theory. Now I'm wondering if I COULD work fashion into your therapy.

Roman: Liliana...

Liliana: Relax. Just bring the shorts.

After a moment...

Liliana: Do you trust me?

I don't even hesitate.

Roman: You know I do.

Roman: I'll be there tonight with pink flamingos on, Doc.

By the time I enter the clinic a few hours later, I've managed to come down from the high of Lily texting me—which is insane, because we've been randomly texting for weeks now, and my brain definitely *shouldn't* temporarily lose mental capacity every time her name pops up on my phone—and figured out what she's probably planning.

Aquatic therapy.

I know she noticed my nerve pain last time I was here. I couldn't hide it very well; not that I even feel the need to hide anything from her these days. She knows anyway; plus, it's a relief to be 100% honest with someone. The nerve pain isn't new, but I haven't had a bad case of it in a while. I got used to the usual sensations that come with an incomplete spinal cord injury—the tingling, burning, pins and needles —but I think with our increased training, my body is protesting. I've barely been able to sleep the past week from the pain. I thought about drowning it with booze, like I have in the past, but...I don't want to do that anymore.

I don't know if being in a pool will help, but I'll try anything.

And even if it doesn't...seeing Lily in a swimsuit might.

I try to not-so-obviously check her out as I approach her in the clinic. She's waiting for me, towels in her hands. I take in her clothes, trying to see if she has that knotted string around her neck that always gives away when a girl is wearing a string bikini, clearly in denial about what professional swim attire probably looks like.

"You better be wearing flamingos under those joggers," she says with a disappointed glare at my legs.

Sighing, I stop in front of her and pull up my shirt to expose the waistband of my shorts.

And I delight in the way her glare drops and her throat moves in a rough swallow when it also exposes my abs.

"There's no need to doubt me, Liliana. Haven't I been a good patient lately?"

Her eyes dart to my face, her cheeks pinkening just a little. "You—I-I mean yes, you've been good lately. *Patient.* You've been a good *patient.*"

I don't bother to control my grin. "Happy to hear it, Doc."

Flustered, she gestures toward the hallway. "Just... just *go.*"

My grin widens. "I don't know where we're going. You're just too entranced by my six-pack to realize that."

Finally, she sighs as she starts down the hallway. "I didn't count, but I'm pretty sure that was an eight-pack, Roman."

"It is. I was trying to be humble."

She flashes a glare over her shoulder, to where I'm already following her, but there's a twinkle of amusement in her eyes.

She's already faced forward again when she says, "Why? Cocky looks good on you."

Now *I'm* the one swallowing roughly.

I try to focus on where we're going before my shorts can get too tight. "Anyway, how are we going to do my PT in the pool if the sight of my abs makes you lose focus?"

Another sigh, this one sounding a little powerless. "No idea. This might be a terrible idea, but..." She turns slightly to look at me again. "I hate that you're in pain. I thought water might help."

And just like that, the air sobers.

We're both quiet as she leads us to the pool. I didn't even know this place has a pool. Aquatic therapy was suggested to me a few times, but I couldn't get over needing to be lifted into the water. That, and the general vulnerable feeling of being unable to kick through the water to stay afloat.

When we reach the pool, Lily stops a few feet from the shallow end. Then she turns to face me.

"Your records said you haven't done aquatic therapy. Was it the lift?"

*She knows me so well.* "Among other things, but yes."

She nods. "I figured. We don't need to use it. I trust both of us that you can safely slide into the water. Any other concerns I should know about?"

I swallow nervously and look around the room. It's a small pool, clearly used for something that isn't swimming laps, and I notice Lily somehow made it so there's no one else here. Any fears I have, anything that happens...it's just us.

"What—" I clear my throat and try again. "What exactly are we doing?"

Lily gives me a soft smile. "Whatever we feel like doing. We can get in and use the bars to practice walking—forward and back, side to side—or we can just get in and float."

Slowly, relief trickles into my bloodstream. "Okay. Can we decide when we get in?"

"Of course. But—" *Here it comes.* "I need to put a flotation device around you." She looks almost guilty as she says it. "I'm certified as a lifeguard, but to be extra safe, I figured I'd tie a pool noodle or two around your chest. Is that okay?"

I have a now-rare negative thought of *none of this is okay,* but I can admit the idea makes *me* feel better, too. I nod. "Yeah, that's fine."

I can see the relief on Lily's face. Setting the towels down on a nearby chair, she strips her shirt and sweatpants off in quick motions, then straightens and waits for me to do the same.

I don't think I can move past the pounding in my chest.

She's wearing a modest one-piece blue bathing suit but...at this point, I'm pretty sure she could be wearing a burlap sack and I'd still think she was the most beautiful girl in the world. She might *have* to wear a sack to cover her curves. Because even a swimsuit that covers her tits and ass is tight enough to reveal them.

"Roman?" she asks. My brain catches on to the humor in her tone, and my gaze shoots to her face.

Her hands are on her hips, lips are pressed together, and those blue eyes are laughing at me. "Payback for the abs," she says casually.

I bark out a surprised laugh. "Touché."

By the time I've managed to wiggle out of my joggers and strip off my shirt, I think I hear her murmur, "Definitely a bad idea."

I don't respond. The truth is, I'm relieved our flirting has lightened the moment. I'm hoping the sensation of being in the water helps the pain, because this is actually terrifying.

Slowly, I climb out of my wheelchair and onto the soft water mat beside the pool. Then I scoot over to the edge.

"Hold on," Lily says from behind me. She's been close enough to touch this whole time, of course. I hear her grab something, then feel as she loops it around my chest and fastens it in the back. I look down to see…not quite a floatie, but some kind of flotation device.

"Here," she says, handing me a pool noodle. "I figured you'd feel better having one to hold on to."

She's not wrong. Holding the noodle tightly in one hand, I scoot closer to the edge and prepare to slide into the water. But then there's a splash, and I realize Lily beat me to it.

I quirk an eyebrow at her standing in front of me, the water up to her collarbone. "You gonna catch me, Doc?"

She's not laughing at my teasing.

"Always."

And when I finally enter the water, it's with a racing heart.

I let out the most relieved sigh when the splash has cleared, and I've settled onto the pool noodle. Even in the shallow water, my legs stretched out before me and feet grazing the bottom, the weightlessness feels...euphoric.

"What the *fuck*, Liliana," I groan up at the ceiling. "Why haven't we done this before? This is the least pain I've ever been in."

I barely hear her soft giggle, but I feel the way she grabs the end of the noodle to stay close to me. "I can look into getting you in here during the week sometimes."

"I'd pay any amount of money for that," I mumble, my eyes closing.

She lets me simply float. I revel in the feeling of being weightless, my nerve pain dulling to barely a hum. After a few minutes, I ask, "Can we go a little deeper? So I can straighten and stretch out my legs?"

I lift my head to see her chewing on her bottom lip as she looks toward the deeper end. The whole pool is barely the size of a living room, and the "deep end" looks like it's barely six feet deep, but I know she's mulling over any risks. Finally, she says, "If you're trying to float, can I put a donut around you?"

I nod. I'll agree to anything.

I watch as she climbs out of the pool to grab something I didn't notice when we first came in. It's...a giant inflatable donut with sprinkles?

"Liliana," I scold weakly. "I thought you were kidding."

"That sounds like a personal problem," she quips as she drops back into the water. "It's not a board-certified therapy tool, but...I had a feeling you'd enjoy a comfortable float today. This way, you can rest on it."

When she reaches me, she looks between the donut and

my body with a frown of concentration. "Can you stand and lean on me so I can switch it out?"

Groaning, I pull my legs under me. Once my feet are planted, I force myself to stand, quickly grabbing Lily's shoulders to brace myself.

She rushes to hold my ribs. "Okay?" she asks worriedly.

*God, she's so close. I wish I could pull her closer.*

"I'm good, Doc," I say with a tight smile in an effort to remind myself where we are.

Once she decides she believes me, Lily nods and slides the first flotation device from my chest, down to my waist. That way, she can gesture for me to put my arms through the donut floatie and guide it down under my armpits.

When I can lower my arms and sink my weight into the pool again, I do it with another groan of relief. Lily was right, this is way nicer. I can use my arms to paddle into deeper water to let my legs hang, and then I can relax my arms and head on the inflatable donut.

"I need to put a pool in my yard," I groan. "I'm pretty sure I could sleep like this."

Lily walks over to stand before me. "You might get a little prune-y," she says with a smile.

"I'll happily shrivel into a raisin if it means this kind of pain relief," I all but slur.

She looks downright delighted. "This better be the last time you question my methods."

I lazily wave a hand. "I will never question you again."

She shakes her head with a chuckle. "Who knew I only needed to get you into the water to placate you." Then she sobers and adds quietly, "I'm just glad it helped. I don't like when you're in pain."

Her comment brings me out of the haze I'd sunk into and back to reality. I lift my head so I can study her.

She's only a few inches away from me, close enough that she can get to me in a second. The water is deep enough that I wonder if she has to stand on her toes at this depth. She seems comfortable, though, her hands moving gracefully through the water as she lets me relax, watching me the whole time. Her blonde hair is in a ponytail, the end dipped in the water, and she has water droplets all over her face from jumping in.

I step a little closer, just so I can watch one slide down her cheek.

*Goddamn, she's pretty.*

I think the water must bring out the color of her eyes because they're *piercing* right now. She's never looked more beautiful. Especially with her attention solely on me, never looking away as I shift a little bit closer.

I can't help it—I might die if I don't touch her. Lifting my hand, I place it gently on her face and wipe a water droplet from her cheek.

Her breath hitches at my touch. I wonder if she'll pull away, or if she'll do me the honor of staying this close. I won't make any move to kiss her, even though every fiber of my being is screaming at me to lean in. I just...want her close.

I watch indecision war in her eyes. She glances at my lips, and I wonder if she's thinking about our kiss, the one that never happened. Sometimes when she looks at me, I swear she's thinking of it too. When her gaze lifts again, her hand comes up to cover mine. And a breath whooshes from my lungs when she leans into my touch, her eyes dropping to half-mast.

"Roman," she murmurs, sounding as dazed as I did a minute ago. It's not a warning, as I thought it might be, though.

My eyes drop to her lips, the need to taste the sound only growing. *She's so perfect.*

But I'm not yet completely out of my mind. I know where we are. I know what's allowed and what's not. It's not like the night she drove me home, when we could pretend...

"I know," I murmur, letting my thumb brush over her cheek again. Just to touch her soft skin, to feel the warmth of the flush.

My gaze moves back to her eyes, finding her staring back at me. She doesn't shy away, our connection staying locked as I crystallize this moment to hold on to for when I have to let her go.

But not before I tell her softly, "Thank you."

My words are loaded with meaning. She knows it, too. But she simply smiles and leans into my hand for another moment before pulling back. "You're welcome."

As soon as there's a little bit of space between us, the water feels cold, and a shiver runs through me.

Lily notices, of course, and jerks her head toward the bars at the other end of the pool. "Want to do a little bit of work? We don't have to stay here for the whole hour; we can plan for half-hour sessions in the future."

I smile again, but this one's tighter. "Sounds good, Doc."

As we move through the water, I wonder if this tension is going to last our entire session, if these moments of *want* are going to become more and more frequent during my time with Lily.

Leave it to her to lighten the moment, same way she always does.

"So...besides flamingos, what other shorts do you have?"

# 27

# ROMAN

"Alright, Doc, what are we doing today?"

Is it a figment of my imagination, or is she nervous?

She lets go of her bottom lip that she was chewing on and says, "I thought we'd try the parallel bars today."

I glance toward the bars and sigh. I hate that fucking harness.

"Without the harness."

My head snaps back to Lily. "What?" When she only gives me a patient and knowing look, I say, "Lily, I just barely mastered standing on my own. And now you want me to walk?"

She nods in answer.

I look around the room, panic instantly rushing through my veins. This is a huge ask, even for Lily.

"Are we using the FES pads?" I ask, looking for *some* kind of crutch.

She shakes her head. "No. You can lean on the bars if you need to."

I gape at her. "*If* I need to? Lily, I'm *going* to need to. I can't walk."

Her eyes narrow at me. She's been getting more and more strict about me not using that kind of language.

Sure enough, she growls, "Don't make me paint a rah-rah motivational slogan on the wall. You know I'll do it."

My gaze slides over to the bars, my heart beating harder and harder against my ribs. I don't know why I didn't see this coming. We've been repping the same exercises for a while now; I should've known I was due for another push-that-feels-too-hard. I guess I got lost in the enjoying-Lily part of therapy.

"So, you want me to just...stand up between the bars and walk?" I ask in a voice that's too shaky for my liking.

"Yes," she answers firmly, walking over to the bars. "We've worked on all the movements separately, and we've built up your strength... so, now it's time to put it all together."

"Why can't we put it all together with the harness?" I'm pleading, but I'm so terrified of what a failure right now might look like that I don't even care.

"Because you've been using it as a crutch, both mentally and physically." She takes up a stance between the bars, one hand on each side, and gives me an expectant look. "We've been putting this off, and you know it. Come on."

I glance toward the lifting area, wondering if I have any shot at convincing her to just do strength training today, to give me one more session before we try for something this big, but she sees right through me.

Her voice is gentle as she says, "Roman, you're ready. I promise."

My stomach clenches, but I nod, albeit reluctantly. Having no more excuses, I spin my wheelchair toward the parallel bars.

Lily waits patiently as I orient myself. Once I'm stationed

at the end of the bars, I lock the brakes on my chair, place my feet on the ground, and take another deep breath to ready myself. Then I grab the bars and pull myself to my feet.

Lily shoots forward to steady me as I do it, her hands bracing on my ribs to both help slightly with a lift and to ensure I don't do a faceplant if everything gives out.

Gritting my teeth, I adjust my white-knuckled grip on the bars and shuffle my stance slightly to feel more balanced.

Then I do it again. And again.

"Roman," comes Lily's soft voice.

My gaze jerks up to meet hers. She's only a few inches from me, her hands still on my sides, her expression one of determination. I don't know what mine is, but whatever it is, it makes something flash in her eyes that I can't read.

"I told you once that I understood why you didn't want to let yourself hope for this, do you remember that?" she asks. I nod once, stiffly. "Do you remember what else I told you?"

I think back to that first heart-to-heart, the one that made me finally commit to giving a shit about my recovery again. But all I can remember about that moment is Lily asking me to trust her.

When I shake my head, that look flashes in her eyes again.

"I told you that it was okay not to hope for it. That I would carry that hope for you." Her voice drops to a near-whisper. "I'm going to carry it for a little while longer, okay? I just need you to trust me."

My chest tightens with so much appreciation, so much adoration for this girl, I almost can't breathe around it.

Forcing the words past my lips, I say, "I trust you."

A smile appears on her face, and she looks so *happy* that I'm filled with a burst of determination. I straighten my back and say, "Alright, let's do this."

Impossibly, Lily's smile gets bigger. "When you're ready, then."

Looking down at the floor before me, I shift my weight onto my left foot, gripping the parallel bars like my life depends on it, and I *will* my leg to move.

It takes a second, and it happens at a snail's pace, but eventually, my quad muscle twitches and my leg moves. My foot slides forward, never fully getting off the ground and without utilizing the proper heel-to-toe motions that Lily has drilled into me, but it does move. It's a step.

"God," Lily breathes out, the word made of wonder. I don't even think she realizes she said it. She's still holding on to me, still looking down at my legs.

I don't let myself feel anything because the left side is the harder side. This next step is the true test.

Sucking in a big breath, I attempt the same thing with my left leg. I shift my weight to my right side, engage my left quad, and try to take a step.

I barely move an inch. My left quad is still weak enough that I can't get my foot off the ground enough to move it.

My held breath whooshes out of me in defeat.

"That's okay. I'll just give you a little bit of help for this one," Lily consoles me, dropping into a squat. She places her hands on my leg so she can better guide me, then looks up and gives me a nod of encouragement.

I grit my teeth...and try again.

Shifting my weight onto my right foot, I attempt to engage my left quad muscle. Again, it barely twitches in response. But when I feel the gentle pressure of Lily pulling my knee forward and lightly lifting by my hamstring, a shock goes through whatever passageway my brain couldn't access before. And my foot lifts the tiniest bit.

"Perfect," Lily hums, her smile visible even from where I'm looking down at her. She emphasizes the heel-to-toe movement as I work on the weight shift, and then I'm taking another step with my right foot. No assistance needed this time.

"Come on, Roman, you can do this," she encourages, her brow furrowing as she holds her hands around my left leg but doesn't touch. She's merely ready to, if needed.

I once again *will* my leg to move, as hard as I possibly can. I visualize my leg working and my foot moving. I picture myself *walking*.

Slowly, my thigh twitching more than once, I lift my leg, my foot clearing the ground. Then I drop it back down a few inches from where I started.

"Roman..." Lily says in wonder. She straightens and takes up the place she started with: standing before me, ready to catch me as I fall but giving me a look that says she believes with her whole heart that I won't. I feel a flicker of disappointment that she doesn't put her hands on me again, while part of me recognizes that also means another crutch has been taken away that I don't need.

"Do it again," she breathes, looking down at my legs.

I take another step, if only to get closer to her before she can back up. Because my eyes aren't on my legs anymore.

They're on her.

I both see and hear the sob that bubbles past her lips. So, I take another step, wanting, *needing* to be closer to her.

And then I take another. And another. And by the time I reach the end of the parallel bars, a tear is running down Lily's cheek.

"You did it," she says on a cry, lifting her head to look up at me. "I knew you could, but..."

I shift my weight slightly to make sure I can let go of the bar with one hand, the other one still holding firmly. And I lift my hand to Lily's face.

"I think I'm ready to carry that hope now," I whisper.

Her eyes fill with tears all over again, and when another runs down her cheek, I brush it away with my thumb.

And then, I kiss her.

It's everything and nothing like our kisses before this. She tastes just as sweet, and I want her just as much, but things also feel...different.

I'm not kissing her to feel something—I'm kissing her because she's *everything*.

# 28

## ROMAN

I didn't kiss her with the intention of escalating things, but there are so many emotions between us that the heat builds on its own. It builds when her hand curls in my shirt, and when my tongue touches her bottom lip. It builds when a breathy moan leaves her lips, and I automatically swallow it with another hard kiss of my own. It doesn't take long for me to cup the base of her neck and tilt her head so I can slide my tongue into her mouth with a groan.

But after a minute, I pull back, chest heaving as I try to suck in air. I also reach down to grip the parallel bar and steady myself so I don't sway forward and fall into Lily.

Thankfully, Lily doesn't read it as a retreat and stays close enough to keep her grip on my shirt. She's breathing heavily, too.

"I—" I swallow thickly and try again, this time dropping my head forward to touch my forehead to hers. "I want to touch you. Can I touch you?"

She's nodding before I've even gotten the question out. "God, yes. Please."

A relieved exhale escapes my mouth at her answer. Then I'm taking her mouth in a quick, eager kiss.

She looks dazed when I pull away, and I think I catch *her* swaying. "Can you...sit?" she asks. "Right here where you are?"

I look down at the soft flooring and nod. Then I slowly, and very carefully, lower myself to the ground, using my grip on the bars to make sure it's a semi-graceful maneuver. I pull myself over to the wall that the bars are next to and lean my back against it. By the time I'm settled and looking up to see what Lily's doing, she's already lowering herself down to straddle me.

My hands immediately go to her waist to pull her closer. "You're incredible," I breathe against her mouth, only a moment before I'm kissing her again.

It's a relief to be able to kiss her like this. I can touch her anywhere, kiss her anywhere, can feel her *everywhere*. I can kiss her, reveling in her taste and her eager response, even as my hands travel over her body, touching as much of her as I can—up her sides, down her back, around to her ass.

When I reach her ass, I grip her cheeks with both hands and *groan* into the kiss. My touch becomes a little harder, a little needier. Thankfully, so does her kiss.

With her arms around my neck, she's already close enough that there's barely any space between our bodies. But when the desire ignites, her hips start to rock against me.

Instantly, I need more.

Reaching for the bottom of her scrub top, I wait for her hands to go up before I lift the fabric over her head. She's wearing some kind of sports bra underneath, so I quickly tug that off, too, wanting her naked more than I want to breathe.

The moment I'm face to face with her breasts, another groan rips from my chest.

"Jesus," I groan, immediately cupping them with two hands. "You're incredible."

"You said that already," Lily says, breathless, giving away that she doesn't really mind the praise.

"I'll probably say it a million more times," I confess absentmindedly, unable to look away from her breasts as I knead them in my hands. Her nipples are pink and hard, my mouth instantly watering at the sight of those tips begging to be savored.

I don't hesitate, I just lean forward and suck one between my lips.

And if I thought Lily's hips felt needy before, it's nothing compared to how they start rocking now that I'm kissing her breasts. I hear her gasp and feel her body press down harder on my growing cock, her hands sinking into my hair to hold me against her. Taking that motion for the invite that it is, I curl my tongue around her nipple and suck harder.

The sound of her moaning my name hardens me to a painful degree. I was too focused on Lily when this started to spare any thoughts—or concerns—for my ability to get hard, but right now, with Lily's taste on my tongue and the feel of her skin under my hands, I'm thinking this might be the hardest I've ever been.

The fact that Lily is dragging her pussy over my cock, clearly turned on by the feel of it, only makes this a million times hotter.

But the thought of her pussy brings a new level of desperation. Because *God*, if her tits taste this sweet...I can't even imagine what her cunt tastes like.

I quickly suck her other nipple into my mouth, refusing

to miss out on tasting *any* part of her, and at the same time, I drop one hand between her legs.

I let her nipple go with a pop. "*Fuck*, baby, I can feel you're soaked through your pants," I groan. I look up at her in wonder, my fingers lazily caressing her warmth through her scrubs. "What made you this wet?"

"I don't know," she breathes, cupping my face and rolling into my fingers. Her eyes are hooded, lips glossy from our kisses, her cheeks pinkened. "It's just...you. It's everything."

*Fuck*, this girl. This beautiful, perfect, incredible girl.

I can't help taking her lips in a kiss any more than I can stop myself from breathing. She kisses me back just as hungrily, her fingers sinking into my hair as she slides her tongue across mine with a breathy moan.

Without breaking the kiss, I slide my hand down the front of her pants, groaning when my fingers slip through her wetness. My kiss becomes harder, needier, as my thumb settles on her clit. In an instant, every one of my thoughts zeroes in on making the angel in my lap come all over my hand.

It takes me a minute to find the pressure and pace that makes her moan, but once I do, the heat between us kicks up to a whole other level. By the time I sink two fingers inside her, she's breathing so hard she can barely keep our mouths connected.

"Go ahead, baby," I murmur against her lips. "Soak my hand. I want to taste it."

She whimpers at that, her hands fisting in my hair. When her face tips up and her eyes slide closed, I drag my lips along her jaw and down her neck, nipping at the place where her neck and shoulders meet. My fingers continue to pump in and out, my thumb never stopping its circles on her clit.

I can *feel* her release starting to build. It's in her labored breathing, and her rocking hips, and the way there's a gush of wetness every time I nip at her skin. It almost makes me wonder...

Taking a chance, I kiss my way down her chest until I can suck a peaked nipple into my mouth. And then I lightly bite down.

Lily *explodes*.

Her gasp echoes in my ears, turning into a soft cry as her muscles squeeze and spasm around me. I try to memorize every sound, every feeling, of Lily coming all over my hand.

When she finally stops shuddering, her body melting in my lap, I begrudgingly pull back, already calculating the time before I can do that again.

"That was..." She's breathless, her expression dazed and sated in a way that makes me want to beat my chest in pride. It takes her a second to lock eyes with me. "That was..."

I can't help it; a slow grin slides across my face. "You said that already," I say, lobbing her earlier tease back at her.

She huffs a laugh, finally recovered from her high. "Something tells me I could probably say it a million more."

"I'm good with that." Lifting my hand, I study the wetness on my fingers for a moment before sucking them into my mouth.

I hear Lily's sharp intake of a breath, but I'm too busy groaning around her flavor. When I pull my fingers out of my mouth, the fire in Lily's eyes has once again roared back to life.

"Delicious," I murmur.

At first, she doesn't move, she just stares at my mouth. Then suddenly, she's a flutter of activity.

She reaches for the bottom of my shirt and impatiently tugs it up and over my head. As soon as she's thrown the fabric off to the side, she's kissing me again, her hands fumbling between us to untie my joggers.

With her half-naked in my arms, having just come all over my hand, I'm still harder than I've ever been, and as soon as my tongue touches Lily's, she lets out the sexiest moan I've ever heard. I feel the moment she gets lost in the kiss, because her hands pause on my pants and her hips start grinding into me again.

But that only seems to make her more desperate, because she suddenly climbs off my lap and stands, then quickly pulls her pants off. Her motions still when she realizes I'm frozen in open-mouthed wonder at the sight before me.

Specifically, the sight of a completely naked Lily.

"You're beautiful," I say on an exhale, trying to memorize every inch of her. My bite marks on her breasts, the cluster of freckles on her stomach, the little patch of hair above her pussy. *Is it too much to ask her to turn around for me?*

Lily, ever the confident woman, lets me look my fill as she says sweetly, "Thank you."

I sound far less sweet when I say, "I'm going to have dreams about you sitting on my face."

She lets out a surprised laugh at that. "Dirty man," she murmurs with a smile. Then she's leaning down and tugging at my waistband.

I push my pants over my hips and let her pull them off my legs, but now the nerves are starting to bubble in my stomach. I haven't had sex in two years, and never with this injury—and plus, this is *Lily.* I'm pretty sure I would've been instantly fighting the urge to come even on that rooftop. There's no way I'm not about to come in ten seconds.

When she straddles me again and I feel her pussy rub along the length of my cock—*without* any clothes between us this time—I mentally drop that time down to two seconds.

Swallowing thickly, I place my hands on her waist and drop my head back against the wall. "*Fuck*, Lily."

But then she kisses me, and this kiss feels comforting, almost reverent—as if she knows the thoughts swirling around in my mind.

"I can't wait to feel you inside me," she whispers against my lips.

And *yeah, she definitely knows what thoughts are swirling.*

"Should I get a condom?" she asks, her hips already starting to rock into me, her wetness making the slide over my cock easy. "I'm clean and on the pill, but if you're uncomfortable…"

I can't help the humorless laugh I let out. "Lily, I haven't even *kissed* a girl since the night I met you. I'm clean. And if you think I'm going to ask for a condom and risk losing this hard-on, you don't understand what's going on here."

She pulls back so she can study me for a moment. "Is that what you're worried about? Performing?"

My exhale is a tired sound. I wish I didn't have to have this conversation, but I also know we need to. "Lily, you know what the science of this shit looks like. I don't need to tell you I'm probably going to go soft or come immediately. My only goal is to make you come again in one way or another before you put your clothes back on and hopefully salvage what's left of my male pride."

Instead of the pitying look that I expect, I'm surprised to see a determined glint enter Lily's eyes. "I think your male pride is more intact than you think it is," she purrs. Then she reaches between us and takes my cock in her hand.

My breathing grows heavy as soon as her grip starts to glide up and down my length. Her movements are slow enough that I don't feel like I'm fighting the urge to come, but they're sexy enough that the air around us becomes stifling.

When she lifts slightly and aims the tip of my cock at her clit, I start to wonder how much longer it's going to be before I'm mentally reciting UFC stats. Because the sight of Lily naked is more than enough to make me lose control, but the sight of her using *my* body to play with herself is... on a whole other level.

I don't think I move a single muscle the entire minute she spends circling the tip of my cock around her clit. We're both staring, enraptured, at the place where our bodies meet.

It's only when she plays with me along the length of her slit that I finally move a muscle. Because the moment she places me at her opening, my grip is tightening on her waist like I'll die if she moves away.

We're both holding our breaths as she slides down onto my cock.

And we're both moaning as soon as she's settled in my lap.

"Oh God," Lily whimpers, gripping my shoulder so hard I can feel her nails digging into my skin. "You're so... *God*, you're so big."

*Big is good. Big can make her come again.*

"You feel so fucking good," I groan. *I'm going to come so fucking quick.*

Once again, Lily looks like she can read my thoughts. Because her hips don't shift even an inch as she moves my hand from her waist to her pussy.

"Just touch me," she whispers. Once my thumb starts to

rub her clit, her hand drifts from mine, up to cup her own breast. She does the same with her other hand, too.

"I touched myself every night for weeks after the night we met," she confesses, pinching her nipples. A moan escapes her lips when I start with the pressure and pace that she likes on her clit. "Some nights, I would come as soon as I touched myself, just from the memory of your kiss."

I all but choke on my breath at her admission. *This woman is a fucking goddess, and she's talking about how even the thought of me gave her pleasure.*

And whether it's what she intended or not, Lily's words spark an old flame of confidence. I forget about my nerves, and my worry that this won't be good for Lily. I stop hating myself for the fact that I can't physically fuck her the way I'm used to fucking.

Instead, I think about how badly she wants me *now*.

I think about how eagerly she kisses me—every time. How her cheeks get pink when she checks me out. How she became soaking wet just from *feeling* my cock.

And with that reminder, I take Lily's mouth in a searing kiss. There's nothing sweet about it, I simply slide my tongue between her lips and kiss her until she's breathless.

Sure enough, when I eventually pull back, she's panting. Which gives me the opportunity to brush my lips over her jaw, pressing a kiss under her ear to the sensitive spot on her neck.

"What did you think about?" I murmur against her skin. "Did you think about what happened, or what you *want* to happen?"

"Both," she gasps, her hands going to my shoulders again.

"And what is it you want?" I ask, nipping her earlobe as

my thumb presses harder against her clit. "Tell me about your fantasies, Liliana."

"Oh God," she moans. Her hips start rolling before she's even answered the question. "This," she gasps. "I think about this."

And then she's riding me, her hips rising and falling as she works my cock inside her.

I bite off a curse at the sensation. *Fuck. Did sex ever feel like this?*

I pull back just enough that I can watch as Lily fucks me, her lips parted with moans of pleasure, her thighs flexing with exertion. Her pussy is so wet, I can see my cock glistening with her arousal every time she lifts up.

*No. I don't think it ever felt like this.*

I kiss her because I can't *not* kiss her.

"You feel so good," she whimpers into my mouth, kissing me back like she's just as eager to feel me everywhere.

As her hips move quicker, I help as much as I can, lifting her up and down with the hand still on her waist, but I can't do as much as I'd like. I can't fuck up into her. It's frustrating, but I also realize that, even without my hips working, she's still clearly on the edge of an orgasm.

"I can feel your pussy squeezing me," I groan into another kiss. "Are you going to come again?"

She nods desperately and rides me harder. "I'm so close," she whispers.

Dropping my mouth to her peaked nipple, I pull the tip between my lips and suck hard enough to make Lily gasp.

"Oh God, *yes*," she breathes out, one hand sinking into my hair. "That's going to make me—"

She chokes on her next word when I worry the tip with my teeth. And when I follow that by pinching her clit between my fingers, she stops breathing entirely.

I *groan* into her skin as her pussy starts to spasm. My eyes slide closed, my fingers dig into her waist, and I try to memorize the sensation of Lily's muscles clamping down on my cock.

When she eventually slumps into me with a sigh, I'm still guiding her hips forward and back, my movements slow and lazy. "Damn, baby," I groan, leaving a trail of kisses across her breast and up to her collarbone. I could keep her in my arms forever, just like this.

But then her hips move in a way that hits the head of my dick, a jolt of sheer pleasure shooting up my spine.

I suck in a sharp breath. "Oh *shit*. Fuck—wait—don't—" My hands dig into Lily's waist to hold her in place.

Her eyes go wide as she freezes. "What is it? Oh my God, did I hurt you?"

I quickly shake my head. "No, it's not that. It's just—" I force my grip to loosen, my gaze traveling down to where my cock is halfway inside of Lily. "I don't know, you moved somehow, and it felt..."

*Like the slickest fucking silk.*

*Like all I want to do is fuck up into you to chase it.*

My throat moves on a rough swallow. Because I *can't* fuck up into her. I can only stay still and revel in this weird, crazy, incredible sensation.

Lily must read something on my face because I feel her grip on my shoulders loosen. She doesn't move, but she asks in a soft purr, "Does it feel good?"

A breath rushes out of me, and I nod. "*So* fucking good."

"How do you want me?" she asks, her voice enough to send a ripple of pleasure through my body.

"I think if you—" I rotate her hips the slightest bit, just until her pussy is squeezing around the head of my cock. The moment she hits the right angle, a groan rumbles through my chest. "Fuck, yeah that's it. Just stay right there for a second. That feels—*Jesus*, that feels good."

Lily stays perfectly still, letting me revel in the feel of her body like this. The only time she moves is when she clamps down on me, which makes me groan and beg her to do it again. By the third time, I'm pretty sure she's fried the pleasure center of my brain.

I don't have to ask her to start riding me again; she just knows. A few seconds of Lily sliding over my length and then I'm coming, giving in to my release with a stuttered exhale.

When it finally ends, the only sound around us is my gasping breaths. My forehead tips forward to rest against her shoulder.

"Holy *shit*," I gasp.

Lily lets out a soft laugh and snuggles deeper into my embrace. It feels like the most natural thing in the world for my arms to go around her, one hand sliding up to hold the back of her neck.

"I might need a cigarette after that," I murmur against her neck.

"Don't even think about it," she grumbles back. But her words don't have any bite to them, especially when she lets out a sated purr as I start to knead the muscles around her neck.

The quiet is a comfortable one. I feel...content. If it wasn't for Lily's hips shifting, my softening cock still inside her, I'd stay here all night.

But the movement has me groaning, the sound making her pull back with an expression of concern.

"Oh God, sorry," she blurts. "Am I too heavy? Are your legs in pain?"

"Lily, I'm paralyzed. I can barely *feel* my legs."

At first, she only blinks at my teasing. But after a moment, her eyes narrow and she lightly shoves at my chest.

"Jerk," she mutters. "I was showing *concern.*"

I grin and lean forward for a kiss. "I know," I murmur against her lips. "It was sweet." Then I lean back against the wall and give her a real answer. "But no, I'm not in pain. I feel fucking fantastic."

That has her faux annoyance melting, to be replaced with a giddy smile that she tries to hide.

But after a moment, reality sets in, and the first flash of uncertainty appears in Lily's eyes.

"We should probably get cleaned up," she says, looking around for some kind of towel.

She lifts off me before I can pull her back down for another kiss. I swallow the disappointed sigh that wants to slip out of me and instead reach for my pants.

I manage to pull them on and get to my feet while Lily is still cleaning herself up. I'm half-tempted to leave my shirt off, just so I can steal her attention for another second, but I know we've already risked too much tonight, so I pull that on, too.

I'm so caught up with the need to be close to her that her scrub top has barely cleared her head before I'm pulling her into my lap, where I'm back in my wheelchair. She drops onto my legs, and I swallow her surprised squeak with a kiss.

The kiss is sweet, but not short. When I feel like I've sated my need for her enough to allow some space, I pull back, but only so far that I can lean my forehead against hers.

"Hi," I whisper with a smile. I can feel her chest heaving against mine.

"Hi," she breathes, a dazed look on her face.

I want to ask her if I can see her soon. Outside of the clinic, before my next appointment. These sessions are no longer enough time with her. I want more.

I wonder if she reads something on my face, because she puts space between us before she says, "Um, don't forget that I'm away with my family this weekend. So, I won't see you until next Monday."

My heart drops. It's Wednesday now, so that feels like an eternity.

"Oh. That's right, I forgot that was this weekend." I force a smile on my face, despite knowing how badly I'm going to miss her. "Are you excited for the break? You haven't missed a day since I've been here."

She softens at that. "Yeah, I am. It's always nice to get some time with my family."

I hum thoughtfully as I brush my lips over her jaw. "I know you'll be busy, but...will you text me sometime?"

She nods, and then I'm kissing her again, so enveloped in bliss that nothing else registers.

It isn't until later, when I'm psychoanalyzing every moment of tonight, that I notice her hesitation.

# 29

## LILIANA

I think I'm in shock for the next hour. Once I leave the clinic, I drive home and immediately start packing for my trip. Somehow, having to decide between taking my red or black shorts is enough of a distraction to keep me from thinking about...anything else.

It isn't until my head hits the pillow and sleep *doesn't* consume me—in fact, it's the opposite: I'm wide awake—that I start to spiral.

I had sex with Roman.

I had sex with *Roman.*

*I had sex with a patient in the clinic.*

Squeezing my eyes closed, I try to wrap my head around that sentence. But all it does is bring the memory into focus.

*Roman's lips on mine, his kiss equal parts hungry and sweet. The urgency he touched me with. The feel of him inside me—*

A shiver runs through my body, and I flip onto my stomach to bury my face in the pillow.

I have *never* had sex like that. That was...otherworldly. Maybe it was the build-up, maybe it was the connection—whatever it was, that didn't feel like just sex.

But that thought also makes my heart ache. Because that makes this so much more complicated than if it was *just sex.*

Flipping onto my back again, I let out an exhale heavy with frustration. This just got so much more complicated.

I should've known this was going to happen. God, I should've known from *day one.* From the moment Roman kissed me two years ago, I should've known there was no way I could be impartial to him.

Or if not then, there were a thousand other moments that should have clued me in. Jesus, how were there a *thousand* moments? The texting? The calling? The dinner date? The flirting? I've crossed so many boundaries with justifications.

When I think about Trivia Night, and the kiss it ended with, shame settles over my skin like a layer of dirt. Even remembering how badly I wanted Roman to kiss me that night, and how nothing could have prepared me for it when he finally did, I have no excuse for not doing the right thing, the *ethical* thing, after that.

Wincing, I push off my bed and grab a towel, hoping a shower might clear the fog from my head. I try to convince myself that I'm not turning the water all the way to blue to punish myself.

Ice-cold water should be the least of my punishments. If I hadn't been deluding myself, sweeping all the signs under the rug, I may have been able to stop this train. Because tonight, it completely tore off the tracks.

Maybe the freezing water does help, because by the time my teeth start chattering, I'm numb both inside and out. I pull my sweats back on with shaking hands and slide under my comforter once again.

The moment I'm enveloped by heat, exhaustion claims me.

The next day is a blur. Between the 5 a.m. flight that's only the beginning of a hectic travel day, and the same-day hike that my dad scheduled for us right after touchdown—in order for us to "fight the jet lag"—I barely have time to catch my breath, let alone think about the ticking time bomb that is my career path.

The canyons are gorgeous. The white sandstone walls look like they're out of a National Geographic picture, and rappelling down them is a rush. When we reach the hike's main destination and look between the canyons at the pond we're about to drop into, the sight is so beautiful that it knocks any other thought out of my head.

The next day is much of the same. We're up early, already half an hour into the hike by the time the sun peeks over the horizon. Today's hike is the big one. It's also the main reason I picked Utah as the destination for this year's family trip. Thankfully, the views are even more stunning today than the ones yesterday, keeping my attention soundly on my next step and nothing else.

That is, until my dad appears beside me during a particularly steep part of the hike and asks, "How you doing, sweetheart? You look tired."

I aim a glare at my ridiculously-in-shape sixty-year-old father, my leg muscles burning and sweat dropping off the tip of my sunburnt nose. "Gee, you don't say. I thought a six-mile hike and rappel would be relaxing."

He doesn't laugh the way I expect him to. Which tells me everything I need to know about how this conversation is about to go.

"Are you not having fun?" he asks, the concern in his voice obvious.

I take a deep breath and turn toward him with a small smile. "I'm having a great time, Dad, I promise," I assure him. But, knowing that's not going to be enough to appease him, I add, "You're right, though. I am tired. Work stress has me a little beat down right now."

He nods at that, having heard me say that a few times in recent years. "But you're okay?" he presses. "With work? And right now?"

My smile becomes a little more genuine, and I reach to give his arm a comforting squeeze. "Yeah, Dad, everything's good." And while the pit in my stomach that tells me everything is *not* good still exists, I mean it when I gesture at the gorgeous canyons around us and say, "This is exactly what I needed. This is incredible."

He looks around, a shimmer of excitement coming back to his eyes. "It is, isn't it? Good pick, Liliana."

We hike quietly for a few more minutes, and I think I'm finally relaxing for the first time all weekend, when my dad curiously asks, "So, your work stress... Is it a specific patient? Or is it your workload in general?"

*And I'm right back to tense and stressed the fuck out.*

"Why do you ask?" is the only thing I manage to say.

"That's Dad's way of asking about that MMA fighter you're working with," Sean interjects from where he's walking behind us.

Predictably, my other brother Colin pipes up from beside him. "What MMA fighter?"

"Holy shit, I forgot to tell you," Sean starts excitedly. "Do you remember that Philly fighter Roman Ward? The one who got paralyzed during his title fight? He's Lily's newest patient."

I turn back to glare at Sean and find Colin gawking at me. "No *way*," he breathes out. "That guy was a freak of nature. He probably would've made it into the Hall of Fame. *That's* your patient?"

Not wanting to engage in this type of conversation, I bring my attention back to the scenery. I hate talking about who Roman *used* to be.

"Alright, you two, you know she can't talk about her patients," my dad scolds. "That's not why I asked."

"Then why did you?" I ask.

"You just seemed...different with him," he answers carefully. "I guess I was curious if he was the reason for your work stress."

*Fuck.*

"I'm not different with him," I argue, wondering if my defensive tone is as obvious as it sounds to my ears. "I mean, he's a tough patient, but that's about it."

I hear my brother's snort behind me. "Lily, you were worried about him being with another therapist for *one* session. I'm surprised you didn't make us shorten or postpone the trip."

I spin in place and send another glare in my brother's direction, my heart rate doubling.

"So, I give a shit about my patients, sue me," I snap. "His recovery is...precarious. I didn't want to mess anything up."

Sean blinks at me in surprise, shocked at my outburst. I'm shocked, too. But if my brother picked up on something like that during one ten-minute visit, then who knows what else I made obvious. And now, I'm panicking.

"Okay, give it a rest, you two," comes my dad's voice. His hand drops onto my shoulder. "Lily, we just wanted to make sure you were okay. That's all."

Sean nods in agreement. "Yeah. Lil...I didn't mean you caring was a *bad* thing."

I wince and swipe a hand down my face. "I know. I'm sorry, that was an overreaction. I'm just tired."

"Do you want to go home?" my dad asks, his worry coming back to the forefront.

I shake my head instantly. "No, not at all. I meant it when I said this trip is helping."

"Uh...the view over here might help even more in a second," Colin comments from a few feet ahead, the awe in his voice obvious.

That effectively ends the entire conversation, because now we're all too curious not to check what he sees. The three of us walk over to where Colin is standing, looking down over the canyon edge.

"Holy fuck," Sean murmurs.

*Holy fuck* is right. It's probably one hundred feet to the bottom, but where I expected the bottom to be sand or rock, it's the prettiest blue water.

"Wow," Dad whispers, in awe. "That's incredible." He looks up at me with a smile. "I'll say it again: good pick, Liliana."

I return the smile with one of my own, the sight before us somehow driving all my panicked thoughts about Roman to the back of my mind.

For a little while, at least.

<hr>

They come flooding back the next day.

When I get a text from Roman that says, *Can't wait to see you on Monday. Hope you're having a fun weekend.*

I drop my head back against the lounge chair, my eyes sliding closed and my heart dropping into my stomach.

It's the last night of our trip, and we're going out to a

restaurant. Everyone else is getting ready, but I needed a minute alone on the balcony of the hotel. Just to catch my breath.

That idea is shot to shit with Roman's text coming through.

Because now, all I'm thinking about is Monday. About what I need to do on Monday.

I was already thinking it, but my family's comments about Roman yesterday made it clear that I can't keep treating him. I'm so far past the point of unprofessional and unethical that even the subconscious reasoning I was giving myself about our relationship not being harmful to Roman's recovery isn't enough. I need to transfer him to another physical therapist.

Fran already gave me the green light when I took him on as a patient. I know I could send her an email right now with a request to have him be treated by someone else, and she would transfer him without a question. This should be easy.

*Should* be.

But in reality, there's nothing about this that's easy. Not the request of transferring, not the process, nothing.

I *hate* this. I hate the idea of not having sessions with Roman. Already, my heart is splintering at the thought of not seeing him, of not helping him on bad days and laughing together on the good ones.

And this could get so ugly. Roman already doesn't do well with hiccups in his recovery, so what's he going to do with a new therapist? Is it going to disrupt his therapy entirely? What if he stops making progress? All I've ever wanted for him is a better quality of life, and I'll hate myself more than I already do if this ends up hurting him in the end.

And I don't even want to *think* about how he's going to handle this in a non-physical therapy sense. I mean, it's obvious there are feelings involved here. There's a strong possibility he's going to take this as a personal rejection. Which could have disastrous effects on his recovery by itself, as well as his mental health.

*God*, this is so bad. This is *so bad*. What was I thinking? How could I let things get this far?

And even as I spiral about *what's next*, I don't let myself contemplate the answer to that question. Because I know exactly what blinded me to my own actions.

Just as I know that I'm deluding myself about Roman being the only one who won't handle this well.

Because I haven't even done anything yet, and my heart is already broken.

# 30

# ROMAN

I'm walking on cloud nine the entire weekend.

I can't remember ever feeling this hopeful, or this light. Between the physical victory of walking and then opening a whole new connection with Lily, I feel like *me* again.

I think about texting Lily way too often, but I don't want to bother her this weekend. I know how close she is with her family, and I don't want to be that guy who pulls her away from that.

So, I try to keep myself busy. I push myself way too hard with PT at home, but I revel in the soreness. Knowing that I *can* walk makes every physical exercise I complete feel that much more valuable. I'm more eager than I've ever been to get back to the clinic.

When I'm not working out, I'm either cooking, cleaning, or hanging out with Mom. I want to *move*. I want to do something. When I move my video game controller as I'm cleaning, I realize it's been a couple of weeks since I've had the urge to waste time with it.

Even still, that only covers a few hours out of my day. And that restlessness only grows.

I find myself thinking about work again, the same way it's been constantly in the back of my mind since the conversation with Lily during Trivia Night. Especially with walking finally being a possibility on the horizon, I need to get my ass back to reality and find a job.

But...I can't quite bring myself to take that question in the direction of Lily's suggestion of school. It's too big of an ask, too big of a change. Despite all my progress lately, I still need *some* things to remain in my comfort zone.

And that's how I end up emailing my old manager to ask if there are any coaching opportunities open anywhere in the organization. Before my injury, I'd heard whispers that they were planning to do more seasons of their reality TV show, and that they were adding more assistant coaches to the roster this time. I might not be able to fight, but I still have more sport knowledge than most of the fighters in the organization. A coaching job, or even a mentorship, could be perfect.

After I've mentally crossed my fingers and hit *Send*, I release a heavy exhale and once again look around my house for something to do. Now I'm restless *and* motivated.

And thinking about Lily more than ever.

Honestly, I'm surprised I make it to Saturday night before texting her. I've been fighting the urge since Thursday, wanting *some* sort of connection with her after a moment like sending my first job application since the injury.

In the end, I keep it simple. *Can't wait to see you on Monday. Hope you're having a fun weekend.* I can wait until then to share the exciting news with her. I don't need to vomit it all through text. I just wanted to let her know I'm thinking of her.

At first, it doesn't bother me that she doesn't respond

right away. I mean, she's hiking a canyon. I don't even know if she has cell service.

But by the time Sunday rolls around, and I still haven't heard from her, my gut starts to churn. Because I know she came home today.

I tell myself maybe she took a late flight home, or maybe she's just busy unpacking. And I shove the worry to the back of my mind. Because I can't imagine that she's not excited to see me tomorrow. There's no conceivable way that what we shared didn't mean anything to her. I saw the look in her eyes, and I felt the way we connected. I *know* how Lily feels about me.

I'm so convinced of it that by the time I enter the clinic fifteen minutes early on Monday, my chest is bursting with just as much happiness as it was when I left last Wednesday.

But when I set eyes on Lily, where she's working with another client, that happiness...dims.

And doubt starts to take its place.

She's working with a little girl. They're doing some kind of wrist exercise, making me wonder if the girl is coming off a broken arm. She'll occasionally wince in discomfort, but once Lily soothes her with soft words and a gentle hand, she looks up at Lily with trust in her eyes.

The sight makes me wonder what kind of mother Lily would be. No doubt an incredible one, with her patience and ability to comfort. In a way, I feel like I'm seeing that future in front of me right now.

And that doubt becomes full-blown dread.

Because even though I'm entirely aware of the fact that I'm putting the cart *way* before the horse, I'm too lost in the growing fear to stop the direction of my thoughts. That I might not be able to give her that family. Or, at the very least, it would likely require the help of a fertility clinic. I may have gotten a hard-on with Lily last week, but that doesn't mean it will be a consistent thing with me, *or* that there's nothing wrong with my semen quality. I wasn't exactly focused on getting that checked when I first became injured.

And when the man who I assume is the little girl's father steps forward and into my view, that dread becomes a mental breakdown.

It's not just that the three of them together complete the picture my mind had already created, of Lily with the family she wants and that I might not be able to give her.

It's also that he's *flirting* with her. And she's smiling back at him.

As my heart starts to race, I take in more details about the guy. He's young and attractive, wearing a tailored suit, his smile bright and his hair perfectly styled.

And he's *standing*.

When Lily laughs at something he says, it hits me that even if I learn to walk on my own again, I'll never be as whole as that guy right there. I'll always be missing something, never again the Roman of before who may have deserved her, once.

In an instant, I'm *angry*. At the unfairness of it all. At the humiliation this injury comes with. At the inferiority I'm constantly battling with. I fucking *hate* it.

I stare at the guy, visualizing taking my anger out on him. Thinking about how good it would feel to hit him, to use him as a relief valve for all these feelings. To just let it *out*—

But then Lily turns, and we lock eyes.

And that anger becomes a sinking black hole of despair.

Because I can see it on her face that she's done with me. Whatever we had—whatever I *thought* we had—is ending before it can even begin. She's going to end it today.

"I'll be right with you, Roman, I'm just finishing up," she says, her tone as flat as the look she gives me.

Fuck. I... *Fuck.* I should've known this was coming.

I should've known she was too good to be true. I should've known *this* was too good to be true.

When she turns back to the little girl, all the emotion, all the sweetness that I was looking forward to today, comes flooding back when she smiles.

"Alright, Alice, I'll see you next week, okay? Have fun on your field trip, but remember to be careful. Your wrist is still a bit fragile."

"Thanks again for rescheduling us this week," the dad says, giving Lily a warm smile of his own. "I really appreciate you being flexible."

"Of course," Lily says as she straightens from her crouch. "I'm happy we could make it work."

Watching their interaction, I think it makes me angrier that the guy *isn't* some smarmy jackass. If he was leering at Lily or making an inappropriate pass, maybe I could write him off and convince myself I'm still better than him, even with a physical limitation. But the guy just seems...nice.

I'm still reeling from the knowledge that Lily is going to end it with me as she walks the two of them out of the clinic. I feel like I'm standing on a boat in the middle of a storm, being flung around and unable to get my bearings. I can't get my feet under me.

When she finally re-enters the room and it's just the two of us, her expression is equal parts sad and wary. Her steps slow as she nears me.

"So that's it, then?" I ask. It's all I can get out.

She lets out a heavy breath, looking suddenly exhausted.

"Roman..." Her eyebrows pull together as she reaches up to rub the weariness from her eyes. "You have to know that what we did was wrong."

Maybe she sees on my face that *no, I don't know that,* because when I don't respond, she locks eyes with me and straightens.

"I don't know how it took me so long to see it," she says in a near-whisper. She sounds sad. "But I can't ignore it anymore. Not after last week. Not after—" Something flashes in her eyes, her throat working on a rough swallow.

Maybe that's what causes my outburst, maybe it's the feeling of my heart cracking in my chest.

"So, you're just going to abandon me?" I ask. "You're going to be like every other therapist and pass me off to someone else?"

"Roman, I *can't* be your therapist," she says, the pain and desperation obvious in her voice. "I'm so far past the level of unprofessional that I can't even *see* the line anymore. You have to understand that."

But I *can't* understand it. I'm terrified of losing Lily, of seeing who I am, and what I might become, without her. Not to mention, the idea of not *being* with her is more than I can stand.

And because I can't accept what she's saying, my brain grasps for some other reason she might be doing this. It has to be because of my injury.

"Was the sex really that bad?"

She jerks back at that. "Was...what?"

I dive headfirst into the accusation, my words snowballing as my head spins and my heart shatters.

"All of this because I can't fuck you properly?" I shake my head with a scoff. "Damn, Lily, if you're going to dump me because I'm bad in bed, at least be honest about it."

Lily's eyes widen. "You *cannot* be serious right now."

"I don't hear you denying it," I say defensively.

I can see the thoughts roiling around her brain as she searches my face, trying to figure out how to respond.

"So, that's what your brain is hearing right now, huh? It's not that I could lose my job, or even my *license*, you think I'm doing this because I have an issue with our physical chemistry? Are you serious?"

Before I can respond, frustration changes her tone. "Do I need to remind you about the night we met? Because you and I *both* know I was just as hot for you last week as I was two years ago. So don't you *dare* bring your injury into this."

Her words have my body heating, lust flaming at the memory. I remember exactly how turned on she was two years ago.

I remember everything about that kiss. The way she tasted like berries, but with a hint of mint. How soft her skin felt under my hands. The way she wrapped her leg around me and rocked against my cock, silently begging for more until I finally lifted her into my arms and ravished her against the wall.

That last detail blasts me back to the present.

Because I can't lift her up anymore.

There's a different kind of heat in my voice when I look at Lily and tell her, "Trust me, I know why you wanted me *then*."

Her lips part to say something, but before she can dispute it, I temporarily lose my mind and tug her into my lap.

# 31

## LILIANA

I fall forward with a gasp, my knees going on either side of Roman's legs and my hands bracing on his shoulders. His hands go immediately to my hips.

"I would've made you come all night long, you know," he growls quietly, his grip on me tightening. "I would've spent hours between your legs, making you come over and over again with my fingers, my mouth. My cock. I would've blown your mind, Liliana."

Despite my anger at Roman's defensive reaction to all this, my chest aches. Because I know it's coming from a place of insecurity, and that he can't help it.

"You blew my mind last week, too," I say softly.

His throat moves on a swallow, doubt and another wave of fear entering his eyes.

"Let me show you," he begs in a gravelly voice, pulling me the slightest bit closer. "Just one last time, let me show you what it would have been like that night."

My pulse pounds in my ears. "Roman..." I whisper.

"Come on, Lily..." His hands guide my hips forward and back, just for a second, just enough that I can feel how hard he is beneath me, how bad he wants this. "You already requested my transfer, didn't you?"

Guilt floods me. Because yes, I sent Fran an email this morning. I didn't trust myself to do it in person and possibly break down crying. And yes, she approved the transfer instantly, the way she told me she would if it was ever needed. All I asked for is to be the one to tell Roman the news tonight.

I knew he wouldn't handle it well, but *this*... I'm not sure I have the strength to put the brakes on, not with the way he's looking at me.

I know Roman can see the answer in my eyes because there's a flash of sadness before he nods and says, "Which means it's not against the rules anymore. Not really." He pulls me closer, our lips brushing as he forms the words. "Please, baby... Just let me touch you."

I open my mouth to tell him we can't, that this is the whole reason I can't be his physical therapist anymore, but then his hand slides along the front of my pants, tugging at the drawstring bow in silent question. The gasp it forces from my lips also wipes every responsible thought from my brain.

"Roman," I say on an exhale, my hips sliding forward of their own accord.

"Tell me to stop," he murmurs. "Tell me to stop, and I will."

And maybe this is how my relationship with Roman went too far. This web we weave around each other, inadvertently creating a reality where it's just us. Where nothing else matters, and where I can't imagine saying anything but—

"Don't stop."

We both dive into the kiss with equal parts hunger and

desperation. There's no easing into it, no teasing or flirting. We both know what this is, and what this means. This is the last *everything*.

And that's exactly what the kiss tastes like.

He coaxes my lips open, his tongue caressing mine in a way that has me whimpering and pulling myself closer. When I grind down on his lap, he makes a needy sound of his own and kisses me harder, his hands pulling frantically at the knot on my drawstring. And the moment his hand slips down the front of my pants and he realizes just how turned on I am, he *groans* into our kiss.

"*Fuck*, Liliana," he breathes, dragging his fingers through my wetness. "You're so wet for me."

I let out a moan that sounds like his name. I feel like I have no control over my body anymore, running solely on my *need* for Roman. Digging my nails into his shoulders, I pull myself closer and grind down harder on his hand.

The action seems to light a new level of fire within him. His hand tightens on my hip, while the other twists so he can press his thumb to my clit. He watches my face as he plays with speed and pressure, waiting for the moment that my chest starts heaving. And then he slides two fingers deep inside me.

"Oh my God," I gasp, my eyes going wide. Pleasure coils between my legs, the perfect feeling of Roman pumping his fingers in and out making it spike quicker than I expected it to.

He bites out a curse. "Jesus, I can feel your pussy squeezing me," he groans, his movements quickening.

I try to get impossibly closer, my lips brushing against his. His touch is one thing, but it's his closeness that I want more of. I want more of *him*. That's what's going to set me off.

"Kiss me," I whimper. "Kiss me like it's—"

He captures my mouth before I can even finish my sentence. His arm slides around my waist, pulling me flush against his body, and he devours me exactly how I was craving. All while his fingers work me ceaselessly toward an explosive release.

"Come for me," he begs. "Just give me that, Liliana. Send me home knowing I could make you happy for a while."

My breath hitches at his words, but the pleasure is already taking over my body. The orgasm rolls through me, drowning me in wave after wave of euphoria as I moan his name, leaving me breathless and shaking in his arms.

"Beautiful," he breathes.

With a stuttered exhale, I drop my forehead to his shoulder, trying to catch my breath. His hand starts to rub circles in a soothing rhythm on my back.

But when his hand bumps his armrest...he stops.

I pull back with a frown. And come face to face with Roman's blank expression.

"What's wrong?" I ask.

He shrugs, an arrogant smirk appearing on his lips. But I can tell he's forcing it, his stiff posture making it obvious to me that he's hiding something.

"You just came all over my fingers. Why would anything be wrong?" He raises his hand in front of his face, rubbing his thumb over the pads of his fingers and studying the wetness coating them. "And that was just my fingers. I bet the single dad couldn't have even done that with his fully functional cock."

I stiffen. *He did not just say that...*

I knew Roman was lashing out at me at the beginning of this conversation, but this is taking it too far. With unease slithering through my body, I climb off of his lap and right my clothes.

"That was a mistake," I say, my tone hardening. I force myself to meet Roman's eyes. "This is why I asked Fran to transfer you to a different therapist."

And this is the moment that Roman's walls crumble. Every façade, every defense he's had up since we started this conversation...it disappears. And I see the true emotions hiding underneath.

Hurt. Fear. Panic.

But truthfully, I'm feeling all of those things right now, too.

"I'm sorry." The words slip out before I can think through the apology. "I never wanted this to happen. I—" My voice cracks, and I have to clear my throat before I can continue. "I only ever wanted the best for you."

"*You're* what's best for me," he bursts out. "*You* made me better. You're the *only* one who made me better. Liliana, please..." Another flash of fear in his eyes. "Please don't leave me to do this alone."

"Roman, I *can't*," I say, pleading with him to understand. "This has gone way too far. It's wrong on a hundred levels, and on top of that, we clearly don't have enough self-control to keep it from happening again. There's just no way I can stay on as your therapist."

He knows I'm right. But he's stubborn, and afraid, and already pushing back with a headshake.

I try to cut off his rebuttal by saying, "You'll be okay with someone else, I promise. I'll have Fran transfer you to someone who I know you'll be able to work with, and without the distraction of...this, you'll be on your feet in no time. You'll see."

"You're delusional if you think that's true," he spits out

angrily. "You know what a dozen failed therapists have taught me? That *you* were the secret to my success. There's a reason you're the only one I made real progress with."

My desperation mounts. "Roman—"

"I won't work with anyone else," he says sharply. "If you transfer me, I'll stop doing my therapy. There won't be any point."

My eyes widen at the blunt threat. I knew he was going to push back, but *this*... this is the worst-case scenario reaction, and it's one I didn't prepare for.

But somehow, it's also the thing that makes me realize, truly realize, that I'm doing the right thing. Because our relationship isn't the only reason that we need to separate.

Roman also needs to stand on his own.

My voice softens as I say, "Then that's even more of a reason for a transfer. Roman, I can't be the only reason you want to walk. *You* have to want it."

His gaze darts away, his throat moving on an audible swallow.

"I told you I'd carry the hope for you...and I meant it. I carried it. I'd carry it forever if I thought it was best for you. But Roman...I can't carry *you*. I can't be the only motivation in your life. It's not healthy, it's not sustainable, and it's just not good for you." I pull in a shaky breath for strength. "So whether you allow another PT to help you with your rehab is up to you, but *you* have to make the decision. No one else. Your life is in your hands now, Roman."

When he still doesn't meet my eyes, I chance a step forward. And then another, until I'm standing in front of him. With tears burning my eyes, I place a hand on the side of his face.

"So what are you going to do with it?" I ask. "Throw it

away because some girl walked away from you? Or take control of it?"

Roman's gaze jerks up and locks with mine. "You're not just some g—" But he cuts himself off and clears his throat. I wait for him to say something else, but when he's still silent a moment later, I realize the fear has frozen him in place.

My thumb brushes over Roman's cheek, my heart breaking for him. It breaks for me, too, which is the reason I throw good judgment out the window one last time and lean down to press a gentle kiss to his lips. Still, he remains frozen, though I can hear the squeak of his hands tightening on the armrests.

I meet his eyes as I pull back, wanting him to see every bit of sincerity in my words. "I hope you know you have something to offer the world, Roman. Wheelchair or not, fighter or not, you're so much more than your injury." I force myself to straighten. "I hope you realize that," I add in a near-whisper, barely holding it together.

I take a step back, and then another.

He doesn't try to stop me this time.

**32**

---

# ROMAN

I go numb as Lily walks out of the room.

I'm numb as I get in my mom's car, and as I deflect her questions about my session ending early. I feel nothing as I enter my house and collapse on the couch.

How is it possible for a person to go from the highest high to the lowest low in the span of an hour? When I left for therapy, I thought I had everything: Lily, progress on my rehab, maybe even a vision of my future. I should've known it was too good to be true.

I thought I had already experienced the worst parts of this injury. I didn't realize losing Lily was going to be my true rock bottom.

And then my phone beeps with a notification.

The alert is a custom sound. I set it up to only work for one specific sender.

The UFC.

Reaching for my phone feels different now than it used to. In the past, when I got an email from the promotion, it was with fight contracts and Fight of the Night bonuses—

that sound used to fill me with excitement and sheer joy. Now, all I feel is confusion and an impending sense of grief.

Which grows as soon as I tap my phone screen and the email subject becomes visible.

*Interest in Ultimate Fighter Coach Position*

Steeling myself, I open the email.

*Roman,*

*Thank you for your interest in the coaching position on the Ultimate Fighter reality TV show. We've reviewed your qualifications and considered the expertise and energy you would bring to the competition as both Head Coach and Assistant Coach, but unfortunately have decided that you wouldn't be a good fit for the show. We believe a coach should not only be a mentor and wealth of knowledge for the fighters, but also an active and challenging training partner on the mat. So, despite your impressive fight record and reputation in the organization, for this reason we cannot accept you onto the show's coaching staff.*

*We apologize for any disappointment this causes. We appreciate your interest and hope you'll still watch and share the show.*

*Regards,*

*The Ultimate Fighter Production Team*

And that's when everything crashes down on me, like one final wave sending me down the abyss.

It doesn't matter if I walk again—I'll never fight again. I'll never have *anything* to do with fighting. I'll never really be able to coach, not without being able to fight. This email just proved that. Applying for the coaching position was my last-ditch effort at staying in the MMA world, my application sent in on a good PT day when my hopes were unrealistically high. I should've known it was too much to ask for.

And if I'm not in the fight world, what the fuck am I doing? *Who am I?* At twenty-eight years old, I don't have a single thing to offer beyond my fighting skills. So, what am I supposed to do? What do I do with my time, and what do I do for money?

And then I think about Lily.

And I realize that even if I could figure out this job shit, I still wouldn't have *her*.

So if I don't have a purpose, and I don't have Lily...then what's the point of anything? *What's the fucking point?*

In a now-unfamiliar move, I grab the whiskey from my kitchen cabinet. And then I yank the cork out and chug several mouthfuls right out of the bottle.

I just want oblivion back. I don't want to exist in my reality anymore; there's nothing here for me but pain.

Moving back to the couch, I wait for the buzz to hit me. When I get impatient, I take another swig.

But it's still not working quickly enough. I don't feel anything, and nothing is dissolving the pain and anger that are raging inside me.

I glare down at my useless legs. At the cause of every single problem in my life. "This is *your* fucking fault," I growl.

With the hand not holding the bottle of whiskey, I make a fist and punch my thigh, ignoring the fact that I can actually feel the strike. I'm too lost in the moment to be rational.

"If it weren't for *you*," I spit out, chest heaving, "I'd be the reigning champion of the world right now and the greatest light heavyweight in the history of the UFC. *You* took that from me. You made me into this... this... this *degenerate*. I'm *useless*. A fucking *toddler* can do more than I can."

Saying that out loud triggers something in me. And in a fit of frustration, I slam the bottle of whiskey on the side table and adjust my feet in front of the couch. And then I push myself up to a standing position.

*Fuck this. I'm going to walk, even if it kills me.*

I sway slightly, but it's my usual attempt at regaining my balance—the whiskey hasn't hit me yet. It always takes me a second to feel like I have my feet under me.

The moment I'm stable, I squeeze my hands into fists. And then I will myself to move.

I barely make it three inches, and I wobble so hard afterwards that, for a second, I think I'm going to do a faceplant.

But I don't. I've taken my first ever—unassisted—step.

I don't think it fully registers at first. Nothing feels different. I still hate my reality just as much as I did a minute ago.

So, I clench my jaw, and I force myself to take another one. And then another. And another.

Four steps later, I'm not even three feet from the couch, and I have no idea how to turn around. I'm stuck. Frozen in a state of shock.

Which is when the whiskey takes effect.

The dizziness hits me so hard that I have to close my eyes to fight against it. But that just makes me wobble, and I extend my arms out to try to regain my balance.

It doesn't work. Before I can even attempt to aim my fall toward the couch, I go crashing to the ground.

I let out a pained groan as I roll onto my back. I managed to keep from faceplanting completely, but I can already tell my elbow and hip are going to be bruised as fuck tomorrow.

*Whatever. It's not like any of this shit matters.*

I stare up at the ceiling in utter defeat. I don't even want to get up right now, because...*what's the point?* I hate everything. I can't do *anything*. And I don't bring any value to anyone else's life, so it's not like I matter to anyone outside of myself. I should stay down here.

Not for the first time, I wish the injury had been a little more complete—a little bit more permanent. At least if I was dead, I never would've known what it was like to have everything and then lose it. To become nothing when I used to be everything.

I look toward the whiskey on the side table not far from me. I've never seriously thought about finishing the job, but feeling like this is why I started drinking in the first place. I just wanted to escape my thoughts, my *reality*, for a little while.

With that, I crawl toward the table, dragging my useless legs like a slug behind me. And I reach up to grab the bottle.

Fuck this. Fuck *all* of this. Nothing matters. Might as well lose consciousness so I don't have to be in my own head. Maybe I can get drunk enough that I'll do something so I don't have to be in my own *body*.

With another swig of whiskey, I think, *one can only hope.*

**33**

---

# LILIANA

A week after my fight with Roman, Tina finds me miserably jabbing at the buttons on our coffee machine.

She bumps me aside to take over coffee duties, and once the air fills with the smell of brewing coffee, she turns around and crosses her arms, fixing me with a hard stare.

"Alright, I think I've given you more than enough time and space. Are you ready to talk about whatever happened last week?"

I pluck at a string on my sweatshirt. "Not really," I murmur sullenly.

She lets out a sad sigh and drops her arms to her sides. "Just *talk* to me. You've barely left the house and...I can hear you crying at night." When I only sniffle in response, she adds quietly, "I already know it's about Roman."

It doesn't even surprise me by now that my feelings for Roman were this obvious to everyone. But I still ask, "How?"

She gives me a sad smile. "Because he's the only one I've ever known to affect you this strongly. Now *and* two years ago."

I let out a shaky exhale and nod. "Yeah, it's about Roman."

Tina's eyes move over my face for a moment before she nods and turns around to quickly prepare two cups of coffee for us.

"Start at the beginning," she says as she slides a mug over to me.

Forty-five minutes later, I've confessed every honest, ugly truth. I've been crying on and off, and I think I've hit every emotion on the spectrum with the chronological retelling. By the time I tell Tina about the fight with Roman, I'm in the same heartbroken state I was in when I walked away from Roman.

"You did the right thing with him," Tina says, her tone gentle. It's the first time she's said anything, so I release a single, somewhat relieved breath when she says that. "There's no way you could have kept working with him after that."

"I know, I just... I can't stop worrying about him. I knew he wasn't going to react well to it, but I didn't think he'd just quit entirely." When I wipe away yet another tear, Tina hands me a tissue. "I wasn't trying to hurt him. But now I'm worried that I ruined everything."

"Lily, you can't feel guilty for Roman quitting," Tina says, her tone somehow both gentle and stern. "*If* he quits, that's his decision. He's a grown man. You're not responsible for his life choices."

But then she pauses, and I look up to see her nervously mulling something over. I know what she's going to say before she even opens her mouth, and my stomach sinks.

The look she gives me is almost pitying as she says, "But you are responsible for *your* life choices. And Lily...you need to come clean to your boss."

I nod miserably. "I know. I've been stressing over this all week. These past few months, I wanted to tell Fran so many times, but every time I almost walked into her office, I just... couldn't. Because of Roman."

Tina gives me a confused look, but I'm relieved to see there's no judgment in it. "What do you mean?"

"Tina, he got *better*," I rush to explain. "Everything I was doing, all the texting and time we spent together, all of it was *helping* him. He was motivated, he was trying—he was finally making real progress for the first time in two years."

"Is that why you did it?"

My gaze drops to my lap, throat tightening up. *Because no, that's not why I did it.*

When I finally gather the strength to look up again, I shouldn't be surprised by the sadness that enters Tina's eyes, because it's merely a confirmation of what I've known subconsciously this whole time.

"Because that doesn't make it okay," she says with an expression that shows just how kind she's being about this. "You have a moral obligation as a healthcare provider, Lily."

"I know," I whisper. "I know, I know."

"So, then you have to tell your boss," she pushes. "For one, it's the right thing to do. For another, it's clearly eating you up inside. This is what you've been stressed about, isn't it?"

I nod silently.

"Tell Fran. Tell her the truth, and deal with this the right way." When she takes my hands in hers, the touch warm and comforting, my eyes fill with tears all over again. "And no matter what happens, I'll be here for you." She gives me a love-filled smile, her eyes also glassy. "We'll figure it out, Lily. You'll be okay, too."

I nod my defeat and fall into her arms. But even as I

prepare to come clean, and to possibly lose my job, my license, my *life*, all I can think about is...

*If he's happy and better off at the end of all this, it was worth it.*

---

I look like a wreck when I walk into the clinic a few hours later. I debated waiting a day or two to hopefully pull myself together a little more, but in the end, I decided I don't want to wait. I need to deal with this.

I enter through the back door at a time when only a few other people are still working, and immediately approach Fran's office. She calls for me to come in as soon as I knock, but does a triple-take when she finally looks up at me.

"What's wrong?" she demands, standing from her chair and coming around her desk. "What happened?"

"Do you have a few minutes to talk?" I ask instead.

"Of course, of course." She gestures for me to sit in one of the guest chairs, and she takes the one beside it. "Tell me what happened."

I suck in a shaky breath. All day, I've been trying to figure out what to say and how to start, but I'm no closer to knowing the right answer. So I just...start talking.

"Fran, I made a mistake. I...developed an inappropriate relationship with a patient."

A wall drops over Fran's eyes, making it impossible to read her. She leans back in her chair as she studies me.

"This is about Roman." She says it as a statement, not a question.

I nod. I had already assumed it wouldn't be hard to guess which of my patients.

"It was only a friendship for the longest time," I explain,

trying to make my voice sound as neutral as possible, and not at all defensive. "But then that friendship went beyond the clinic. I knew even that was wrong, but..." I swallow thickly. "I felt that I could help Roman as more than just his physical therapist."

The words taste bitter on my tongue. Because while that's true in a way, none of what I did was solely because I wanted to help Roman. I didn't give him my pity friendship.

I wanted *his* friendship.

"I see," Fran says, still giving nothing away. "And I'm assuming this friendship later developed...feelings?"

I'm grateful for her wording. If she had asked me relationship questions, or—God forbid—questions about whether a physical relationship developed, I probably would have given everything away and expired on the spot.

Again, I nod slowly. Then, deciding to be honest about *my* feelings, I admit, "It was impossible not to. With him."

That finally elicits a reaction I can decipher. Fran softens the tiniest bit before letting out a heavy exhale.

"Lily, I've been a manager within the healthcare space for almost twenty years. I've known *you* for almost ten. I'd like to think I can read people well enough to not be completely oblivious." Sliding her glasses off, she massages the bridge of her nose. "To be honest, I should take partial responsibility for this. I had a feeling something was going on."

I drop my gaze, shame rolling through me. I've known Fran since I was a senior in high school—she was my dad's physical therapist and became something of a mentor for me way before she ever hired me as a PT. The last thing I ever wanted to do with all this was hurt someone I respect so much.

Fran continues her thought. "But I, too, was amazed by

Roman's progress. I just figured whatever friendship you two had struck up was working. I should have realized that wasn't the end of it." She pauses, and when she speaks again, the disappointment in her voice is obvious. "You know better, Lily."

I choke on the sob I've been holding back. This feels almost as bad as my conversation with Roman.

"I know," I say, a tear running down my cheek as I look up to meet Fran's eyes again. "And I am so, *so* sorry. You're right, I should have known better. I should have told you sooner. I just— I don't know why—"

I feel Fran's eyes on me as I once again try to compose myself. I have no idea what she's thinking, or where she's going to take this. My future really is in her hands at this point.

As if reading my mind, she says in an even tone, "I should fire you."

I flinch at the harsh statement.

"I should report you to the state board, too. On paper, this is an abuse of power and any future patient in your care would be at risk."

My stomach sinks. I knew this was the most likely outcome, but I never really thought—

"But I won't."

My head snaps up in shock. "You... *What?*"

"I'm not going to report you, Lily," Fran says in that same even tone. "Or fire you. But I *am* putting you on probation."

My head is still spinning. "Why... why would you do that? I don't understand. I broke so many rules. I did the most unethical thing I can think of in this profession, I... I don't understand."

"If it were any other therapist, or any other *patient*, I would." Her tone eases. "But I know you. I know your soul,

Lily. I know that you wish every day that you could take your patients' pain from them. I know that if you did something like this, there was an *irrefutable* reason for it. Not to mention, I also know Roman. I saw how he changed, between his first day and now, and I saw how much your care meant to him. How much it affected his recovery. How *you* helped him. I think that's why I didn't ask you more often how things were going."

When she hesitates, I look up at her with a confused frown. She's studying me. "I was also scared of what would happen to him if I disrupted your process with him. Which I was apparently right about."

My frown deepens. "What do you mean?" I ask with a sniffle.

Another hesitation. Then, "He hasn't been back to the clinic since I reassigned him. He never showed up to his sessions with the new PT last week."

And after everything, maybe that cuts the most. Because regardless of what I fucked up, regardless of the mistakes *I* made, the only thing I ever wanted for Roman is a better quality of life. "Then none of it helped," I say, my voice thick as tears start to fall again. "He's right back to square one. Everything I did, everything I justified—it didn't work."

"Oh, Lily," Fran says with a sigh. "Did you really think his recovery wasn't going to have some highs and lows? When I admitted him in here as a patient, I expected him to quit twice as many times as he has. He's not back at square one, I can promise you that." She waits until I meet her eyes before saying, "You know just like I do that that man has more fight left in him."

And I realize...she's right. My guilt hasn't allowed me to see how much hope I still harbor for Roman's health and happiness. But the truth is, I believe in his ability to better *himself* far more than I'm letting myself admit.

I reach for the tissue box on Fran's desk to wipe the tears off my face. "Even still," I murmur, still nervous about this part of the conversation, "I can't be the one in his corner anymore."

"No, you cannot," Fran agrees, standing from her chair and rounding her desk to settle in her own office chair. "I would have pulled him as your client." Her focus has already locked back on her computer screen, but it flits to me for a split second. "But I'm glad you recognized that before I needed to act on it. If nothing else, that tells me that you're still somewhat clear-headed enough about this whole thing." Her gaze moves back to her screen. "I'll deal with Roman. But as far as *your* next steps…"

I stiffen in my seat before hanging my head. "I'll accept any punishment you see fit. Just tell me what you want me to do. Anything is a blessing compared to losing my license."

"And don't ever forget that. No, you're not losing your license or your job. But I'm officially putting you on probation for the next six months. I will be in complete control of your case load, and you will do a weekly debrief session with me to review every single one of your patients. If I see any unprofessional behavior, any at all, you're gone. I'm not doing a repeat of this, Lily."

I shake my head rapidly. "Never. This will *never* happen again, I promise."

Fran nods her approval. "Good. There's one more thing."

My brow furrows with confusion, but I say anyway, "Anything."

She holds my gaze, imprinting the importance of whatever she's about to say.

"No one can know about this. As of right now, what

happened between you and Roman Ward does not leave this office."

My eyes widen. I know she's right because I know how badly my professional reputation would be tarnished If something like this came out even as a rumor.

It's just hitting me a little hard that this also means—

"That also means you two cannot have *any* kind of relationship right now," Fran confirms. "It would be far too easy for people to put two and two together if you two remained friends. It's easier to say you two hit a wall in his recovery and he transferred clinics to continue his physical therapy elsewhere."

I nod, feeling miserable. "You don't have to worry about that. He wants nothing to do with me anyway."

Fran gives me an odd look. I expect her to comment on what I just said, but she only shakes her head.

"Regardless, we just need it to be quiet. I've taken care of the rest." Her expression becomes stern. "Are we clear about everything?"

I nod once more. "Crystal. I can't thank you enough, Fran." My voice cracks as I add, "I don't deserve you, but I'm grateful for you."

At that, Fran releases an exhale and stands from her chair, then comes around to lift me from mine so she can wrap her arms around me.

"You're a good person, Lily," she whispers in my ear. "Don't lose sight of that in all of this."

I don't know if I can agree with her at the moment, but I return the hug with a squeeze anyway.

**34**

---

# ROMAN

I wake up with a raging hangover.

I shouldn't be surprised, considering the amount of booze I've consumed in the past week, but it's been so long since I've drank enough to pass out that I'm caught off guard by the way my head is pounding.

Dragging myself out of bed, I set to showering and cleaning myself up. But even washing the smell of whiskey and regret off my skin does nothing to fix my miserable mood. I throw myself onto the couch with a frustrated shout into the void.

Suddenly, electronic beeps fill the air. When they're followed by the sound of a lock disengaging, I turn my head to see who's walking unprompted into my house.

It's Mikey. Of course, it's Mikey.

He struts in like he owns the place, merely glancing at me before he plops himself down on the other end of the couch.

I wonder if he's going to comment on my current hungover state, especially because it's been weeks since he's seen me drink more than the occasional beer. But the only reaction he gives the whiskey bottle and empty beer cans is a raised eyebrow. Then he looks at me and asks simply, "So, what are we playing today?"

Clearing my throat, I sit up into a more comfortable position. "Uh, I don't know. Call of Duty sound good?"

He nods and reaches for the controllers, throwing one of them over to me as he asks, "Don't you have PT today?"

My throat tightens at the memory of Lily, and the knowledge that I gave up on the clinic entirely. I haven't been back in probably two weeks now; not that I'm keeping track. My voice is hoarse when I say, "Nah, I'm done with that shit."

Mikey's brow furrows, though he's still not looking at me. "Why?"

My shrug is stiff. "Bunch of reasons."

"Such as?"

"Jesus, what's with the interrogation?" I explode, uncomfortable and at my wit's end. "You've never given a shit about my rehab."

Finally, Mikey turns to me with a frown. "That's not true. I just never pressured you about it. You got enough of that from everyone else."

I look away from him, shame heating my face. He's right; he's never been one to nag me. It's one of my favorite things about him. Who am I to blow up on him the first time he shows concern?

"Although that doesn't mean I haven't thought you're a moron about some things," he says casually.

Now I'm the one frowning. Turning to face him, I ask, "What do you mean? What things?"

He shrugs, as if this isn't the most serious conversation we've ever had. "Your PT, for one. I won't say I know anything about what it's like to be paralyzed, or to go from one of the greatest athletes in the world *to* paralyzed, but even I can see that you're being a pussy about your rehab."

I almost laugh at that, his resemblance to Lily uncanny with that statement.

"You could've been walking a year ago, and you know it."

*That* makes my amusement disappear.

I look down at my lap, fidgeting with the controller as I grumble, "Anything else you'd like to unburden yourself with?"

"Yeah. What are you *doing?*"

My head rears back, confused. "What do you mean?"

He throws his arms out, clearly at *his* wit's end. "I mean, what *is* this? What's your plan here? Every time I come over, you're sitting on the couch, watching TV or playing a video game." I wonder if he can feel the way his words burn me, because after his focus shifts to me, and he watches me for a moment, his voice is gentler when he continues. "Don't get me wrong, there's something to be said about being able to rely on you as an escape from my everyday bullshit. But *you* should also have everyday bullshit, man. This can't be all there is for you." He hesitates, shooting me a curious look. "You seemed to be doing better for a while but... I don't know. I don't know what's going on with you."

I can sense him waiting for me to give him an answer, to react in some way to what he's saying. But when I don't, he sighs. "You know, sometimes when I'm typing in the code on your keypad, I catch myself wishing you're not home. That you found a job, or a hobby, or something that lights you up the way fighting used to."

I swallow roughly and finally speak. "I don't think that exists, man. Fighting was everything to me."

"Maybe," Mikey says. And my gratitude for him grows that he doesn't simply wave me off as being dramatic the way I have been in the past by doctors and therapists. "But people can have more than one thing that fulfills them. Family, hobbies, careers. You keep thinking of fighting as the only thing that could ever be your reason for living, and it's keeping you from moving on, man. You're stuck in this limbo that you don't need to be in."

"So, what am I supposed to do?" I demand, my frustration peaking. "If I don't have fighting"—*and I don't have Lily,* I add silently—"then how do I figure out what fulfills me? I'm almost thirty. I feel ridiculous even asking that question out loud."

Mikey shrugs. "Same way a twenty-year-old figures it out. Just think of it as a midlife crisis."

I blow out an exasperated breath. "So, what, buy a sports car and start dating models?"

"Well, you can't drive, and you've already done the second one, so both of those are out."

I glare at my supposed best friend. "You're terrible at this."

"Hey, this is why people pay professionals to be their therapists," he says with a shrug. "It's not my fault you've been too stubborn to ask. Now you're stuck with my amateur version of therapy."

My sigh is tired. He's right, but one step at a time.

Then something occurs to me, and I ask curiously, "How did you decide you wanted to be an accountant?"

"Same way a lot of people find their career path. I was in college and liked my math classes the most."

Instantly, my thoughts flash back to Lily's comments about school, about being good at history and the career options that talent might come with. *Should I go back to school? Could I go back to school?*

"Look," Mikey continues, "All I'm saying is you have

more options than you think you do. And you don't have to do anything today, but whatever you eventually decide on, you have to just *do* it. You can't keep sitting around here; you're going to go crazy."

Dropping my head back against the couch, I let out a heavy, tired exhale, a million thoughts spiraling around my head. But then I notice Mikey looks a little pleased with himself, and I lift my head as my eyes narrow in suspicion.

"So, how long have you been waiting to say all that?"

As if he really has been holding everything back, a breath whooshes from his chest. "You have no idea. I wanted to throw it in your face every time you started your woe-is-me bullshit."

I let out a bark of laughter, shaking my head. I can't even really blame him for it. "Then why the fuck did you hang around?"

He shrugs. "Because you're my friend. And you helped me get through my family shit in middle school, even if you never realized it. I figured you needed someone to just be *your* friend."

My chest squeezes at his admission, and the easy way he says it. No feelings, just easy truth. And I think about how I have no reason to doubt him, how everything he's said, everything he's done for me this past year has proven that he wants nothing from me. How I've always felt like he just wanted to bring back the same friendship that two middle schoolers had almost two decades ago.

And then I think about how *that*, that easy friendship, kept me sane a lot of days. How he made me feel normal, made me feel wanted, how he kept me busy.

And I become overwhelmed with gratitude.

I clear my throat, trying to get rid of the tightness in it. I want to tell him I appreciate him, that he probably saved me more than once, but it's also Mikey—he'd probably just get uncomfortable and run from my house.

So instead, I toss him the controller in my hand, the one I know he loves because of how smooth the buttons feel. And then I grab the shitty one from his hand.

We don't exchange any words. I know he knows what I'm doing because of the way his eyes go wide, but he doesn't say anything about it. He just grins and settles deeper into the couch cushions.

"Don't think I won't still kick your ass," I taunt. "A shitty controller won't save you."

Mikey rolls his eyes. "Let's revisit this conversation in twenty minutes when you realize a controller was the *only* thing giving you those W's."

# 35

# ROMAN

I don't waste any time getting my shit together. I've wasted enough as it is.

The next morning, after I've kicked Mikey out of my house and sent him off to work like a 1950s housewife, I set up my computer at my dining room table and start in on my to-do list.

*Number one: register for college.*

I don't go crazy with it. It's just community college, a steppingstone toward what is hopefully figuring out what the fuck I want to do with my life. But Lily and Mikey were right; I need to start somewhere. And what better place to start than with an array of General Education classes in an Associate's program.

The timing is perfect, with the registration for the college's fall semester still open. It takes me a bit to fill it out, mostly because it's been a decade since I've done anything education related, and I can't even remember what classes I took during the one semester I was in college. But what I find as I dig for my old details and trudge through the application is that my excitement—for something new, for something *challenging*—is mounting.

In fact, by the time I submit my application, I'm riding a high that demands *more*. So, I pull up Monster.com and start to browse.

It's useless, of course, at least for me. I have no degree, no experience, nothing to offer. But scrolling through job listings gives me that same rush that the college website did.

Which is how I end up on a resume builder website.

That one dulls the excitement, putting me face to face with the yawning void that is my credentials, but I feel accomplished by the end of it, nevertheless. I have a rough draft that I didn't have an hour ago, and for now, that's enough.

When I'm done, I close my laptop and suck in a deep breath. Now comes the hard part.

The clinic.

I debated for hours yesterday about what I should do with the clinic. If I should fight for Lily to take me back, to make her a promise that I'll try harder this time, or if I should just cut my losses and transfer to a different clinic. But in the end, I realize Lily *shouldn't* take me back—that she was right about me needing to do this myself.

So, I'll do it myself. But I need to mend some bridges first.

---

Mom and I are both quiet on the drive over to the clinic. Me, because I'm lost in my thoughts, and Mom, because she has no idea what's going on. I can tell she wants to ask because she keeps glancing at me, but I think she's just relieved I'm not drunk on my couch anymore and instead asking to go to the clinic on a Tuesday afternoon.

When she pulls up in front of the building, I unclip my seatbelt before turning to her and saying, "Thanks, Mom."

She smiles. "Of course, sweetie."

"No, I mean...thank you. For everything." I shift more toward her, desperate to make her understand just how *much* I mean it. "For putting up with me, for never giving up on me—for being there even when I didn't deserve to have your support. I..." I swallow roughly, the backs of my eyes burning. "I wouldn't have survived without you. And I've done a shit job of showing just how much I appreciate you. But that stops now. I'm so grateful for you, Mom, and I just... I love you so much."

Before I can brace for it, she's throwing her arms around me and sobbing into my shoulder. "Oh, honey. I love you, too. But I'm your mother; of course, I'm going to be there for you. You don't need to thank me for that."

Returning her hug, I squeeze her to me. "Yes, I do. I should've said it every day, but I'm saying it now. Thank you."

When she pulls back, she takes a second to wipe the tears from her cheeks. "I don't know what's gotten into you, but whatever it is, I'm glad. You seem...happier."

I think about what I'm feeling for a moment, then admit quietly, "Not yet. But I'm working on it."

She smiles and cups my face. "Good. I'd like to see you happy again." Then once she composes herself with a shaky breath, she glances at the clinic and says, "Now go do whatever it is we came here for."

I pull in a deep breath of my own, gathering all the courage I can muster. And then I head into the building.

I didn't time it this way on purpose, but part of me is

relieved that Lily doesn't work on Tuesdays. I'm not convinced my reaction to seeing her right now wouldn't be throwing myself at her feet and begging her to take me back.

When the receptionist sees me, her brow immediately furrows. "Mr. Ward. Hi. I'm sorry, Lily's not here. Did you... reschedule your appointment?"

"Actually, I was hoping I could talk to her boss. Is Fran here?"

Her confusion grows at that. But she nods and says, "She is... If you give me a minute, I can check to see if she has time to talk to you right now."

"That would be great, thank you."

She rushes off, leaving me in the waiting room. Thankfully, though, she doesn't make me wait long. Only a minute later, Fran appears, the receptionist standing behind her with a curious expression.

"Mr. Ward, what a surprise," she says. She gestures toward the hallway she just came from. "We can talk in my office. If you'll follow me?"

I nod and turn toward her, sending the receptionist a nod of appreciation.

When we enter Fran's office, she lifts one of the chairs away from her desk in order to make room for my wheelchair. Then she takes a seat in her own chair and trains a stare on me that tells me exactly nothing about what she knows or what she's thinking.

"So," she starts. "How can I help you, Roman?"

I decide on a no-nonsense approach, since Fran has always seemed like a no-nonsense type of woman.

"Am I right in assuming patient transfers don't happen without your knowledge? That you already know Lily asked me to be moved to someone else?"

She nods. "Your assumption would be correct."

That still doesn't tell me what she knows, but after a moment, I realize it doesn't matter. Anyone could've guessed that my rehab failing was going to be my own fault.

So, I simply settle on an apology.

"I want you to know that none of this was Lily's fault." I pause to take a deep breath. "You should know that you're lucky to have her on your staff. Her energy, her knowledge, her ability to read what people need—she got me further than anyone else has in two years. She's...an incredible physical therapist."

"I know she is," Fran says, her voice just barely softer than it was before. "I knew it the day I hired her, and I know it now. Whatever happened between you two doesn't change that."

I nod as I look down at my lap, my chest squeezing at the memory of what happened between us. I'm relieved, at least, that it didn't have an effect on her job or how her boss sees her.

"I apologize for upsetting her," I say quietly, my voice tight. "And for any trouble I've caused for you and this clinic. I never meant to, I just..." I clear my throat with a swallow and look up at Fran. "Dealing with this injury has been hard. It hasn't exactly made me the best person. Which doesn't excuse my behavior, of course, but...I just want you to know that I am truly, deeply sorry."

At that, she softens. "I appreciate that, Roman. I accept your apology. And I know Lily would accept it, too."

Knowing that she's right only makes my heart hurt more.

"Is that why you're here?" Fran asks. "To tell me that?"

I straighten in my chair. "One of the reasons. The other is to ask for a referral to another clinic."

Her eyebrows rise in surprise.

"If I'm not working with Lily, I don't think it would be a good idea for me to stay here under another PT," I explain. "But...I would still like to continue my rehab. So, I'm hoping you can give me a recommendation."

I can see the thoughts roiling in Fran's head, and after a moment, she says, "I can do that. Actually, I have an old colleague who specializes in SCIs working at our sister clinic on the other side of the city." There's a flash of amusement in her expression. "He's ex-military, though, so a bit of a drill sergeant when it comes to his therapy methods. Is that okay?"

I huff a laugh. "More than okay. Thank you."

Chuckling, she pulls a notepad over and starts to scribble on it. When she looks up, she asks, "Is there anything else I can help you with?"

I take another steadying breath. This is the hard part, but it's probably also the most important one.

"Yeah. Can you recommend a psychologist, as well? I think it's about time I talk to someone."

**36**

---

# LILIANA

*Four Months Later*

"Thanks again, Lily. I'll see you next week!"

I wave at my last patient of the day with a smile. "Sounds good, Dave, see you then! Have a nice weekend!"

Once he's gone, I organize my area. With back-to-back clients all day, this is my first chance to do any cleanup. Nowadays, my schedule is jampacked like this. I don't mind it, though—I've come to appreciate it as a reliable distraction from my own thoughts.

Not that my boss doesn't try to lighten my load. Even now, I can tell what she's going to say before she reaches the gym.

"Are you sure you don't want me to transfer Dave to Sandy?" she asks, her hands on her hips and a concerned look on her face. "You know he'd be happy with any young female PT. He's not picky. It doesn't need to be you."

I roll my eyes as I continue to clean up. "Well, that just makes me feel all warm and fuzzy and appreciated."

"You know what I mean. I'd just rather you have a few less clients. You're working yourself too hard, Lily. You're going to burn out."

My throat tightens. I know I'm working too hard, but I also know it's the only thing keeping me sane these days.

She sighs, her hands dropping to her sides. "Well, it was worth a try. I'm leaving now but don't stay too late, okay? You need to get some sleep."

I force a smile onto my face as I wave her off. "I won't. I'll see you next week, Fran."

She starts toward her office, but before she can get very far, she snaps her fingers and turns back around.

"I almost forgot. I had a feeling you'd say no to a smaller workload, so I left a little something in your locker. Do me a favor and at least *try* to use it."

My brow furrows. "What did you leave me?"

She's already walking toward her office again as she calls out, "Just use it, Lily!"

I'm too curious not to go immediately into the break-room to check my locker.

She left me a ticket to the movies tonight.

My chest tightens, partly because I'm affected by her thoughtfulness, but mostly because of the person who comes to mind when I think of anything movie related.

It's been four months, and yet there isn't a day that passes when I don't think about Roman. On good days, the thought is a fleeting one, something along the lines of wondering how he's doing and hoping he's okay. But on bad ones, I end up in a downward spiral of overthinking.

Despite how firmly I ended things, I never stopped second-guessing my decisions. Not just my decision to leave him, but every single other one, as well. I questioned the unconventional way I handled his therapy, my decision to get involved with him, my reasoning for leaving him. I also debated if not calling him *now* was the right idea. No matter how I painted the months with Roman, I could never go more than a day or two convinced of my decisions being the right ones.

The worst part of all my second-guessing is feeling like I gave up on him. When I think about how I promised Roman to help him every step of the way, and then about how *I* was the one to end things, I want to vomit. I've lost more nights of sleep over it than I ever thought possible. I wish I could know that he's at least doing well, but I refuse to butcher my medical oath any more than I already have just to find out how his therapy is going. The only thing keeping me sane is knowing that he had asked my boss for a referral. The fact that the recommended PT is a really good therapist who has a lot of experience with SCIs is a bonus weight off my shoulders I probably don't deserve.

Swallowing past the knot in my throat, I slide the movie tickets into my purse. And since I'm already torturing myself with guilt, I give myself a second to think about what it would have been like to go to the movies with Roman. He probably would have mocked me for the giant tub of popcorn I'd order, but he'd also insist on paying for it and then steal a few kernels when he thinks I'm not looking. He would probably pair it with a dinner date *after* the movie, so we could take our time talking about and analyzing the movie. I bet he would know an annoying amount of behind-the-scenes movie facts.

My heart aches at the thought of it. Because the hardest part of the hard days is simply that...I miss *him*.

I let out a bone-weary sigh as I pull my jacket out of my

locker. I had been planning on distracting myself with a deep clean in the gym, but since the ticket is for tonight, I guess my plans are changing.

I've reached some new state of unfeeling by the time I park at the movie theater. It's probably a good thing that Fran bought tickets for a showing only an hour after she presented them, because even that twenty-minute drive gave me too much time to get lost in my own head. Specifically, to get lost in memories of when Roman and I won tickets to the movies.

I'm too busy thinking about how this probably would have been the movie we would have picked to pay much attention as I walk toward the movie theater entrance. It isn't until a tingle runs over my skin that I think to look around.

It's...Roman.

I think my heart stops beating at first glance—my breathing definitely stops when I see him. Because he's here, yes, but also because...he's *walking*. He's standing on his own two feet, using two forearm crutches to brace himself, and he's moving slowly but steadily toward me.

My eyes go wide at the sight of him, desperate to take in every new detail. And there are a *lot*. It's not just the lack of his wheelchair, it's differences in his appearance, and in his vibe. He looks like an entirely different person.

His hair has grown out, no longer the lazy buzzcut he had a few months ago. There are no bags under his eyes, no sallow tint to his skin. And he looks *big*. His chest and arms have filled out with even more muscle than he had before, and his legs look strong now, too. Physically, he looks more like the Roman I met that very first night.

But as far as his aura...he doesn't feel like the first *or* second Roman I got to know.

There's a calmness in his eyes now, a confidence that

feels more like self-realization than the arrogance it used to be. He seems sure of himself. There's no anger, no self-hatred, nothing in his expression that makes him look like a lost little boy. He looks like...a *man*. A self-assured man who knows who he is and what he wants.

And he's looking at *me*.

"Hey, Doc," he says in a deep voice that sends sparks scattering beneath my skin. He keeps his eyes trained on me, a soft smile just barely visible on his lips.

"Roman," I say on an exhale. I clear my throat and try again. "Oh my God...you're *walking*."

He looks down at his crutches, his smile growing. "I am. I had a bunch of great therapists, so I guess it's about time."

My heart starts to beat so powerfully at that, I lift my hand to my chest and subconsciously rub the space where I can feel it hammering. My eyes are also burning, and it takes me two tries to get any words out.

"So...the PT my boss recommended worked out then?"

Roman watches me for a moment, but in a way that I can't read. After a moment, he nods and says, "Dr. Martin, yeah. He's great." His lip quirks with amusement. "He hurt my feelings a lot less than I'm used to in a rehab environment, but we've accomplished what we set out to."

A wet laugh bursts out of me. "I feel like I should apologize, but I don't really want to."

The smile he gives me is warm, and it does things to me I can't understand in this emotional whirlwind. "I don't want you to, either," he says.

I hesitate for a moment, then slowly take a step toward Roman. "Are you still working with him? I mean, where are you in your PT?"

He studies me, and this time, I can read his expression. It's adoration.

"You can't help yourself, can you?" he asks softly. "You go right back to caring."

I'm already moving, already one step closer to him. "I never stopped caring," I whisper, close enough now that I need to look up to meet his eyes.

His throat moves with a swallow, his eyes dipping to my mouth before meeting mine again, emotions flickering in his gaze. But he still answers my question. "Yeah, I'm still working with him. I like his methods. I'll probably keep him for a while."

Relief warms my body. "Good, I'm glad," I say with a smile.

And then all small talk, all softness disappears from the air, and everything sobers with the intensity of his eyes on me. He leans his crutches against the wall, then turns back to me and says simply, "You were right, you know."

I suck in a breath. I have no idea what he's about to say, but I'm hoping so hard that I was right about one thing in particular that I can't breathe around the feeling.

His smile his sad, his voice tender. "I needed to do it on my own. You were right to make me."

And if I thought my relief was great before, it's nothing compared to what I feel when he says that.

"I'm so, so grateful that I had you with me in the beginning," he starts, taking a step closer, "because I was in dire need of a kick in the ass. You were exactly what I needed at that point in my life. And I appreciate you so much for it. But..." His eyes take on a shine that just makes my eyes burn again. "But I needed to take that final step on my own."

He lets out a stuttered exhale, and I wonder if *he* feels relief, too. Like maybe he's been wanting to say this out loud.

And now that they're out, it's like the dam has broken, and all the other thoughts come rushing out.

"At first, everything felt meaningless," he says. "I knew I'd never get back to the life I had, so even trying felt pointless. I couldn't wrap my head around what a life without fighting looked like and, honestly, a part of me didn't want to. But...then *you* came around, and you made it feel like a rehabilitation goal was not only worthwhile, but achievable. You gave me *hope*, Liliana. You...revived me." He smiles and reaches up to tuck a strand of hair behind my ear, a hurricane of emotions swirling in his eyes. But just as quickly, his hand drops and he looks away. "I should've realized sooner that I had subconsciously started to convince myself that walking would magically fix everything. That if I could just walk, I would feel like myself again, and that I would regain everything I had lost. Because I still felt like I was missing myself."

He pulls in a shaky breath, seemingly composing himself. And this time when he turns back to me, he's wearing the same look I noticed when he walked over: the look of a self-assured man.

His voice is quiet but strong when he says, "It took the kick in the ass that you gave me to remember I was already whole. To realize that I had become so focused on what I lost that I forgot to look at what I have. *You* reminded me how much good I have in my life. I just needed to give myself permission to explore it. To start living again."

The need to hug him, to tell him I'm *so proud* of him, is becoming overwhelming, but I also don't want to interrupt him.

"And I'm sorry you ever felt like that pressure was on you," he says in a near-whisper, his voice rife with emotion. "Your only job was to help with my physical rehab. I never should have let you feel like you needed to carry the burden of my mental health problems, or—God forbid—

my self-worth. And I'm so, *so* sorry you ever felt like you needed to."

"I would have," I admit, unable to stay quiet at this point. "If I thought it would help you, if it would have brought happiness into your life, I would have. In a heartbeat."

He smiles, his hand coming up to cup my face. His thumb brushes over my cheek, the touch leaving a trail of warmth on my skin. "I know," he says affectionately. "It's one of the reasons I fell in love with you."

I suck in a startled breath. I don't know if I'm more caught off guard by his casual confession, or the look in his eyes as he says it.

Part of me wonders if he even realizes what he just said. Especially when his next words are, "It's also one of the reasons I hate myself for putting your job in jeopardy. I was a selfish prick for risking your career like that, and I'll never forgive myself for it."

"Roman, *no.*" I reach up to cup the hand still holding my face. "We did that together; that's not on you. *I* don't even hate you for that."

His lips lift in another warm smile, his thumb smoothing over my cheek again. But after a moment, he sighs and drops his hand. "I'm just glad nothing happened. Partly because I never could have forgiven myself, but also because I didn't deserve the privilege to have you like that. And..." An intensity flares in his eyes that takes my breath away once again. "I don't know if I deserve it now, but I think I'm dying without you. I couldn't go another day without seeing you and telling you thank you and, *God*, you're just so beautiful."

I choke on a sob, my hand coming up to cover my mouth. I'm too overwhelmed to respond, so Roman takes this opportunity to take my face in his hands—both hands, this time—and look down at me with a level of longing that I never thought I'd see again.

"Liliana…" The sound of my name on his lips is the best thing I've ever heard. "I miss you. Every single day. And I'm so grateful for you. You saved my life. And hopefully, I'll never be able to return the favor, but I'd love to return it with other things, instead. Happiness. Comfort. Excitement. Love. So, Liliana…" He smiles then, so much love and tenderness in his eyes that I think my heart might fly right out of my chest. "Will you do me the honor of going to the movies with me?"

A laugh bubbles past my lips. "*That's* your question? That was a lot of buildup for a movie invite."

Grinning, his hands drop to my waist. "I thought I'd start with an easy one."

Chuckling, I tell him, "I would like nothing more than to see a movie with you. And it's perfect timing because my boss already got me a ticket."

Somehow, Roman's grin grows even bigger. "She may have been the one who gave it to you, but…"

My mouth drops open. "You set this all up?" Then, with even more shock, I exclaim, "Wait…are you saying my boss was your *wing woman?*"

Roman lets out a loud laugh that makes my heart triple in size. "I never thought of it like that, but yeah, I guess she was." He sobers, and adds, "She's been very helpful since I last saw you. With a number of things."

I start smiling and shaking my head at that, but Roman seems to have the opposite reaction. As if he's suddenly reminded of something, all humor drops from his face and his hands tighten on my hips.

"You didn't get in trouble with anything, did you?" he asks, concerned. "It was obvious that she knew about us, but she also implied that you still had your license and your job, so I'm assuming nothing too terrible came of...all of this." His concern shifts to mild panic. "Am I right? You're okay at work? Because if anything happened to you because of my bullshit, I'll—"

I gently press a hand against his mouth, unable to stop my growing smile. *God, I've missed him.*

"I'm fine, Roman, I promise," I tell him. "I came clean to Fran and we worked it out. Everything is good."

Relief fills his eyes. Before I can remove my hand from his mouth, I feel the gentlest kiss against my palm.

I feel warm all over just from that light touch, and when his gaze drops to my lips, a heat flares in them that makes it suddenly hard to breathe. I drop my hand from his mouth to rest on his chest.

"Am I allowed to kiss you?" he asks. "I refuse to do anything anymore that's not by the book, so if it's inappropriate—"

I cut him off with a kiss of my own.

He sinks into it with a groan of relief.

I cling to him, my hands fisting in his shirt as his wrap around me, the feeling entirely mutual.

I don't know which one of us eventually pulls back, but Roman's forehead drops to mine, his eyes sliding closed. It lets me look at him, lets me truly take in this moment of contentment. And I can't help asking in a whisper, "Did you just tell me you love me?"

His eyes open and he straightens slightly, though his hands stay on me so he can keep me close. "I did. You don't need to say it back, that's not why I—"

"I love you, too, Roman."

His eyes widen.

"And I missed you. So much."

And then Roman is the one initiating the kiss, his lips taking mine with a desperation that wasn't there a minute ago. I give into it with a sigh, comforted by the need thrumming beneath Roman's touch.

We're both breathing a little heavier when we pull back this time. He only moves so far as to lean his forehead against mine before saying, "So, about that movie..."

# 37

# LILIANA

I don't know how I make it through the movie.

Roman keeps his arm around me the entire time, seeming to want the physical connection as much as I do, and yet it's still not enough. I want to look at him, run my hands over him, convince myself he's really *here*. I glance at him more times than I can count during the movie. But it's okay, because he's doing the same thing. And every time our eyes meet, he cups my cheek and kisses me.

Thank God, the movie is only an hour and a half. It's good enough that I can tell I'd be really into it if not for... everything, but it's not enough to make me pay attention beyond a few gasps at the gore and laughs at the comedy. I'm mostly just counting down to the moment the credits start rolling.

When they do, it takes everything in me not to jump up and pull Roman back to the sunshine, back to reality where we can really talk. Instead, I force myself to stay in my seat and turn to Roman so I can ask cheerfully, "So...what'd you think?"

His eyes lock on mine, heat flowing through them. "I think we're probably going to have to rewatch that at home another time."

A heavy breath whooshes from me. "Oh thank God, I thought it was just me. Can we leave now?"

Chuckling, he pulls me to him for another kiss. "Yeah, Doc, we can leave."

I smile at the reminder of his nickname for me. "Mmm... I missed that," I whisper.

He kisses me again, seemingly unable to stop. "Me, too," he whispers back. "More than you know." But then he's reaching for his crutches and pushing to his feet, getting his bearings before extending a hand to me. "Come on, let's get out of here."

We're both quiet as we walk out of the theater. It's so bizarre to think about how much has changed since I left the clinic, how three hours ago, I was merely existing, and now... now I get to see and experience and be with Roman in a whole new way.

"So...I don't want to assume," Roman starts as we slow in the parking lot. "But I'm hoping if I invite you back to my house, you'll let me make you dinner." He pulls me in front of him and cups my cheek. "And we can talk," he says softly. "I want to hear all about your trip with your family. And whatever other insane adventures you've had since then."

The simplicity of the suggestion, combined with the knowledge that I finally get my time with Roman back, has love blooming in my heart like a flower. I press up on my toes to plant a quick kiss on Roman's lips, noticing our new height difference for the first time.

"Then let's go," I say, my smile feeling like it's going to crack my face. "I want to hear about yours, too."

The drive back to Roman's house is a different kind of quiet from the theater. Back there, I was in shock. Here, I'm in awe.

It's not just the sight of him driving—though the casual way he's reclined in the seat, his right hand switching from the hand controls beside the steering wheel to taking a possessive hold of my hand, definitely does something to me. It's more the sight of him being so confident. In the six months that I worked with him, I never saw him this comfortable in his body, this devoid of the hatred he's always had for it.

My amazement only grows when we reach his house and he kisses the back of my hand before telling me to wait for a moment. And then he pulls his crutches from the back seat, gets out of the car, and walks around the hood of it to open my car door.

I don't bother trying to hide the smile from my face as I step out. "Such a gentleman," I say happily.

"It's a new quality I'm trying out," he says with a smile. Before he starts toward the front door, he takes my lips in another quick kiss, and I wonder if the excessive amount of kisses are his way of keeping our physical connection since he can't hold my hand as he walks.

I follow behind him as he walks down the path, taking the opportunity to admire his legs, his gait—and his overall mouth-watering physique. While his clothes don't look as tight as they did that one night at the restaurant, they're still tight enough to show off his increasingly muscular body. Not to mention...Roman Ward has a delectable butt.

I'm trying to hide my grin at the observation when Roman lets us into the house, but he catches it anyway.

"What are you smiling about?" he asks as he sets his crutches against the wall and walks stiffly into the kitchen.

Leaning against the counter, I chew on my lip for a second before going for the honest approach. "I was admiring your butt."

He shoots me a smirk as he opens the fridge and pulls out a few ingredients. "Oh yeah? Does that mean I get free rein to do the same?" Heat flashes in his eyes as his gaze drops over my body. "Give me a turn, Doc."

Feeling suddenly self-conscious about the fact that I am absolutely *not* dressed for a date—I left the clinic in jeans and an oversized hoodie—I make a quick, awkward turn. And yet when I face forward again, meeting Roman's gaze, all I see is...awe.

"Beautiful," he breathes out.

Blushing, I look down to hide my smile.

When he starts back on dinner prep, I look over at the ingredients.

"What are you making?" I ask curiously.

"I don't know if it's going to be anything like your grand-mother's, but...I've been playing around with the classic Hungarian meals lately." He glances up at me, his hesitation obvious. "I was going to make us goulash."

My chest warms with affection knowing he chose that recipe specifically for me. "That's a great recipe," I say tell him.

The tension in his shoulders disappears. "Okay, good." His smile twitching with amusement, he jerks his head toward the rest of his house. "Go ahead, look around. I can tell you're itching to."

I let out a laugh and push off the counter. "You know me too well."

As I stroll over to the living room, I take in how clean and neat everything is. There are books *everywhere*. I spot a journal on the couch and pick it up. I don't open it, but I'm too curious not to pick it up and hold it for Roman to see. "You started journaling?"

He looks up from the carrots he's started chopping. "Yeah. My therapist recommended it." He huffs a laugh. "Who knew she'd be right."

I'm sure my delight is obvious, but even still, I wave at the stacks of books. "And the books?"

He straightens and locks our gazes. "For school," he says. Simply. As if that isn't a huge deal.

"Did you start already?" I ask him, putting the journal back down and drifting back toward the kitchen.

He nods and goes back to chopping. "About a month ago. I enrolled in community college so I could get started quickly and get my GenEd classes out of the way."

"And how is it?"

His movements slow as he mulls over the question. "It's…new. Different. I haven't been in school for over a decade, so it's going to take some getting used to. But I kind of like it." He glances up at me. "I'm glad I enrolled."

Distantly, I wonder if a person can explode from too much pride and happiness.

Especially when he goes back to chopping with a small smile on his face, saying, "I have this one class that I think I'm really going to like. It's history, obviously, and only a GenEd class, but the professor is awesome. He's really well-traveled and he's done a bunch of insanely cool expeditions, so sometimes I'll stay after class to talk to him about it." His expression *oozes* giddiness. "He actually told me about this adaptive scuba diving program that he was involved with. They work mostly with veterans, but he said I'd fit in perfectly. I was thinking of signing up."

"Are you serious?" I squeak. "Roman, that's amazing.

You'll have to tell me the organization. I'll check if they offer dive buddy certifications."

Eyes lit up, he nods before focusing back on the cutting board, then starts animatedly telling me about the program.

I'm mesmerized as I watch Roman. I can't believe this is the same man who, on bad days, wouldn't let himself attempt even the simplest task because he didn't want to deal with the reality of his injury. I always knew he was capable of this kind of healing, but to see it is...

My desire to love him becomes suddenly overwhelming. I don't question the urge, I just round the counter to gently take the knife from Roman and set it down. He gives me a questioning look at first, but once he meets my eyes, there's no more question.

I cup his face in my hands, and then I kiss him.

He *melts* into it. With a stuttered exhale, his arms come around me, clutching me to him in a way that tells me he needs me just as much as I need him. One arm stays around my waist and the other comes up to cradle the back of my head. We can't get enough of each other, can't even pause long enough to take a much-needed breath, and because of it, the passion grows.

And then it ignites. When Roman angles my head to deepen the kiss, I moan and feel myself go weak in his arms.

The sound must break the spell because, in the next moment, he pulls back, breathing heavily. For a moment, his gaze travels over my face, cataloguing every inch of it, but then he takes my hand and leads me out of the kitchen.

In the time it takes to reach Roman's bedroom, I've managed to calm myself just enough that I don't jump him as soon as we're in the vicinity of a bed. I *want* to go at Roman's pace, for both of our sakes.

I let him pull me to him, let him lead us in the sweetest kiss. It almost feels like he's pausing the heat for just long enough to stamp this as a moment to remember.

But then he's reaching for the bottom of my sweatshirt, his kiss developing teeth and sharp edges, and suddenly there's nothing sweet about us anymore.

## 38

---

# ROMAN

I pull her tank top off in one swift move. By the time I'm lifting her sports bra, I'm letting out a growl of frustration at the layers that keep interrupting my ability to taste her. It isn't until she's finally naked from the waist up, and I can take her lips in one more deep, seductive kiss, that I'm finally satisfied.

I'm still kissing her as I lay her down on the bed, and I both feel and taste the sigh of contentment she lets out when my weight settles on top of her. She wraps one leg around my hip, pulling me impossibly closer.

Her obvious hunger makes my own desperation ratchet. I've been fantasizing about this for months, replaying our one time together and thinking about what I would do differently if I ever got her to touch her again. And now that, by some miracle, she's here with me, I'm dizzy with need. I want to do everything. Want to make her *feel* everything.

I take her mouth once more, hard, before letting my kisses drift over her cheek and down to her neck, where they become nips and bites and make her arch even harder into my body.

"*God,* I missed you," I groan into her skin, my hand sliding up to cup her breast as I brace my weight on the opposite forearm. When I give her nipple a harsh pinch, a moan spills from between her lips.

The sound drives me into a frenzy. Sliding farther down the bed, I kiss my way down her body, only stopping for a few seconds to cover first one nipple, then the other, with my mouth. Then I'm impatiently tearing her jeans off.

I feel her freeze as I'm reaching for her thong. "Wait, Roman, I just realized I haven't shaved. You don't have to—"

Her words break off in a gasp when I *rip* the fabric from her body and lick from ass to clit.

"*Oh my God,*" she moans. Her hands sink into my new, long hair, and her legs tighten around my head.

I'm fucking *starved* for her. After two and a half years, I finally get the taste of her directly on my tongue, and already I'm wondering if I'll ever get enough of it. My hands come around her thighs so I can hold her against my face, my tongue swirling in circles around her clit. I hear her moan and feel the way she arches against my mouth.

It isn't until I slide one long finger inside her that my lips finally leave her skin. "Christ, Liliana, you taste like paradise," I gasp, my finger working in and out of her as my thumb settles on her clit. I watch her force her eyes open so she can look down at me.

"That's going to make me come," she whispers, her hips starting to roll against my finger. She whimpers when I add another.

"Not yet," I order in a deep growl, then drop my mouth to her skin again.

With two—*three*—fingers fucking into her, my lips suctioned around her clit, and my brusque command, I feel the moment she starts to shake. Out of the corner of my eye,

I see her grasp the sheets beneath her, can hear her gasping for more air.

"Roman, I-I can't—"

"Not yet," I growl, the vibration of my words making her legs clench tighter around my head.

"Roman," she cries. "Pleasepleaseplease*—*"

Driving my fingers deep inside her, I lift up just enough so that I can murmur, "Come for me, Liliana."

She detonates.

I watch, mesmerized, as the orgasm rolls through her, as she clamps down on my fingers and moans through the pleasure. My fingers don't slow until she finally drops, limp and trembling, back to the bed. After placing a gentle kiss on her hip, I lift up so I can quickly strip my shirt off. Then I shift up the bed until I'm lying on my side beside her, propped up on one elbow so I can look down at her.

"Beautiful, perfect woman," I whisper, brushing my thumbs over her cheeks to wipe the tears away. When she wraps her arms around my neck and pulls me closer, I immediately drop a kiss on her lips.

"You couldn't—" she starts, but it's more of a croak than anything. Laughing, she clears her throat and tries again. "You couldn't have gone easy on me the first time?"

My mouth twitches with a smile. "Not a chance."

But then the nerves hit me. I knew they would, despite hoping and mentally preparing for this day. It doesn't matter that Lily and I have already done this, that I've put in days, weeks, *months* of physical work to get my body where I want it to be—this injury is always going to have lingering effects. Sex is one of them.

Swallowing roughly, I admit the hard part out loud, wanting to be honest with Lily. "I...wasn't sure what the sex would be like, so I wanted to make sure the part I was confident in would at least be good."

She pulls back slightly so she can look at me as she asks, "What do you mean? We already know the sex is great."

Gently, I push her back into the pillows and lift up, wanting to give us both space for this conversation. She lets her arms drop from around my neck.

"I loved you on top," I start. "Watching you ride me, and seeing you come apart from that angle...it was amazing. But...I don't want that to be the only position we can do. Because even though I can kind of walk now, I'm still limited for sex, specifically. And I can't...fuck you the way I want to."

Despite everything, all the work I've done and recovery I've accomplished, that fact still hurts me. It might not always, but for now, I let myself acknowledge the pain of that limitation.

And then I work my way around it.

"I did some research," I continue. "Who knows what will work, but if I got you back, I wanted to be...ready."

Before I can explain my *research*, Lily cups my face and pulls me down for a kiss. And I can feel every ounce of love that she pours into it.

"We'll figure it out," she whispers against my lips. "Together."

My answer is another all-consuming kiss, and before long, I'm dropping down onto my side and pulling Lily onto hers, looping her leg over my hip in the same motion.

"Supposedly, doggy is the second-best position," I say when I'm done kissing her senseless. I watch her dazed eyes try to focus on me. "Especially if I can wrap something around your waist and pull your hips into me. But I don't want to do that this first time." Another time, definitely. The idea of fucking Lily from behind, watching her ass shake as I pull her into me—

"So, then how do you want me?" she asks, her words breathless.

At that, my grip tightens on her thigh, my fingers digging into the muscle. "An intoxicating—and distracting—question, Liliana," I growl.

She huffs a laugh and pulls herself even closer. "Sorry. Continue."

I loosen my grip on her thigh and brush my touch down to her knee, then back up to her hip, then her ribs.

"I actually think this position might be the best right now," I murmur, my gaze dropping over her naked body. "I want to see your eyes, but I don't completely trust myself for missionary, so..."

What I wouldn't give to see her tits shake as I drive into her from above. But I know my hips would tire quickly, if they'd even be able to fuck her the way I want to...

Lily places a hand on my cheek and kisses me. "This position is perfect," she whispers.

I smile against her mouth. "I bought some toys to make sure I can get you off," I murmur. Because there's no way in hell I was getting Lily into my bed and not making her come hard enough to see God.

A loud laugh bursts out of her, but before I can be offended, she says, "I'm sorry, did you not see how hard you just made me come? Unassisted?"

My lips stretch into a grin. "I believe someone once accused me of only knowing how to underachieve or over-achieve."

Chuckling, her hand slides down my neck, down to my chain where her fingers hook through it to pull me closer. "Well, at least you're consistent."

The moment her lips touch mine, the heat between us increases once more, and all teasing disappears. Without another word, I roll onto my back and reach into my bedside drawer.

I don't care that my movements become hurried after that. Once I've grabbed what I need, I quickly strip my pants off and roll back toward Lily. I pull her close and hitch her leg over my hip again.

She watches, wide-eyed and chest heaving, as I slide a cock ring over my length. It's not a fancy one, just something to hopefully keep me harder for longer. Because two and a half years later, my dick still has a mind of its own when it comes to orgasms and sensations.

I'm attempting to shove my worry about it back when I hear Lily breathe, "*God*, I forgot how big you are."

I have to tamp down on my smirk, any remnants of my hesitation disappearing. "I should probably be offended that I'm forgettable, but—" I slide the tip of my cock along her pussy. "Right now, I don't really care."

I love watching her as she stares at me playing with her wetness. But I don't think I can stand another second without her taste on my lips, so I hungrily take her mouth in a kiss, my tongue diving deep to tangle with hers.

The moan she lets out is my undoing. And in one smooth move, I slide inside her.

Her moan turns into a gasp. "Oh my God. The cock ring—"

I thrust again, and again she gasps.

"Can you feel it against your clit?" I groan.

Her nod is jerky. I didn't quite trust myself with a vibrating cock ring, but I couldn't help getting one with a little extra clit stimulation on top. Every time I slide all the way inside, the textured bump hits Lily's clit.

She whimpers when I change angles slightly. "Yes, yes, right there."

My brow furrows in concentration as I take her hips in both hands. While still thrusting into her, I move her lower body forward and back to meet my drives. The added assistance lets me go deeper, and harder.

"Oh *fuck*," she says breathily. Then she's wrapping her arms around my neck, bumping her hips forward, taking over the motion from my hands. I keep one hand on her hip still, guiding her motions, but the other I slide into her hair at the nape of her neck and kiss her.

"You feel fucking incredible," I breathe out against her lips. I have a bizarre moment of gratitude that my injury wasn't a complete SCI, that I can still feel the mind-bending sensation of Lily's pussy dripping down my cock, her muscles squeezing me every time I slide all the way in.

But it registers that she doesn't seem mindless with pleasure, the way she did when she was on the verge of an orgasm. So I quickly grab the second thing I pulled from my bedside table.

The moment I press the buzzing vibrator against Lily's clit, she jolts from the sensation, her eyes flying open. "What—?"

My mouth moves to her neck, nipping and sucking the sensitive skin there. "Overachiever, remember?" I murmur.

It doesn't take her long to recover from the shock, because a second later, her hips start rolling faster, chasing the small vibrator. Her breathing becomes shallow, and a sweat breaks out on her skin.

*Now* I can feel her spiraling. She frantically grabs for my face, pulling my lips back to hers. She's gasping for air too hard to actually kiss me, but the bump and slide of our mouths against each other is a comfort in itself.

"You're going to make me come," she whispers. "Roman, I'm about to—"

Her admission wrenches a sound out of me, and I press the vibrator harder against her clit. My grip on her hips tightens as I pull her into my thrusts with desperation.

I know she's on the verge of coming, so I'm surprised when she reaches down to knock the bullet out of my hand. "I want you," she gasps against my lips. "I only ever want you." I can feel her muscles clamping down on me as she shakes and moans. "I want you and I love you and I—"

My orgasm slams into me so hard, I think I black out for a minute. Between Lily's words and the feeling of her absolutely losing it all over my cock, I'm bowled over by a tsunami of pleasure.

When the air finally settles, we're both trembling, both breathing heavily. Still wrapped tightly in each other's arms. I think I'd be happy to stay like this for the rest of the night.

"Holy shit," I breathe. "That was..."

Lily laughs softly at the repeated line. "I wonder how long it'll take us to stop saying that after sex."

Smiling, I kiss her lips. "I'm guessing never."

She lets out a sweet hum against my mouth. "I can live with that," she whispers.

I think I could live in this moment, right here. With Lily in my arms and love shining in her eyes, the only thing that makes it less than perfect is when the discomfort of the cock ring registers.

Wincing, I roll onto my back and slide the ring off, then place it with the vibrator on my nightstand. When I turn back toward Lily, she's lifted onto one hand and is staring down at me with a frown.

"Are you in pain?" she asks.

I shake my head with a smile and pull her down onto my

chest. She braces her forearms on my chest as she waits for my answer.

"I'm fine, Liliana," I reassure her. "I'm just not exactly used to the sensation of a cock ring."

That at least earns me an amused smile. She drops her chin on top of her hands and stares up at me. "Have you used other sex toys?"

I shake my head as I prop an extra pillow behind my head. "I was a bit of a purist. Before."

She lets out a thoughtful hum. "Same. But that just means we get to experiment together."

I'm smiling as I tuck a strand of hair behind her ear, lost in the knowledge that she's just as beautiful on the inside as she is on the outside.

She's the sunshine I needed to illuminate the dark parts of my life, to show me just how not-scary they were.

Something catches her eye, and she pushes up to her forearms again with a pinched brow. Then she places her hand on my shoulder.

"Is this a new tattoo?" she asks.

Realizing what caught her eye, I only nod in answer.

Her touch moves over my skin. "Is it...a phoenix?"

Another nod.

Biting her lip, she asks curiously, "But aren't they supposed to rise from the ashes?"

Placing my hand over hers, I guide it along the lines of the tattoo. Over the beautifully intricate fire-color bird, to its tail, down to the white lily blooming open on my chest. Her eyes meet mine, glassy with realization.

"They are. But mine rose from a lily."

# EPILOGUE

## ROMAN

*2 Years Later*

"You ask him!"

"No, *you* ask him!"

"I bet he's an assassin with that cane. Maybe it's a secret weapon."

A smile stretches across my face as I'm looking over some papers at my supervising teacher's desk. The kids are supposed to be discussing the question on the board in small groups, but...I'm realizing middle schoolers have a fairly short attention span. Especially when a teacher walks in with a cane.

"Mr. Ward?"

I look up, surprised that one of them actually worked up the courage. By the end of the day, I'll learn that middle schoolers are also shamelessly blunt.

"Yes?" I ask patiently.

He glances down at my cane that's leaning against the

desk. He seems to stumble over his question for a moment. "Why— Uh, why do you have a cane?"

"Because sometimes I need help walking," I answer simply.

His brow furrows. "But...you're not even that old."

My lip twitches with amusement. "Old people aren't the only ones who might need help walking." When that doesn't clear up his confusion even a little, I nod toward his glasses and add, "You know how your glasses help you see better? That's all my cane is, too. Some days, my legs just need a little extra help."

All three boys make a little *oooh* sound at my answer. It's why I decide to wink at them and add, "I like to think of it as my super-secret weapon."

Their eyes widen, but I'm already standing and calling the class to order. Hopefully, their reactions mean I'll be getting more questions about the cane after class.

A few hours—and a million questions—later, I'm finally leaving school grounds and driving home. I'm still smiling when I walk through the door.

As soon as I'm dropping my keys in the kitchen bowl, Garfield rises from where he was sleeping on a barstool and climbs onto the counter. He lets out one demanding meow that I can already translate.

"I know for a fact your automatic feeder just went off, so no, I'm not feeding you," I scold him, scratching behind his ear. "I'm not Tina. You don't get treats just because you're cute."

"I'm telling Tina you said that."

I'm already smiling, even before I set eyes on my girl-friend. You'd never know it's been almost a year of living together because I *still* can't get over the feeling of walking into the house and knowing she's already here.

I look up to see her walking into the kitchen, wearing jeans and a t-shirt, her hair still wet from her shower. She's smiling as she steps up to me, her arms immediately circling my waist. "Hi," she greets sweetly. "How was your first day of school?"

I ignore the question, but only for long enough to slide my hand into her hair and take her mouth in a kiss.

"Hi, Doc," I murmur with a smile.

I feel her lips tip up in a smile of her own. "Hi," she whispers back.

But when I accidentally bump her with the cane still in my hand, she frowns and pushes me back. Looking down, she asks, "Are you having a bad pain day?"

Once again, I ignore her question and instead tip her face up for another kiss, setting my cane aside in the same motion. "What did I say about leaving your PT hat at the door?"

She nips at my lip. "That wasn't my PT hat, you jerk. But fine, I won't ask." As she starts to turn away from me, I wrap my arms around her waist and pull her back. "Not a pain day," I murmur into her neck. "I just wanted to get the cane distraction out of the way with the kids."

Again, she pushes me back so she can look up at me, this time with excitement in her eyes. "And? How were they?"

I try for a nonchalant shrug, but I'm not hiding anything. Lily knows how excited I've been for the student teaching part of my undergraduate degree.

"Exactly the way I expected them to be. Curious, easily distracted, and predictably unfazed."

Lily props her chin on my chest, sunshine radiating from her expression. "I love that," she says. Then softer, "I love that you love this."

I take her mouth in another kiss, because I can't not. "I love *you.*"

Her smile widens, and before I can let my feelings completely adle my mind, I tap her thigh in a silent request that she jump up on the counter. She lifts herself immediately. And once she's closer to my level, I can lean both hands on the counter by her hips and drop my face down to her neck, letting out a breath that releases all the tension from my body.

"I can already tell I'll need the vacation we booked at the end of the thirteen weeks, though," I murmur against her skin. "I'm glad we timed it that way."

Sometimes, I look back at how worried I was that I wouldn't fit into Lily's life outside of the clinic, and I laugh. Because that fear couldn't have been further from the truth. In the two years we've been together, we've taken plenty of trips, some with just the two of us and some with her dad and brothers. They folded me into their family so seamlessly, I forgot I was ever concerned about not being able to keep up.

This upcoming trip we're taking, the annual Davis family trip, is the perfect example of that. Because they let me pick the destination, and when I suggested a scuba diving trip after becoming certified as an adaptive scuba diver, not only did they agree to the idea, but they also became certified as adaptive support divers. Even knowing it was enough safety-wise for Lily to be my support diver, they still took the time and money to go the extra step to make me feel included.

"I think we're both going to be ready for some time off by then," Lily comments, her hands brushing along my ribs. "I swear Fran is trying to overload me with patients lately."

I smile against her neck. "It's because she knows you're

the best physical therapist." I press another kiss to her skin. "Although I might be slightly biased."

Lily lets out a laugh, her arms going around my body to pull me closer. But when my phone rings with a call, she reaches into my pocket and pulls it out to show me *Mikey calling*.

I accept the call with a gruff, "What's up?"

"Hey, man. You home?"

I straighten with a frown and look around. Because I can hear the question from the phone, but it also sounds like—

"Are you *here*?" I demand.

A pause. "Maybe."

I sigh. "You're insane."

"Is that Mikey?" Lily asks with an amused smile.

I nod. "He probably sussed out that we're having our breakfast for dinner date with Mom tonight."

"I did," Mikey confirms. Another pause. "So...can I come in?"

"Just get *in* here," Lily sighs into the phone. We hear the door opening, and a moment later, Mikey is strutting into our house and throwing himself onto the couch like he owns it. Lily rolls her eyes and goes to move off the counter, but I box her in and keep her where she is.

"I thought having my girlfriend move in with me would put a stop to your pop-ins, but I guess that was an ambitious dream," I call over my shoulder at my best friend, even as my attention turns back to Lily.

"Hey, I stopped walking in. I call more. That's all you get."

I shake my head, but I'm smiling. Lily chuckles.

"Do you want me to get started on dinner while you shower?" she asks when we hear Mikey turn on the TV. "Your mom said she's coming over in an hour. Apparently, her book is riveting. She talked my ear off for twenty minutes when I walked over to ask."

My smile widens at that tidbit. Not that I would've expected anything else, but the fact that Mom fell in love with Lily the same way I did never ceases to make me happy. Some days, the two are inseparable. They bonded instantly, over books, traveling, and of course teasing me.

It's one of the reasons we decided to keep Mom in the cottage on my property. I would've paid for a new place if she wanted to live a little once I no longer relied on her as my safety blanket, but in the end, I realized that was never why she had been there in the first place. She *likes* being close. And I love having her around. Lily, too.

"Do you want to get started on that stuffed French toast that she loves?" I answer Lily. "We haven't made that in a while."

She nods, just as Mikey calls out, "Oooh, stuffed French toast, nice."

Lily and I roll our eyes at the same time. But after a moment, she sobers and peeks up at me. "Sure you're okay today?" she asks softly.

I haven't needed my cane in a while, so I know that's what's making her worry. Because that care she treated me with from day one has never faded, never dulled.

I nod and take my time reassuring her with a kiss, the same way I do every time. Even though I still have bad days, days when the nerve pain gets bad again, or I need the cane to walk, I'm no longer in a place where those things can send me into a spiral. Nowadays, I know those things don't determine my worth.

I pull back so I can look at Lily, this beautiful woman who saw that worth even when I was in the darkest period of my life. The woman who never gave up on me, who revived me and helped me find a new version of myself. And I wonder, for the millionth time, what I may have done in a past life to deserve her.

I want to tell her that I'm always okay when she's around. That my legs never hurt when she's kissing me.

That I'm so madly in love with her, my physical therapy has been solely focused on one specific exercise lately.

Getting down on one knee.

But I'm not quite there yet, so instead, I smile and tip her chin up for another kiss.

"Never better, Doc."

# ACKNOWLEDGMENTS

I want to start by saying that this book is, by far, my favorite book I've ever written. The pride I feel for it is immeasurable. And I also know that it would not exist without the help of many, many people.

To my husband, who had a glimmer of an idea several years ago for a love story in which an injured fighter falls for his physical therapist. For years he's been pressing me to write it, convinced it was going to be THE book for me. I hate admitting you were right, but... I think you were right.

To my editor Kenzie, who continues to be the most integral piece in my writing process. This book definitely put us through the wringer but in the end, I think the months of rewrites and 4-hour brainstorming sessions and voice messages talking me off the ledge were exactly what we needed to create something special. And this one is so, so special.

To my beta reader and friend Nicole: I've lost count of how many books we've worked on together but the truth still remains that your feedback is invaluable, every single time. Thank you for always being my most reliable friend and beta reader.

To my friend Erin: I'm having a little bit of a surreal worlds collide moment because what do you *mean* I got to work on this passion project with one of my best friends from college. I can't thank you enough for answering my million random texts and for helping to shape this story. I love you!

To my sensitivity readers Candice, Tori, and Becca: I don't think I can properly express my gratitude to you. I was out of my depth with this story but wanted so badly to do it justice, and I never would have been able to do that without your help. You not only assured me that my research and approach to the story were valid, but you were also the first ones to make me feel like I wasn't alone in thinking this story was special. A million times over, thank you for helping me shape this story into its best possible version.

To my family, friends, readers, *everyone* who has supported me throughout this writing journey, all I can say is *THANK YOU!* As I say with every book, without you, a book is just some ink on a dead tree. Thank you for loving this story as much as I do.

# ALSO BY NIKKI CASTLE

**The Fight Game Series**

Book One: 5 Rounds

Book Two: 2 Fights

Book Three: 3 Count

Book Four: 1 Last Shot

Book Five: 4th Degree

**The Just Tonight Novella Series**

The Stranger in Seat 8B

The Waiter at Table 6

# ABOUT THE AUTHOR

Nikki Castle is a wife and dog mom from Philadelphia who writes spicy love stories about alpha MMA fighters and the women that melt their badass, playboy hearts. She's a full-time romance author during the day and spends her evenings running a Mixed Martial Arts (MMA) gym with her husband, who is also a retired fighter.

Nikki has been writing in one way or another since she was a teenager. She pursued an English and Philosophy degree in college, and finally decided to sit down and fulfill her longtime dream of writing a novel when quarantine began in 2020.

Nikki loves to hear from her readers on Instagram or through email. Message her on any social media platform @nikkicastleromance or email her at nikkicastleromance@gmail.com!

www.ingramcontent.com/pod-product-compliance
Lightning Source LLC
Chambersburg PA
CBHW022307310726
48973CB00001B/254